The Letter

Valverde Maclean

Also by Valverde Maclean

The Disappearance of Merry

A young woman disappeared. Her brother was killed in a car crash. It's an old mystery but someone still doesn't want questions asked. Suzie and Peter must travel Australia to find the answer. All the while avoiding death as they relive their own pasts.

Magenta

In a remote region a young woman's body vanishes, only to re-appear fifteen hundred kilometres away. A road trip across the north and the west of Australia brings unexpected revelations, romance, danger and uncertainty that will change relationships forever.

Visit **www.valverdemaclean.com**

DEDICATION

To

Erin and Tay

For showing me the value of

Determination, Effort

And

Following your Dreams.

CONTENTS

ACKNOWLEDGEMENTS

Thank you to all those readers who are interested in my novels.

Firstly, thank you to Bryan Hughes for his honest advice on my first draft. His wise and thoughtful comments and suggestions have made the story a much better read.

Thanks also to the extended Taylor Family for their hospitality over the years I have been visiting the far reaches of Queensland. Special thanks to Esmae Taylor for her assistance.

I must also mention another Taylor, this time Sandy Taylor, for his knowledge of the history of Western Queensland and the life of its people. He made sure the background to my story reflected the times accurately. I only wish I could have included more of the interesting, and entertaining, stories that are local history.

Thank you to Geena Carroll, and to Joshua and Tristen Lindner for their assistance in the current idioms used by the younger generation.

I must also mention Jeanette Hauf. Changing one small word can make a great improvement to a story. I would also like to acknowledge Maria and Jack Carroll for their comments on the story and the cover design.

Thanks also to Kylie Owens of Barcaldine with whom I had an interesting and informative conversation about past and present life in Central Western Queensland. Fact can sometimes be more interesting than fiction.

As always, very special thanks to my ever patient wife whose comments, and use of a pencil, make for a far, far better story.

Once again a thank you to Nahum Szumer for his advice and his skill with graphics in developing the cover design.

Finally, thanks to Gemma Brown for her diligence in editing and proofreading the penultimate draft. Her comments, and many corrections of my errors, are greatly appreciated. Any errors remaining are due to my subsequent alterations.

1 The Little Box

It all began with my mother's death.

Even the day seemed to suit the occasion. It was a Melbourne day of changes, at times grey, miserable and overcast, at other times bright and sunny, but always with that chill that can come on a late April afternoon. Little did I realise how that day would change my life, or where it would take me.

For the three of us Finley children, it had been a day of high emotion. We'd cried. Well, we two girls had cried, not so much my brother. At other times we'd laughed. We'd relived memories of good times and bad, of holidays and of school days. And of our parents, especially our mother. After all, that was why we were here in her room at what the management referred to as a Lifestyle Resort but our mum disparagingly called "a halfway house for half-deads". Considering how bright and active, although frail, she had been until the last weeks before her death, it seemed an inappropriate, but typical, comment from her.

Now, we three siblings had the job of removing her possessions so the next eager and hopeful person on the waitlist could take up residency. Our mother had been very strict on what she had taken with her when she had moved into the aged care home. The family had already been given the best of her furniture and most of her treasured possessions—whether we wanted them or not. "I'll not have my children fighting over my effects like some families I know." Our mother had always been an organised and practical person, rarely emotional, although we had never had any reason to doubt her love for us.

It was the old brown cardboard box that started my search. It was a shoe box, the sort that people once used to store memories, which changed our lives. My sister, Margaret, remembered once seeing it being carefully transferred as my mother had moved from the family home to come to live with me. Neither my brother nor I had ever seen it. Margaret had not given it much thought at the time, but was a little puzzled as our mother had been insistent on not wanting to take "all those knick-knacks and junk with me to Elizabeth's". Yet she had taken the old shoebox. And she had kept it with her when she'd moved into the aged care home. It was so unlike her.

"What are you going to do with it? Does it go in the pile for the rubbish?" It was John, my brother, who as usual, was looking for a quick decision.

"John, we need to open it and see what is in there before we throw it out." I agreed with Margaret. I pulled on the end of the bow, the twine released and the lid lifted away. The small box was only half full. Inside were a few coloured photos from years long past, and a collection of older black and white photos. Photos of us as children, our first days at school, on holidays, our weddings, and three faded photos we recognised of our parents on their wedding day. There was a dog-eared photograph of the first car my father had ever purchased, and there were others of the days when our parents were young and obviously in love. A few photos were even older.

"I'm sure that's Nan's mother when she was young. I remember seeing that photo once. Years ago. You girls were away overseas and mum was showing me some photos of her parents. I'd asked mum what our grandfather used to look like. I wanted to know if he ever had a bushy beard. I was considering growing one."

"John, you'd look ridiculous in a bushy beard. You would be like a grey-bearded Ned Kelly." I had to agree with my sister.

Somehow our mother had become known as Nan to all the family. To everyone. To us, her own children, to her grandchildren, and even her four great grandchildren; the oldest was now nineteen. Even some of her friends had taken to calling her Nan. It somehow suited our mother.

Underneath the photos were some cards: invitations to weddings and parties from long ago, thank-you notes from names we'd never known. Then, two small envelopes containing treasures that our mother had collected: a brown lock of hair from my first haircut, another blonder lock from my sister. There were tiny swatches of fabric. Some I remembered from dresses my mother made for special occasions for my sister or myself, and others from old dresses I recalled her discarding from her wardrobe when she had moved from the family home. Hidden away in this small box were memories our mother had held close to her heart.

At the very bottom of the box was a tiny packet of letters tied together with what had once been red ribbon. The red had long ago faded to pink. The once white paper was yellowed and had become brittle.

"Do you think they are love letters our father wrote to Nan?"

"Maybe, they look old, and why else would she keep them?"

"Maybe they're from an old boyfriend before our father?"

"John! I don't think that is likely!" I couldn't imagine my mother keeping letters from an old boyfriend. But then children, even mature-aged children, are not always the best judge of their parent's youth. "It's more likely they're from our father, but that last one looks much older."

"Open them and find out." We followed Margaret's suggestion.

The first letters were from our father. An invitation to a concert in the Wodonga Town Hall. Perhaps it was the first date? Then, as their relationship and love blossomed, the letters became less formal. There were older letters. Letters from her mum, our grandmother, to our grandfather telling of our mother, Nan, growing up while her father served in the army in Europe during the Second World War. From the creases they had been cherished, read and reread: sad letters of separation, of longing, but lacking much detail because of wartime censorship. By the look of them they must have been carried for years before being returned to the writer.

There was one more letter. A faded envelope with a distant address. Only a page. But it meant nothing to us.

"It must be important. Why else would it be in the box?

Nan wouldn't have kept it otherwise."

We looked at each other for an explanation. None of us had an answer.

2 The Letter

June 18, 1877

My dearest Bessie,

I am sending this letter addressed to you care of the Aramac Post Office. I hope that somehow it will find you, or someone who knows where you are who can pass it along to you. Recently I heard a travelling drover speak of Aramac. He gave me a little news but had no knowledge of you, so I decided I must write to find out your wellbeing. I was distressed when I heard of the fire. I hope you are safe and have found a home for you and your precious one.

I am as well as can be expected. I

am hopeful of finding a permanent position soon. We are both making our new lives far away. Please don't try to find me but be assured I am well and happy. I will never forget the special times that we had together.

Your everlasting friend

Annie

3 A Mystery

"It must have been important to Nan."

I agreed with my sister. We had never thought of our mother as a sentimental woman, and yet here in the box were her secret treasures.

"Do either of you girls know anything about a Bessie or Annie?"

We both turned to John and shook our heads.

"I've never heard the names mentioned." Margaret turned to me. "What about you Liz?"

"Me neither."

"Well, knowing our mother, it must have been important for her to have kept the letter. She didn't just keep things."

"John's right, Liz. For mum to have kept this letter for all those years it must have held some special connection. But I have no idea what it could be. If she kept the letters from her mother to her father, perhaps this could be something similar?"

"But we don't have any Annies or Bessies in our family. To my knowledge they are not family names. We don't have any cousins or aunties with those names."

"But you could be a Bessie! Elizabeth, that can be contracted to Beth, or Bess, or Bessie."

Margaret was right. I'd just never thought of my name in that way. I was always Liz, or Elizabeth. I had never had anyone call me Beth, let alone Bess. Yet of course there was Good Queen Bess and she was Elizabeth.

"Look at the date. June 1877. That goes back well before our mother's birth. I know Nan, our mum, was born in 1934. That's at least another two, or even three generations further back. There would be our mother 'Nan', her mother our 'Granny J', I think she was born about the time of the First World War, and then there would be at least another two generations, maybe even three, to get back to someone writing in 1877."

John's calculation of the timeline made sense of the dates. It also made me realise how little I knew of our family history. John continued. "By the look of the letter, it was written by someone other than Annie. She just put her signature at the end. I suspect Annie couldn't write, apart from her name, and maybe she couldn't read either. For some people that wouldn't have been unusual at that time. Your schooling could be very limited unless you were wealthy or fortunate."

"What about the envelope?"

John turned the envelope over and looked at the address. "Mrs Bessie Buckley, c/-The Post Office, Aramac, Queensland. I've heard of it. I think it is somewhere out in western Queensland. Not sure exactly where. The postmark is Warren. I think that's a town in western New South Wales. They would be a long way apart."

It was Margaret who pointed out the next puzzle. "What does she mean by 'finding a home for you and your precious one'? Is that a baby or a loved one? What do you think Liz?"

"To me it is probably a baby, but it could be a husband I suppose. Then there is the bit about 'new lives far away'. That's in the plural. It really doesn't give you any answers."

It was John who raised the next peculiarity. "There's no address on the letterhead. It's as if Annie didn't want Bessie to know where she was, and yet she wanted to find out about Bessie's wellbeing. That's really strange."

"I think she was concerned about Bessie and wanted to let her know. It was moral support. A reply wasn't really needed. Perhaps she had some reason for keeping her location secret."

"Nan, or someone, must have got the letter from Bessie because it couldn't have been returned to Annie—she didn't put an address on the envelope or the letter. It looks as if the postmaster, or somebody, must have passed it on to Bessie."

"Do you think they were sisters?"

"No." Neither Margaret nor I felt they could be sisters.

"A sister wouldn't sign a letter with 'your everlasting friend'. She would use 'your sister' or a special familiar name."

I thought even cousins would be unlikely, and yet the two women were obviously very close. For that reason we decided that Annie was unlikely to be an Annie Buckley.

" 'As well as can be expected'. That sounds as if there's been some major sickness or trauma in her life. What do you think, John?"

"Yes. Obviously Bessie must know something about Annie's past experiences, but we can have no idea what they may have been from the letter. 'Finding a position' sounds like Annie was hoping for some sort of job. Did married women work, for pay I mean, in those days?"

Both John and Margaret had raised good points. It was a puzzling letter. The more I thought about it, the more I wondered what was the story behind the lines. Then there was 'the fire' and 'the special times', 'your everlasting friend'. It was a brief note, but it raised so many questions.

As we left what had once been my mother's unit, now bare and empty, cleaned out and ready for a new occupant, we divided the contents of the box. Each took the items most precious to them. The box and the last, puzzling, letter remained with me.

.

4 Thoughts

Driving back to my home in South Melbourne the thought of Annie and Bessie remained in my mind. What would their lives have been like back in eighteen seventy-seven? What were the two women like? How had they reached such far away and distant places? How had our lives changed in the almost one hundred and forty years that had passed since the letter had been written? There were so many questions I would have liked to ask them about their lives and the letter.

Thinking of them, I realised I really didn't know much about my own family's history. Were they related to me, way, way, back? Were they sisters or cousins? We'd decided that was unlikely. It must have been a major event to cause them to separate. But then, since Annie still thought of the other woman as an everlasting friend, it must have been a deep relationship.

Arriving home, I put the thoughts out of my mind and again became immersed in my daily life. My mother's funeral had passed without drama. My brother and sister and I had a good relationship, not really as intense or close as some families, but still close enough to share and have a sense of being family.

I had my son and daughter, and my four grandchildren,

with the great news of another on the way.

Yet somehow, I was feeling a greater sense of emptiness and loss than I'd expected. My mother had had a good and interesting life, and had survived to old age without too many serious ailments. She'd remained bright and alert, even as her body became frailer. With her age I could hardly say her death was unexpected. But it was more than that.

It was not that I was unfamiliar with death. The empty space left when my husband, Matt, had failed to return from work one evening had been huge, but in the six years since his accident I'd made my life alone. I was fortunate. I had my family, and we'd had a good life together. I was financially secure after his death—unlike some of my friends whose lifestyle had suffered badly with the loss of the breadwinner. I had arranged it so my daughter and her husband could buy our home in Beaumaris from me. It was where Matthew and I had raised our family, and where Meg and her brother had grown up. Then I bought myself a smaller townhouse closer to the city. I was ready to move on. I'd considered moving out of Melbourne, to perhaps Gisborne, or Macedon. I'd always loved those areas but I finally decided I would be better in the city. Now my home was in a pocket of quiet, yet only fifty metres away from the bustle and the rush of the city. One side of the leafy street was filled with the tiny single-fronted houses that were once workers' cottages. Behind their nineteenth century facades they had been renovated and modernised into fashionable inner-city pads. My townhouse was on the opposite side of the street. It, and the neighbouring apartments, lacked the charm of the older houses but were comfortable and convenient, and I had a balcony with a view of the city CBD and its high buildings. The Botanic Gardens were minutes away, the centre of the city a short walk or tram ride. All the benefits of a big city were at my finger-tips, yet I was in a little pool of green with a park and playground half a block away.

Normally my townhouse was peaceful and quiet, but what I'd overlooked was that each year the Formula One car race came to town. It was as if a swarm of angry bees had found a microphone and their screaming and buzzing was magnified and broadcast out at top volume from loud speakers all around Albert Park Lake. I had enjoyed a brief respite one year when the engines of the race cars had been changed and the noise level had dropped. However the lack of noise had so disappointed race fans that the next season the exhaust systems of the cars had been modified and the noise was back. The fans were thus satisfied and could hear the 'proper' noise of a race car! At least it was only for three days and it did add a sense of excitement to the city.

I missed my old Art Deco home with its fireplace and the garden that Matt and I had created over so many years. I had loved the green of the trees in the neighbourhood, and the walk along the cliffs where the tang of sea salt mingled with the smell of the native bushes. I enjoyed watching the walkers and children on the beach, or looking out across the bay with its boats and shipping. The arrangement with my daughter and her husband had suited all of us and I could still enjoy the house and its memories whenever I visited them. My granddaughter had only to walk around the corner to attend the same school that her mother had once attended. Even the aging family beagle, Barky, had remained in the same house as my daughter took over care of him. I'd been concerned how an old dog would cope with a move to a new neighbourhood. It had been a fortuitous arrangement of family affairs for all of us. Then Nan had come to share my townhouse until she decided she was an imposition and would move to the retirement village. She had never complained, but I suspected she was finding the stairs of my townhouse a problem as she became frailer.

I had the freedom to fill my time with friends and groups. Bridge, garden club, volunteer work and Meals-on-Wheels. There were talks at the Gallery and the Botanic Gardens. There was Tony. I had plenty to fill my time.

And I had my two children, Sam and Meg.

It was Meg who was waiting for me as I drove into the garage at my townhouse. With her was Sass, her daughter. "How did the clean-up go, Mum? Did you find the family jewels?"

"No my love, you should know by now there are no family jewels. I don't think our family has ever had any." Over cups of coffee I told her of my day and mentioned the various letters and photos.

"I'd love to see them. Do you have them?"

I explained that we had shared the photos and letters between the siblings. She could certainly read the ones I had. I also told her of the oldest of the letters.

"That sounds interesting. What are you going to do about it?"

"Nothing." I replied. "I know nothing of the people, I've never heard of them. They may not even be family."

"Nan wouldn't have kept the letter if there wasn't some link. Maybe you should do some research."

We finished our coffee and hugged as Meg and Sass left. Time was important to them this year. Meg had started a new job that was proving a greater challenge than she had expected. As well, Sass had started her first year at university and Meg needed to keep her working on her studies. I suspected that would be a big task. Like so many of today's teenagers, Sass seemed to consider her mobile phone far more important than study. I knew Meg worried about how committed Sass was to her studies.

Alone with my thoughts Meg's comment returned to me. I really knew so little about my family's background. I doubted if my sister or brother knew any more than I did. The thought hit with a clap. I was now the eldest of the family; the holder of family memories and history, and yet I had so little. I wanted to ask my mum, but that was no longer possible.

Perhaps it was my own sense of mortality but at that moment I decided I would try to gather together what I could of our family history. For me, for my children and grandchildren, even for the as yet unborn, but growing, fifth grandchild. I would start with my brother and sister. Perhaps we each held some small parcel of knowledge that the others didn't know. I phoned and arranged for them to come for dinner, just them, no spouses or children; hopefully together we would start to discover our past. I doubted it would be exceptional. After all our family was unexceptional, but it might still be interesting.

5 Tony

Tony rang to invite me to a fundraising dinner to aid a cancer fund. It was a cause close to his heart as his wife had sadly died from a rapidly progressing form of the disease.

I'd first met Tony when we were rostered together on Meals-on-Wheels. I'd signed up through my garden club to do one day a month but sometimes did more if they were short of volunteers. Tony was more eager and had signed up for two days a month. But that was Tony. He was always enthusiastic, particularly for seventies music, and for bowls which he played three or four times a week.

I was never a sportswoman. I had tried golf with Matt and enjoyed the casual walk around the leafy course. To me, chasing a little white ball was an intrusion to the stroll amongst the trees and water hazards. I enjoyed the shrubs and trees, and the rolling slopes of the course, but had never seriously taken up the sport. Bowls, for me, lacked even the beauty and interest of a golf course. I tried the game several times at Tony's request but it did nothing for me. Even as a youth I had never been a sporty person. I'd visited a gym at the insistence of some girl-friends and I had tried Pilates and yoga, again without any great interest. My idea of exercise was a brisk walk in the early morning or late afternoon depending on the weather and my mood. Even brisk was a misnomer. Usually I would find a flower or a plant that caught my curiosity, and sometimes with a tweak of the fingers I had a cutting to try to strike. Other times I would meet a few fellow walkers and pass the time of day with them. Bike riders were different. Usually they would pass with their heads bent low over the handlebars, legs pumping, deep in thought of their heartbeat or aching legs, or perhaps lost in the sound playing in their ears from their electronic devices. I had to admit to myself that my favourite activity was to be settled in my favourite lounge chair, a good book in hand, and a cup of coffee or a glass of red wine close by.

Tony and I had established a friendship and he often called to invite me to a movie. We would meet and have a coffee before watching the latest recommended film in the local multiplex, or perhaps we would watch the movie then go on for a meal. He was great company and I enjoyed the time I spent with him. We'd started by each paying our share but for convenience decided to take it in turns paying. I could always rely on Tony to remember whose turn it was. I was much less organised.

In February he'd taken me to a concert by his favourite band, and while I enjoyed The Eagles playing all their big hits I couldn't share his excitement. I remembered their songs, especially 'Hotel California', but I found I was more interested in watching the variety of people sitting around us in the Rod Laver Arena than in the band on stage. Our musical tastes were quite different. I loved Carole King and Janis Joplin, and of course Helen Reddy with her anthem of the times for women. At least we agreed on Led Zeppelin and 'Stairway to Heaven'.

He and his wife had both been school teachers. They'd met at university and had taught at a wide range of schools across both country and city, including a stint in an

Aboriginal community in the Northern Territory. His stories of that time and the people he met were fascinating. He'd also come through the exciting sixties with its protest movements and feminism. I'd been a nurse and all those social movements had been distant to my life. I was too late for burning bras and I had never been a part of the full-on sexual freedoms of the times. I wasn't sure whether it was my latent Scottish Presbyterian genes or an innate conservatism. Not that it mattered when I met my husband. On marriage I had changed to Anglican but neither Matt nor I were particularly pious. We were more Anglican in name and Christian by cultural background. Even then, our religion, when we rarely discussed it, was of the social enlightenment movements rather than the mystical version of the High Church or the excitement of the happy clappers.

I enjoyed my outings with Tony but that was all I wanted. Tony, I thought, hoped the relationship would develop further. I couldn't see it happening, and I wasn't sure I wanted it to happen. It wasn't his looks, or his thinning hair that he hid by keeping it shaven, or his enthusiasm for whatever he was doing. There was something else. I didn't know what it was, but a friend, yes, lover, no. I used to wonder what would happen to our friendship. Would we gradually stop meeting as often, or would he soon decide to find a more approachable woman? I expected the latter. While I would miss his company I could only wish him well.

This time it was his choice of film and the movie he had chosen was 'The Woman in Gold'. It was the story of a woman recovering the Gustav Klimt painting of her aunt looted by Nazis from Vienna during the Second World War. It was a good pick and we discussed our opinions of Helen Mirren's performance and our viewpoints over coffee and cake, occasionally disagreeing but often agreeing. That period in Europe was important to Tony's family. In the difficult times following the War they had migrated to Australia. It was after seeing that movie that he asked me to go with him to Bright. It was the Bright Autumn Festival, a beautiful time when all the deciduous trees were changing to their autumn colours before the bleakness of winter set in. Tony had family in the area. His parents had arrived as immigrants and worked as sharefarmers growing tobacco at Myrtleford. He still had many cousins living in the area and the Festival was a time for the extended family to get together. He would love to take me.

It was a generous invitation, and the thought of seeing the trees in their autumn colours was appealing, but I hesitated. I think it was the thought of meeting his family that made me hesitate. I wasn't sure that I was ready for that step, even if they would be cousins not parents. I felt foolish. I was behaving like a young girl being taken to meet the boyfriend's parents for the first time. I was hardly a young girl anymore.

Tony made it clear that we could stay with a cousin who had lots of bedrooms available. His children had all left home and only two would be back that weekend. I would have a room all to myself. Then I wondered whether his discretion was concern for me, or for him. I thought if we had gone anywhere else the suggestion may have been for a shared room and bed.

His description of the trees had been accurate. Indeed, if anything he had understated the masses of browns and golds, and the range of reds, yellows, and honeys on display. The streets and the parks were a riot of colour depending on the variety of tree, the microclimate and the stage of desiccation and death. Already the dropping leaves would crunch underfoot as we walked over them. The thought of the leaves undergoing death but displaying such beauty in their final stage of life had always seemed rather sad to me.

Tony was, as usual, exuberant, excitable and noisy in everything he did, and now I was in a house full of Tonys. Cousins and relatives, children, I never exactly established all the connections, seemed to appear and disappear at any time during the day and night. So did the wine and the tables laden with food. It was a noisy happy atmosphere and the cousins were welcoming of me. It was impossible not to be carried along by the banter and chat around the large table set up in the garden. These days all those present had been born in Australia but much of their Italian heritage remained in their love of wine and food and especially family and company. It was so different to my upbringing in a family that stressed quietness and reserve in behaviour, reserve that I had carried to my children and grandchildren. While Matt and I had loved to laugh and enjoyed life fully, it was in a quieter manner. Life with Tony could be exhausting.

On Monday morning we returned to Melbourne. I had enjoyed my visit to Bright for the weekend and meeting his family. I'd enjoyed Tony's company. Now I better understood his life and our relationship would continue. He was happy to go to the movies with me, and I was happy to accompany him. Yet deep down I knew he could never replace Matt. We could be good friends but only time would tell if it would be more.

6 A Family Dinner

My plan for a small sibling dinner to discuss our family's history was not a good idea.

Enjoyable and interesting, yes. But not conducive to discovering more of our family story. Perhaps our problem was the wine!

My brother, sister and I had sat around with an excellent glass of sparkling wine and talked of our childhood. A second glass followed and more stories came flooding back. We moved to the meal table and continued our story telling. Another glass or two of red and even more stories flowed. It was interesting to discover how our recollections sometimes differed. Some of my memories went back further than theirs. Although my sister and I were only a few years apart, I could remember events that she was too young to recall. She and I shared recollections of our brother as a young child and especially of him as a baby. We could recall events of which he had no knowledge. Then my sister and brother shared memories of times with our parents after I had left home to go nursing. Even memories of times spent together could sometimes be at variance. Some we put down to the passing of time, but on other occasions it seemed to be more a personal viewpoint of events. Happenings that were of deep shame or pain to my sister and I were considered of no importance and sometimes not even noticed by my brother.

Similarly, we girls had no sympathy for the time that my brother had stupidly broken a leg in an accident. We thought he should have been more careful and deserved it, but to him, it was a mortifying loss of face to have fallen off his pushbike in front of our father.

We spent a long night reliving the days of our youth and our varied memories, and we often spoke of our parents. Even there it was interesting to compare our thoughts about them. John's view of our father and mother was sometimes at odds with the view of us two girls. We'd never considered the importance our father had placed on our 'little brother'. To us he was a walking, talking doll we could play with, at least until he had grown old enough to oppose our plans for him. Then he became uninteresting until much older. However it was a difficult position for him: the only son, but the youngest child in the family. As the eldest child I was often considered 'bossy' by my brother and sister, even though there were only three years between my sister and myself. At other times I hadn't realised how much a 'big' sister meant to Margaret. I guess I had, in some ways, prepared my parents for another teenage girl and smoothed her transition through 'best friends' and boyfriends.

Our father had died when I was twenty-eight. By then I was married and had my two babies. It was more traumatic for my brother. John was only eighteen at his father's passing and he had missed growing up in his presence and sharing his entry to manhood with his dad. At the time of his death I had thought my father was old. Now I was even older. I guess old age depends on the age you are when you think about it.

My father had rarely spoken of his family. I knew he had been a country boy who had never returned to that life when he came back from the Second World War. I remembered my mother saying it was on a brief visit to his family in Wodonga when he met her and they quickly got married. I had never heard him speak about his wartime experience. There were no mementos of that time on display in the house and he had never taken part in the usual Anzac Day events. Nor had he ever spoken of rural life, although I remembered once when my mother had bought rabbit as a special treat and he had refused to eat it.

My memories were of a quiet, self-contained man. On returning from the war he had found a job in a large factory that could use the trade the army had taught him, and there he remained. I remembered my mother once telling me that Dad had started to save for a house as soon as he had returned from the war. After marriage they had continued to save and scrimp, and finally bought their house and it was there that my mother had continued to live, even after Dad had died, until the day she moved to join me in my townhouse. We had never doubted his love, but it was not a demonstrable love, more a quiet security of knowing that you were, and would always be, loved

My mother was different. She was one of those short, active women that were always busy. From her we would get a scolding for bad behaviour; from our father—a quiet word. It was his word that we, his children, dreaded most.

Our mother was younger than our father. She always said he was her first and only boyfriend. It was a whirlwind romance and marriage, and baby. She told us she was only young when she married but I had never considered the matter seriously. I wasn't even sure of the dates, but now as I thought about it, I realised she would have been younger than my nineteen year old granddaughter when she had me.

Jean, or as we called her Nan, had been raised by her mother. She remembered little of her father, apart from what her mother had told her. Like his future son-in-law he had fought in the Second World War but he had not survived. He had left for the War when Mum was only five. Two years later he was dead. It was a year after his death that the man who would marry his daughter joined the army as a young man. I'd never really considered the dates and ages, or realised how much of an effect the war had had on my family. I had always assumed, without thinking about it, that each war would have claimed a different generation. It surprised me to realise that two generations could have fought in the same war. Nor had I considered how young both my mother and grandmother, Grannie J, had been when they had married.

I remembered Grannie J. She had lived to a fine old age, and my children had memories of their great grandmother. Unlike her daughter she was a thin, angular woman. Perhaps it was our unknown grandfather in the photo we had seen with a younger, happier, Jessie. He was certainly more like our mother, shorter, more rotund, with a sense of mischief and vitality in his eyes. Grannie J had eventually come to live with my mother. If it was a sunny morning she could usually be found in a chair on the veranda of the house watching the world pass by. In the afternoon she would change her position to near the vegetable garden at the back of the house where she could catch the last of the day's warmth. To me she always seemed a grey lady, usually clad in black or dark dresses. It was as if she spent her whole life in mourning. I had made a promise to myself that I would never be like her.

Talking together we shared many of our recollections of our family's background but so much still remained a mystery. John recalled once seeing some war medals in the bottom of a drawer and when he asked our father about winning the War, and the medals, he had been given no details. All our father had said was, "There were no winners in war, son, everyone lost. The waste of life, the suffering, and the destruction is terrible. The cost of defeating evil is so great." He had told John of the time when our side was advancing and shelling a position held by the enemy. By the time they finally took the village the huts were destroyed, the land around the village was turned to mud and unexploded ordnance lay somewhere in the gardens that had once grown food for the villagers. The enemy had retreated and the local inhabitants were returning, finally able to bury a baby boy who had died during the shelling. It was a memory that had never left our father.

Margaret recalled our mother once telling her that when our father was young he had lived on a small farm near the Murray River. It was his job to milk cows before he went to school and again after he came home from school. Life had been very hard: there was food and a roof over his head, but not much more, certainly not enough for shoes. If he was lucky he might get a pair of boots for good wear, passed down from an elder brother who had outgrown them. After that, the army, even with its dangers, seemed like luxury and he never wanted to return to milking cows.

Of Grannie J we knew even less. Our last memories were of a silent old lady who rarely spoke. Her name was Jessie, Jessie Palmer. Although to most people who knew her well she was Grannie J, just as the family called her. We had no idea of where she'd come from. We believed her husband, Stan, had worked building roads and we thought that they had moved around the countryside. Work had been difficult to find and she'd ended up in Wodonga when war broke out. After our mother had married she had lived there alone until she'd moved to Melbourne, and then later she had come to live with our mother. Margaret thought Grannie J's maiden name was McGregor and she was a Scot, but when she had come to Australia, or if she had been born in Australia, she didn't know. For some reason that I couldn't place I thought she had had some brothers or sisters but that was all we knew of her background.

I wished our mother had shared any knowledge she had about our family with us. Now it had disappeared with her death.

"I reckon you will find that we're related to the Bessie in the letter."

"Why do you say that, John?"

"Well, it was in Nan's little box of treasures. So it must have been important to her. She didn't just keep 'stuff'. I think that means it was probably something to do with family. She wouldn't have kept it if it was just some curiosity from way back then."

My brother's reply did make sense.

Then he continued. "You're Elizabeth, a Bessie. That's another link. I don't know how or where but I reckon it's there if you search for it. I'd put money on it."

It was my sister who took up the bet. "What do we get if you're wrong?"

"I'll take you both out to dinner at any restaurant you nominate."

"You're brave. I know Liz is dying to go to a very fancy restaurant in town."

"If I lose then you have to take me out for a coffee at one of those coffee shops that Liz's friend, Tony, likes to take her to."

John had only met Tony twice but I had sensed he was not impressed. Not complete disapproval, but certainly not enthusiasm either. While my brother and Matt had been quite different personalities and had never been close mates, they both had great respect for the other and had enjoyed each other's company. I couldn't see that happening with Tony—not that it really mattered.

"But I've never heard any mention of the family ever coming from Queensland. As far as I know we've always been in Victoria, and I've never heard of a Buckley."

"Margaret's right. I've never heard Nan or Grannie J mention Queensland or Aramac."

"Well you did say that Grannie J and our grandfather had moved around before they came to Wodonga."

"Yes John, but that's hardly Queensland."

It was a great night of family recollections but we had done little to track the family line very far. We had discussed our parents. We'd made brief comment on our grandmother on our mother's side, but that was all. Most of their backgrounds, where they had come from, their joys and sorrows, and any secrets they may have hidden were still a mystery. I had a few names, a little history, some stories, mostly stories about our lives, but not much more. Certainly nothing about Annie or Bessie. I decided that we would have to meet again. This time for morning tea, and no alcohol. Perhaps I really was the 'bossy' one.

A few days later I was visiting my daughter. As usual Barky Beagle was pleased to see me. When he was a pup he would always greet new arrivals, vigorously sniffing their leg and tripping them up. Today, with increasing old age he was content to simply eye them off with his bleary eyes, and then settle at the feet of his preferred companion. Today it was me. It was lovely to be able to visit the home where I had so many happy memories. So much of it was the same as when Matt and I were raising our family. While some of the furniture was now a little different, and Meg had put her touch on the décor, the house still held the warmth of our time together.

It was over a cup of coffee that Meg made the suggestion.

I could try doing some searches of Births, Deaths and Marriages. Perhaps there, I would be able to get leads to our family history. She offered to come over to my townhouse one afternoon and help me with an online search. She also suggested War Service records. Perhaps we could find where Grannie J's husband had died during the war. I had no real reason to make a connection but I was becoming even more intrigued by the letter and the link to Aramac. What would it have been like in eighteen seventy-seven? Western Queensland was so far away that it was unlikely I would ever find out.

It was my granddaughter, Sass, who briefly lifted her head from her mobile phone and made the suggestion. "Just Google Aramac and 1877."

7 Aramac

The name Aramac had puzzled me. Most names of towns and other place-names seemed to fall into various groups. There were places named after English aristocrats: Brisbane, Melbourne, Adelaide, Sydney. Some places were named after English or Scottish towns: Perth, Morven, Melton, Liverpool and a favourite name that had amused me in my youth, Chipping Norton. Then there were the aboriginal names: Wagga Wagga, Walla Walla, Wangaratta and Mooloolaba, Gayndah and Goomeri. The name Aramac didn't seem to fit any of those categories. I discovered the answer in my internet searches.

In the 1850's a pastoralist by the name of Robert Ramsey MacKenzie travelled through the area. On a tree he cut his initials 'R R Mac'. Thus was the future town named. Two pastoral stations were established: Bowen Downs in 1862 and Aramac Station in 1863. In time, and after Queensland had become a separate colony, MacKenzie went on to become the Premier of Queensland. By eighteen sixty-nine, after the original bark-hut store on the Aramac creek had been expanded to include a pub, the site was declared a town: the first in the region. Eight years later a letter posted by Annie in Warren arrived for Bessie.

My thoughts were of a rough wild town, more a scraggly

village, of shanties lost in the vast featureless interior scrub of Australia, but then I found an article published in an early Rockhampton Morning Bulletin that described Aramac and its surrounds as 'one of the emporia of the West'.

'The place is known to so many by name only that the visitor feels himself travelled. Moreover, he has become acquainted, however slightly, with the great western country, of which we have all heard so much. "He has been on its threshold, having traversed the desert, and beheld, not without surprise, broad rolling downs stretching away to the horizon, with an open landscape, sparsely mottled with trees, the whole presenting a vivid contrast to the dense scrub and scanty herbage of some of the more easterly districts. He has, in a word, seen an oasis In the 'Sahara' -one which, to him, has a beginning, but is boundless on the western side. Besides this, if the visit has been made during Show week, he has come more, fully to appreciate the great pastoral interest, as represented in the persons of men of intelligence and energy -the pioneers of the, colonisation, the promoters of commerce.'

The article went on to describe the township, one year after the posting of Annie's letter, as one of 'neat weatherboard structures, painted, and comprising four stores, three hotels, and three butchers' shops, with a post office, bank, court house, and surgery'. By then a government school had also opened. My research found that the post office had opened only a few years before Annie's letter had been posted. It was strange to think that Annie and Bessie must have been early users of the new postal service in what appeared to be a remote but thriving and growing town.

Then I found the census figures. Aramac's fortunes as the

chief town of the region changed when the main railway line heading west bypassed the town. Today the town was more like three hundred residents, perhaps even less. I wondered what had happened to the three hotels and three butchers' shops, the surgery and the hospital. What would the town be like today?

While the history of European occupation was painted in glowing colours I also discover a dark side. Relations between the new arrivals and the old occupants were fraught. Attacks on whites were followed by reprisals, and the guns were much more destructive than spears. After one attack where a travelling jeweller, and his wife and child, had been murdered by some of the indigenous population reprisals had once again occurred and one tribe sought refuge in the country of another tribe. This resulted in tribal warfare between the two indigenous groups over occupancy of land, with more deaths resulting.

Perhaps the most surprising claim to fame I discovered in my search for Aramac was the story of the white bull from Bowen Downs. The bull and some other cattle were stolen in this far distant part of Western Queensland and the herd driven overland to South Australia to be sold. However, the bull was recognized in South Australia and the thieves apprehended. It was like some extravagant story from the wild west of America.

My granddaughter had said "Google Aramac" and I had. Of course the ever useful Wikipedia came up, but was it trustworthy? I'd heard stories of people putting false information on the site, but who would do that in this case? I doubted a rival town or village would seek to belittle its neighbour. Maybe someone with a grudge against the town could put disparaging remarks on line, but that seemed unlikely from what I'd read. Short of visiting the town to check what I'd found online the information appeared true. I could picture Annie sending a letter to her 'everlasting friend' hoping the postmaster would pass it on to Bessie. Why had they separated? I still didn't know. Was it something to do with the aboriginal violence? Then again I had found no mention of a fire. Perhaps there was more to find. I suspected, unconsciously, that I had hoped to find some old secret or scandal but nothing was obvious.

I had not expected to learn of the fate of a jeweller and his family as they travelled through the outback regions of Queensland in the mid to late eighteen hundreds. Nor had I expected to read of a thriving growing town so far inland from the coast. Australian history to me was Captain Cook and the First Fleet. Sydney and convicts. I'd read of the early explorers, Blaxland, Wentworth and Lawson in 1813 crossing the Blue Mountains, and of Charles Sturt finding the Murray River and, of course, of Burke and Wills and their disastrous travels, but there my knowledge of explorers ended. I knew of the Gold Rushes but had never considered the spread of enterprise across the land as the country was opened up to graze sheep and cattle. Yet Aramac was an established township, centre of a thriving region just fifty-six years after the Blue Mountains had first been crossed by Europeans.

Aramac was a long way from Melbourne and I knew no one anywhere near the town. Until I found it on a map I hadn't even known where it was apart from somewhere in Queensland. I decided I would make more enquiries. Maybe I would find something that would be linked to Bessie, or Annie, but first I would have another try with my brother and sister, then I had a special date with my 'precious one'.

8 Tea and Scones

At our second gathering I took care to guide the subject to our grandparents. Grannie J had lived to the good age of seventy-eight.   Our memories were of a woman, rather severe with her daughter, but warm to us, her grandchildren, and even more so to her great-grandchildren.   We had indistinct and vague memories of visiting her house before she had come to live with our mother, especially John who remembered being allowed to play with an old box of painted lead soldiers she kept in a hall cupboard. As little girls we used to love trawling through a big drawer full of old clothes and playing dress-ups, usually tripping over the long skirts and dresses that tangled beneath our feet. In her later years we mostly remembered her seated in her chair, either on the veranda or placed in a sunny position in the back garden, or in her room which had a musty smell of age and old perfume,. By that time we were all too busy with our own lives to spend much time with Grannie J.

It was Margaret who recalled, "She was born just before the start of the First World War. I remember seeing the year of her birth on the order of service for her funeral. She died in nineteen ninety-two." The year of birth we had never considered but the birth date we knew. Our mother always had us prepare a special handmade card for Grannie J. Margaret continued.   "I'm sure her husband's Christian names were Stanley Alfred. He was Stanley Alfred Palmer and he was a soldier. I think he died in the Second World War. I'll find the old order of service. I know I put it away somewhere. It might give more details."

My Grannie J would have had a hard life. Born before a war, then a depression, and then another war which claimed her husband. Raising a child alone. It wouldn't have been easy. None of us had memories of her husband who had died before we were born; before even our mother had met our father.

"What about brothers and sisters? Did she have any? Did she have any other children?" John asked.

"I don't know. I never heard her speak of any." Nor had John or Margaret. Much of Grannie J's life had disappeared. All we could recall of her earlier years was an old lady living alone in a tiny weatherboard house until she had come to live with her daughter, our mother.

It was Margaret who answered. "Well, she had our mother. Grannie J would have been twenty-five when the war broke out. Nan was born in nineteen thirty-four...so she must have married young. She could've had other children before the war started."

"But we've never heard of any. I'm sure Nan would have spoken of brothers and sisters." John was right. None of us had ever heard our mother speak of any other family. Only the once she had said something about how hard it was to lose a child. We'd thought she was talking about a friend. Perhaps she was speaking about her mother. We were sure she was not speaking about herself.

"It must have been hard bringing up our mum as a single parent."

"I'm sure there would have been some sort of government support for a war widow but I doubt it would have been very much. I remember when we visited her there was always a clothesline full of washing and baskets of ironing. I drooled over the beautiful white blouses and the gorgeous underwear hanging on the clothesline with its two wires running from the arms on each post. Yet I never remember her wearing such beautiful blouses. Hers were much more basic and simple."

Ever practical John provided the answer. "I suspect she took in laundry to support herself and our mum. It would make sense. She could work from home, and I'm sure her mother would have made sure she had the ability. Life on a pension wouldn't have been easy"

"What about her parents?" We all shook our heads. Grannie J had appeared from nowhere with no history.

"She was living in Wodonga when our mum met Dad. I'm not sure when she moved to Melbourne."

I could add a little to Margaret's knowledge. I had vague memories of my first visit to a tall, straight woman that I was told was my grandmother. "I think I was about five when I was first taken to meet her at the cottage in Port Melbourne. So it would have been about nineteen fifty-seven. I guess that was when she moved from Wodonga."

It was John again who worked out the dates. "Grannie J would have been about forty-three and Mum would have been twenty-three and married, around five years. You were born in fifty-two weren't you Liz?"

"So you think Grannie J came from Wodonga to Melbourne to be closer to her daughter?"

"Seems probable, but where did she meet our grandfather? Was he a Wodonga boy, or did they move there from somewhere else? It would seem that she was living there after the war when Mum met Dad. Perhaps they had been living there when he enlisted? On the other hand I suspect our father was probably a local who didn't like milking cows on cold mornings. When he had the chance he left for the big city. He must have met Mum on a return to the region to visit his family. The military records might help and it may be possible to track down his family in Wodonga."

I was the one who got the job of searching Births, Deaths and Marriages for Grannie J, her husband and our father. Margaret would try the military records of our dad and our unknown grandfather, and John would put his kids to work on searching old newspapers on Trove.

Where to start? I decided to start with Grannie J. We already knew of her death so I would try marriage. I really wanted to find out something about her unknown husband. When I was a small child a nasty girl in my class at school had taunted me for not having enough grandparents. I knew I should have four but I only had one. She would taunt me with the chant, "Your grans must be in jail." I knew it couldn't be right. My family was not like that, yet I couldn't face my parents and ask them. That would be too dreadful. I ignored her chants but it took years for the worry and suspicion to fade.

My first search was the website of the State Library of Victoria. After trawling through page after page but not finding, or really knowing, what I was seeking and becoming more frustrated and confused, I decided that I would visit the Library and take up the invitation to speak to a librarian who could assist my search.

It was a short tram ride into the city to the big building occupying a whole city block in Swanston Street. The magnificent portico gave the impression you were entering some ancient classical seat of learning. I certainly had that feeling as I entered the building. The library was already packed with visitors reading magazines and newspapers, students doing research, and others on computers or microfiche readers. I was amazed to find that in a library, which to me was about books, almost every person had a computer open in front of them or beside them.

I found the enquiry desk for the family history and newspapers at the rear of the large circular room. In response to my enquiries about marriage records I was advised to try an online search. I typed in the address for Victorian BDMs and searched for 'Jessie Palmer', but nothing came up. Did I have the correct name? I tried Jessica Palmer, Jessie MacGregor, Jessica MacGregor, McGregor J. Nothing. I tried my mother, Jean Palmer. At last I had a result. Jean Elizabeth Palmer married Francis Finlay in Wodonga , January 23, 1952. Her parents were Stanley Alfred Palmer and Jessie Palmer. I returned to my helpful librarian with my puzzle. She explained the records I was searching were only for Victoria. Perhaps Jessie was married in another state, or perhaps the marriage was not registered. I admired her discretion regarding marriage. Modern society would certainly provide challenges for future genealogists searching out a family history. With the decline in marriage, and the increase in children born to undocumented partnerships, family trees could have some very tangled branches. It brought to mind the comment of a friend whose elderly father had commenced a relationship with an equally elderly lady. It would certainly not add a new branch to the family tree but she wondered if she should record it as a leafless twig. At least births and deaths would still be recorded and they may hold some answers. I decided births would be my next search but if Grannie J's marriage was not in Victoria then perhaps I would need to look elsewhere. Should it be Queensland? Where would I find those records? Since I had a letter posted in Warren, New South Wales, perhaps I should try that state? I decided to quit for a coffee and take a break. I found the coffee shop attached to the library and sat down to review what I had found or not found. It was not proving quite as simple as I had expected.

I next decided to try deaths. I knew Grannie J had died in Melbourne. I should find that record. This time I was successful and I found more than I had expected. The names of her parents, including her mother's maiden name, her father's occupation, plus her place of birth. I'd definitely started looking in the wrong place.

Births, deaths and marriages. I was dealing with history. Yet all those people had once been alive. They had loved and married with dreams of a happy future. They had faced births with anticipation and hope, and perhaps with a sense of trepidation and fear if things went wrong. And finally they had faced death, sometimes like the two soldiers during the war knowing it could occur at any moment, at other times facing the inevitable in old age. Like those alive today they had laughed and cried, dreamt and feared. Those thoughts suddenly changed the way I felt about them. For me they were no longer dead but alive, around me, and part of me.

It was late in the evening a week later when my sister phoned. I could tell by her voice she was excited. She was still working on Grannie J's husband but was full of news about our father. Her search on the website of the Australian War Memorial had led her to the National Archives where she had unearthed our father's war record. He had enlisted at Wodonga at nineteen years of age. His occupation was shown as labourer and after training he was sent to New Guinea.

"Was he on the Kokoda Track march?" I asked.

"No. That was when the Australian forces were retreating from the Japanese invasion of New Guinea. He had joined up, but by the time he did his training and was sent overseas it was after the Battle of the Coral Sea, and the tide of war had turned and it was the Japanese who were withdrawing. Our dad was involved in the retaking of Lae."

I had been puzzled by John's story of Dad telling him about the shelling of villages and gardens. I'd thought of Europe and it hadn't really made sense to me, but of course villages and food gardens made sense for New Guinea. After Lae his division had returned to Australia for a break, but then were sent to Borneo towards the end of the war. Eventually he came home and was demobbed. That must have been when he moved to Melbourne. Margaret had also found that he had an older brother who was in the army as well. He had died before dad joined up. "At his age Dad must have had permission from his parents to join up. If you were under twenty-one you needed parental permission."

I thought of our father. Only a boy, the same age as my granddaughter, joining the army to fight a war that was coming closer and closer to his country, and of his parents giving him permission to join knowing what could so easily happen to him. I was grateful that I had never been in that position, but then there was Korea and Vietnam, and Malaya, and now Afghanistan and the Middle East. It seems there is always a war.

"I found out more."

I could tell from the sound of Margaret's voice she had something interesting to tell me.

"I decided to check the phone book for Wodonga to see if I could find any Finlays. My first call was no help. The second I spoke to a woman but they had just moved to Wodonga from Sydney. My third call hit pay-dirt. I found a cousin! He was the son of Dad's next older brother, Fred. There were six brothers and sisters. Dad was the youngest. Cousin Alan and his sister still live in Wodonga, the rest of the family have moved away and he has lost track of some of them. Our father's parents are buried in the Wodonga cemetery. Our grandfather died the year Dad married Mum, our grandmother had died a year earlier. They were English migrants, Bert and Mary Finlay. They came out after the First World War and got a job on a local farm. Later Granddad became a share-farmer, milking cows on the farm. Apparently it was a tough life during the depression. The kids were expected to work at whatever they could find, if they could find anything. Money was scarce but they had lots of milk, vegetables from their garden and rabbits were plentiful on the river flats. I guess that explains Dad not eating the meal of casseroled rabbit that Mum made for him. Alan said our grandfather had quite a temper, and he liked a drink, or more than one according to Alan. I got the impression he could get aggressive. It was not a happy house."

I'd always loved my father and I held him in high respect. Margaret's news had explained so much. He'd always been quiet and caring. Perhaps he wanted a family unlike the one he had grown up in. It explained his desire, his need, for security and a regular wage. Mum had spoken about how important buying a house had been to him, and how he wanted to have a home for his wife when he married. I also remembered his concern when my brother and his mates went through a stage of Friday night beer drinking sessions. It explained his reticence about his family, and why he had never shared them with his children and why we had never known them. With Margaret's news so much of our father's character could be understood. I loved him even more.

"I also asked if he knew if our grandparents had ever had any connections to Queensland and he told me he doubted that they had been further north than across the Murray River to Albury. So I guess that counts out our father's side of the family for Annie and Bessie."

We had still not found any reason for the old letter to be a treasured possession of our mother, yet I was growing more and more convinced that the answer was almost within reach. I also had a sense of trepidation that I would not like the answer. Then my phone rang again.

9 Discoveries

It was Tony. "Are you OK? I've been trying to get you for the last hour and the phone's always engaged. Is everything alright?"

I suddenly remembered. I was supposed to phone Tony and confirm a date. He'd heard of a new tiny restaurant in Brunswick and had invited me to go there for lunch with him. There had been some uncertainty about what days each of us were free. I didn't have my diary with me at the time and I knew I had some commitments but wasn't sure of which days. I'd promised to phone him and confirm but in the hunt for my family I had forgotten all about it. I apologised and we tried to find a suitable day for lunch or dinner. Unfortunately it was soon obvious that it wasn't going happen until my return from Sydney. I went to bed that night still thinking of my father, and how much the things he had never discussed with his children had affected his life. But then, my family's history was the past, and Tony was the present.

My brother called me the next day.

"I've got some news. I put the kids to work on the family history. It's a bit hard keeping Ben on the job. All he wants to do is discover a bushranger in the family. I think he reckons because we called him Ben we must be secretly related to Ben Hall the bushranger. I'm sure he would have preferred it if we had called him Ned. Failing that a convict or two would do. Ally is a bit more reliable. She's been searching old newspapers on Trove. The only problem is you need to know names or places so she hasn't found anything. Anyway, Ben was using Ancestry.com at the local library and found a match for a Jessie MacGregor, Grannie J. She married a Stanley Palmer and the dates seem to fit from what I remember. Her parents were Sidney MacGregor and Jeannie MacGregor, and her father's mother was an Annie. It looks like I will have to take you girls out to dinner. I'm still hoping Bessie will turn out to be family. I was looking forward to going to one of those fancy coffee places your friend Tony rabbits on about. I can never work out what to order. I get lost with lattes and macchiatos and cremas and shots and mochas. Even when I just ask for a cup of tea they want to know if I want this one or that one."

My brother had inherited my parent's taste in good simple food. Like them, and many of their generation, he was a meat and three veg person. Steak made a meal great, and seafood was a treat for special occasions. While I enjoyed my outings with Tony, discovering new restaurants and different styles of food, I lacked his passion for the latest 'in' flavours. Still, under his guidance I had learnt a great deal. I was much more knowledgeable about food, and I had learnt to pick the difference between Arabica and Robusta coffee beans. While I especially loved the aroma of freshly ground and brewing coffee, I had no interest in whether the beans were organic or free trade, or came from Guatemala or Ethiopia. For Tony, the more obscure the bean the more interesting they became.

"Anyway that's all Ben has found out so far. It's hard to

keep my boy on the job; he'd rather be out with his mates. Without a convict or a bushranger it's not very exciting. You don't think we would have one, do you?"

I'd never heard mention of a convict or bushranger in the family but then I suspected my mother and grandmother would have kept such information very secret. These days, to have a convict ancestor in the family is almost a badge of honour, but for them it would have been a badge of shame. Having a bushranger in the family would be like having a bank robber or drug dealer in the family. Thinking about it, these days, from all the problems we see on television, there must be lots of families with drug dealers among their kin. A 'gentleman bushranger' might appeal to some romantics, but they were just robbers, and I was sure I would not appreciate being robbed, any more than I would having my house burgled.

For me convicts were a bit different. It was hard times in Britain and for some stealing was the only way to survive. For others it was a trade, just as we have thieves and fraudsters among us today. At least Australia was spared from the worst of humanity: the murderers and rapists. Britain hanged them. Then, there were those driven to political protest by the social conditions of the time and who incurred the full wrath of the established legal system. They only made up a small percentage of the convict arrivals but for them I had to admit some compassion. Still I had no knowledge of any sort of convict in the family tree. "I don't know of any convict forebears. Do you know of any, John?"

"No. Nobody has ever mentioned it. I don't even know when our family came to Australia. Do you know when the last convicts arrived?"

John's question made me realise how poor my knowledge of Australian history was. I knew of the First Fleet and the convict settlements in Tasmania and Norfolk Island. Convicts had been sent to Moreton Bay in Queensland, but I had always just thought of those early days in the late seventeen hundreds. I had no idea when the last convict arrived. Even less, the date the last convict, or ex-convict had died in Australia.

I decided to put my granddaughter to work on improving my knowledge of Australian history. I knew she had even less knowledge than I, and I thought it would do us both some good, besides she was much more familiar with computers than me. She soon came back with some answers. Sydney had been the first penal settlement, then Norfolk Island. Queensland had first received convicts at Moreton Bay, now Brisbane, in 1824, but had ceased receiving convicts fifteen years later. Transportation had ceased to Sydney in 1840. Tasmania had continued as a penal settlement until 1853 and the last convict ship to arrive in Australia was to Western Australia in 1868. Sass had found a newspaper article about a man called Samuel Speed who had arrived at the Swan River settlement in 1864 as a twenty-five year old. He'd been sentenced to seven years for arson. He was still alive in an Old Men's Home in Perth in 1938. He was considered to be the last convict transported to Australia still alive.

I thought it unlikely that a convict would move from Western Australia or Tasmania to Warren or Aramac, although a young convict sent out to Brisbane or Sydney at fifteen years of age, and some were only that age on arrival, would be a man or woman of forty-nine by the time Annie's letter was posted. It could be possible for the two women to have been convicts, but it seemed unlikely. I just had a feeling the letter was between two young women, not middle-aged women. There was no reason for my belief but that was how I felt. Still, without knowing their ages or the dates of their arrivals it was impossible to be sure. I decided to encourage my niece and granddaughter to continue their hunt.

We now had an Annie. Grannie J's father's mother: Annie MacGregor. But what was her story? What was her maiden name and where was she born? Where had she lived and why didn't I find her in my search at the library? Each answer led to another puzzle. I waited for Ben's email to arrive with the details.

The details I already knew about my parents, plus the little I knew of Grannie J, fitted the information in Ben's email. The dates of death and birth seemed to match. I had been warned by a friend who had been researching her family for many years to take great care with the information discovered. It was very easy to find a person with the name you were seeking and whose information was close to what you expected and then decide they were your ancestor—but there could be a lot of Bill Smiths, or Annie MacGregors, and it was easy to side track to a lineage that was not related to you. She warned me to check, and cross check, before taking any record as accurate.

Unfortunately Ben's email only gave me a little more information. What was interesting was Grannie J was shown as having three children. I knew of my mother but the records showed she had a brother five years younger than her. I knew nothing of this uncle. I had never heard my mother or grandmother speak of him. Was this a family secret? But sadder, I found Grannie J and her husband had lost a son at two years of age. Suddenly the references to the sadness of loss made sense.

I returned to my searches of Births, Death and Marriages, but I could get no further than the information I had previously discovered. Even with the dates Ben had supplied my searches still came up empty once I reached Grannie J and her husband.

We had found an Annie. It seemed probable she was the Annie who had written the letter. But there was no sign of Bessie.

Still, as a genealogist I had made a little progress in finding some of my family. As a detective I'd not discovered any secrets or scandals. No convicts. No bushrangers, but I had found an uncle I never knew I had, and a young child whose death was never discussed.

I was still puzzled by the letter in the cardboard box. Annie and Bessie must have a story. I couldn't explain why, but for some reason I was sure it was important to me. I would have to search for the answer in different places, but that would have to wait until my return from Sydney.

10 Sydney

Although I'd lived all my life in Melbourne I'd often been to Sydney. If the sun was shining I always felt a thrill at flying in over the water; hopefully seeing the harbour spread out beneath the aircraft. If I was lucky the flight would take us directly over the harbour and I would see the Bridge, the tall city buildings, and the boats moving around on the blue waters below us. When my husband was alive and he had business meetings or conferences we would have a good vantage point at the front of the aircraft. After his death and I had to pay for the ticket with my own money I economised and moved further back in the plane. Nowadays the wing often interfered with my view. Usually we had stayed in hotels in the centre of the city or somewhere on the North Shore close to his meetings. Occasionally we'd travelled to Sydney for pleasure, perhaps a stage show or a concert, sometimes just as tourists. I had really enjoyed our visits.

These days I was seeing another Sydney. My son had moved there for his work but it was far from the harbour and beaches that I had known. I soon discovered a very different city on my travels west to his home. It was only after he and his wife had purchased a house near Parramatta that I realised how much of Sydney was far away from the beaches and harbour that we would see on television. It was a different world.

The reason for this trip was a christening. When my son, Sam, and Tayla, made the decision to live together I had accepted the arrangement without any qualms. After all it was the usual way of the world these days and I was pleased he had finally settled on Tayla. She was a lovely, vibrant, sensible girl, unlike a few of his earlier girlfriends, and before they had their first child they had decided to marry. That was a relief to Matt and me. Even though times had changed from our parents' day, and some of our friends had lived together for years, we were both conservative and felt the order should be dating, engagement, marriage then children. These days it seemed that divorce often came after children and before marriage—well an irrevocable separation as divorce required a marriage that often never happened.

Sam's work rarely took him to the CBD. The clients of his legal practice were businesses based in the far western reaches of the city. I had seen and heard terrible stories of life and housing in the west and had visions of him representing clients in court on various drug and violence charges. I'd imagined him fronting the police watch-house to arrange bail for another aggressive, bedraggled layabout picked up outside a pub or nightclub on Saturday night. Fortunately these stories seemed as far from my son's life as the harbour. His practice was corporate work advising companies on compliance with the myriad laws that they needed to meet. He and Tayla had a network of friends and business associates that were great company. Already their son, Matthew, was attending a private school and from my impressions at a school concert the education was excellent. I did pick up murmurs from their friends that certain areas were best avoided and some suburbs were not to be considered when looking for a home. However other areas were highly sought after. Western Sydney was now the geographic centre of population for Greater Sydney and far more diverse than the images often shown on television. Sam had also mentioned that there were a few local enterprises he did not wish to work with. Fortunately they didn't want to work with him as his practice had a reputation for integrity, a quality that did not fit their business methods.

While I was surprised, I was pleased that they had decided to have both boys christened. True there was an age difference, Mathew was already seven and James was only fifteen months but at least it was happening. I realised I was becoming more conservative as I became older. It brought back to me Sass's remark about sex the afternoon she and her mother had taken me to the airport.

I had been puzzled by the choice of name for the baby. James Sidney. Both were good old-fashioned solid names. I despaired at some of the names chosen by loving parents at my grandchildren's classes. While certainly creative and original, maybe even cute for a small child, I was sure they could become a burden on an adult. Hopefully some would be replaced by nicknames, or perhaps the child would just decide they wanted to be called something less peculiar. It certainly complicated the work of teachers trying to get the correct spelling for the class roles.

Now I had two James in the family with both my children naming sons James. It wouldn't be a problem really. Meg's James had always been a favourite name she loved, and Sam's James was named after his wife's grandfather. I had puzzled over the name Sidney and asked Sam about it. It was a name he had once heard his grandmother mention. She had told him a story about an uncle out bush that she hadn't seen for years. He had liked the name and decided to give it to his second son. My mother had never mentioned her Uncle Sidney to me.

"I have a surprise for you Mum. I've found your great uncle, James Sidney. I've asked him to the christening. It happened by chance. I was out in Bathurst and talking with a lady from an aged care home, the home is a client. It was after you sent me the family tree with Grannie J's parents on it. There was a name that I recognised. I mentioned it to the manager who took me to meet this old man. I asked if he knew a Jessie MacGregor. That's Grannie J. Apparently he is Grannie J's younger brother."

I had seen a James Sidney MacGregor on the family tree that John's son had discovered but after just burying my mother and memories of my grandmother's death so many years ago I had not thought of Grannie J having a living sibling. We had certainly lost sight of that side of the family.

The christening service had taken place without any tears or dramas, either from one small child being splashed with water or his older brother running off at an inappropriate moment. It was a moving service in the beautiful old church. I loved the square sandstone brick towers dating back to the earliest days of the settlement of the colony and the development of Parramatta. Over the years many changes and additions had been made to the church, but the twin towers had remained, even as a new Norman style church reappeared between them.

After the service we had moved to the garden of my son's house. It was a split level cream brick building like many others in the neighbourhood. The driveway ran down to a double garage but what had appealed to Sam and Tayla was the big backyard for the children and the location close to a school that had a good reputation. In Sydney I knew that the location had made the house a costly purchase and it involved a sacrifice on Sam and Tayla's part.

Tayla and her sisters had laid out a spread on a long table and arranged chairs round the patio and pool for the luncheon guests. Finally Sam had the opportunity to introduce me to my Great Uncle James. Some aged people become heavier with age, others go the other way and become frailer and slighter. Great Uncle James was the latter, and I could see the family resemblance to his sister. He was a tall thin man, totally bald, and standing with a slight stoop. He was accompanied by a young woman. After Sam had introduced me to him he introduced his granddaughter, Colleen. He had asked her to bring him to meet some of the family, and he would stay with her before returning to Bathurst. "It's nice to be with some young people for a change, all the residents are so old."

Grannie J has been seventy-eight when she had died. That was over twenty years ago. I decided that the old man must be at least ninety.

"I think Grandad needs to sit. His knees are not so good."

We found three chairs and formed a circle. I thought that this might be the last opportunity I would have to find out more about my family.

"I know a little about your sister but she rarely spoke of her family. I guess when I was young I was not very interested and then I became involved with my own children and never paid much attention to the past. She always seemed a rather severe lady, although she was good to me."

"Jessie always was. She was the oldest. She used to be very strict with me and Andy. We were younger than her you see. She was ten years older than me and fifteen years older than Andy. Mum was often sick so Jessie sort of brought us up. Andy was just a wee lad when our mum died. I guess Jessie thought we were bits of tearaways. Perhaps we were."

"Your mother was Jeannie?"

"Yes."

"And was her mother Annie?"

"Yes. Why do you ask?"

"My mother had an old letter from an Annie. I thought it might be your grandmother."

"My grandmother was Annie. My father was Sid, like me. My grandfather was Rohan. It's nice to see the young will grow up with an old family name."

"What do you know about your grandmother?"

"I never knew my grandmother. Her name was Annie. I think she died quite young. Had dad, and I think there was another baby. Don't really know. There was never much talk about it."

"What about a Bessie?"

"Bessie? No don't know about that. Who was she?"

I explained the letter we had found in my mother's little box of treasures.

"No, means nothing to me. I don't remember her."

We chatted on and I learnt of other distant relatives

scattered throughout New South Wales and Sydney. My great uncle would spend two nights in Sydney with his granddaughter before returning to his room in an aged care village in Bathurst. We then parted, me to circulate with my son's friends and Tayla's family. Great Uncle James to remain in his chair and chat to those who visited him.

Most of the people attending the celebration were friends of Sam and Tayla. I was the only one from Sam's family present but Tayla's sisters, her parents and two of her aunties had come to the party. One I knew from my school days. Jane was a year younger than me and had been in a class behind me. We hadn't been close at school but sharing a link through Sam and Tayla we had become friends until she had left Melbourne and moved to Noosa. We hadn't seen each other for a number of years but immediately fell into old ways.

Like me her husband had died: hers with a long and painful condition. For both of us our lives had changed. I wasn't sure which would be worse. To live with the knowledge of the inevitable death from a prolonged illness, or the unexpected phone call on a fine sunny day. Each of us had had to make our lives anew without our partner. She had decided to make a complete break and move to Noosa. With an aging mother, a daughter, and two grand-children close by I had decided to remain in Melbourne. Now with my mother gone I was wondering about my decision.

"Why don't you come up for a week? The weather is beautiful. There are some good restaurants. There's a lovely walk through the park and I'm sure we will have a great time."

I passed over the invitation with a, "Sounds great. Maybe, one day."

Guests were already leaving when Colleen came over to me.

"Grandad wants to talk some more with you. He thinks he has remembered something about Bessie. He sent me over to ask you to smoko tomorrow morning. Can you come? He seems very keen to tell you something."

I wrote down the address Colleen gave me. In Great Uncle James I'd found living confirmation I had an Annie in my family, and it was very likely she was the Annie who had written the letter. However she was still just a name, a label, I'd not found anything to lead me to the life of a real person. Perhaps tomorrow I would also learn about the mysterious Bessie. At the very least I would find out more about my distant family and what I realised was my largely unknown background.

11 Family News

The address was in a newish housing estate. All the houses looked as if they had been built at the same time. Perhaps they had: a job lot by a developer. Each house had a large double garage door facing the street. In front of it a paved parking area could hold another two cars, provided you didn't mind obstructing the footpath. A short garden path led to the front door. The houses spread out over the tiny blocks so their eaves almost touched the neighbouring houses. There was not one large tree or any shade in the street. It made me realise how fortunate I was to live in an old established suburb with large spreading shady trees. Even the falling leaves that I complained about each autumn were a small price to pay for the green the trees brought to my life in spring and summer.

Tayla dropped me off at number one twenty-eight with a promise to return on my phone call. I pressed the button on the doorbell and heard the patter of a dog's feet and then Colleen opened the door. "Hello. Come on in. Grandad is ready and waiting to talk with you. I haven't seen him so excited for years. I think he is pleased someone actually wants to hear his stories."

Great Uncle James was already sitting at a table over which was spread a pretty floral cloth. Colleen and I joined him

"Would you like a cup of tea? Gramps likes tea but I can do coffee."

"Tea would be fine, thank you."

"I'll make a pot."

That was another thing that had changed in Australia. When I was a child tea was the drink of choice. I remembered the signs I had often seen, usually beside a railway line, for Robur and Bushells, and Lan Choo Teas. When did coffee replace tea as the drink of choice? Was it the arrival of Greek and Italian migrants with their Mediterranean food that replaced the traditional English pot of tea?

"You mentioned Bessie. It didn't seem familiar but it has come back. I'm an old man, my memories a bit vague sometimes. You know when you get old it doesn't work so fast. Like I said I didn't know my Mum much but I remember hearing Dad occasionally talk with his old mates. They were all bushies that lot. I remember hearing him say 'poor Bessie'. Only ever said it when he was with the old fellas, and even then I only heard it a few times. I don't know who 'poor Bessie' was or why she was 'poor', but they would all go glum like and say things like 'it was so sad'. Lived to be an old lady somewhere in the country. They thought life had treated her harshly. I don't know if she was a relation or not. Perhaps she was me Mum's friend. Although from the way they spoke I thought she must have been older."

"What do you remember of your mother, Uncle James?"

"Not very much. She died when I was young. I was only a little tacker. It was my sister, Jessie, who brought me up really. Dad was always at work."

"How old would Jessie have been when your mother died?"

"She was ten, almost eleven years older than me. I think she was about seventeen when mum died."

"Do you remember anything about your mother?"

"Not much, she always seemed to be in bed. I guess she must have been sick with somethin'. I don't think I was ever told what it was. Dad didn't like to talk about Mum. He would get very quiet and upset. I guess he really missed her. Times were tough then."

"What about your grandparents? Do you remember much of them?"

"No, not much. On my mother's side they were English. Her dad had come out from England on his own as a young lad. He married an English girl already here but I never knew them. Only their names and listening to my mum talk. On my father's side I only saw my grandad a couple of times. He was somewhere out west. He worked on sheep stations until he got old. Then I think he lived in Bourke. I never knew my grannie, his wife. They said she'd died before I was born. I only knew her name. It was Annie. Annie McDonald, she was a Scot. She married my grandad. So she became Annie MacGregor."

Whilst Great Uncle James was a living connection to 'Annie', it didn't look as if it would take me much further in my search to discover what Annie's life had been like. "Where did you grow up?"

"I first remember living in Moree. I must have been a

little kid at the time. Dad had a job with the railway and we lived there for a long time. He was a fettler on the tracks. He lived there all his life. Well since us kids were born. Never left. I left, I went working on stations. Anything I could find. In the woolsheds, fencing. I never became a shearer though, just could never get me count up. I was a shed hand and worked on the wool table. We've still got relatives out that way. More me dad's family and Andy's. We only had Jessie and me and Andy."

"Who's Andy?"

"He was me younger brother. He died about ten years ago."

"But you now live in Bathurst according to my son."

"Yes. Moved there when me and Mary had kids. Working around sheds is hard on the wife and kids so I got a job with the council. Mostly road work."

What about your sister, Jessie, she was my grandmother. We used to call her Grannie J."

"She got a boy-friend and got married. She was pretty young. Me and Andy used to live with her when our dad was away. He'd be away in a camp on the line. Her daughter was only a bit younger than me. Reckon she would have been about ten years younger than me. Then when Dad got a permanent job in town and we were old enough, she and her husband moved. They went down south to Victoria somewhere. I sort of lost touch. We weren't great letter writers or that. I do remember her little girl. She was a lively little kid. My sister always had her looking smart."

"Her daughter was my mother, Jean. Jean Palmer until she married my father Frank Finlay. My mother had two younger brothers. I've only just found out one died at a very young age. The other I never knew. I believe he died in the late nineties. My mum had three children, me, my brother John, and my sister, Margaret.

"I don't know anything about Jessie's family. Once she moved we sort of lost touch."

I passed on news of his sister to her brother. What little I knew of her time in Wodonga, the death of her husband in the war, and her move to Melbourne and eventually living with her daughter. "Do you remember anything more of your grandmother Annie?"

"Like I said, nothing much. I think she died about the turn of the century. The last one, not this one. I reckon she would have been a reasonable age. I think originally she had been somewhere out west or south of Moree. In the bush. Don't know any more than that."

"Could she have lived in Warren?"

"Warren's out west, but I don't know."

It seemed I was not going to find any more answers to the story of my great great grandmother from Great Uncle James. I was still amazed by the overlap of generations. I had never expected that, but a late child in one generation, and a young mother in the next, could certainly cause an overlap. Great Uncle James was living proof.

Over a second pot of tea we chatted until Colleen brought out lunch. The conversation continued with stories of his life in the bush in the forties and fifties. I think he quite relished his new-found position in the family. Jim, he'd asked me to stop the 'Great Uncle' bit and call him Jim like his friends, was full of stories. I told him of my side of the family about which he had no knowledge, and he told me of his children and their partners and kids. Then the family of his brother Andy with whom he had kept in touch. "One of them is claiming she is Aboriginal. Comes from her great-grandmother. I know our family background. There was some Aboriginal blood. Andy did marry a woman whose family was part aboriginal. She was a good sort that one. Hard worker, good wife. Probably better than Andy deserved. He was a bit of a problem. He gave her a hard life. She deserved better. Still this young girl reckons she's Aboriginal. I reckon she's one-sixteenth. That makes her fifteen-sixteenth white. I'm darker than she is."

"Is there any Aboriginal blood in you?"

"Nah. Nothing. Not in my parents and it's not likely to be on my mother's side. I told you they was English. Never any mention of it in my dad's side either. They were Scots. Doesn't look it to me."

It was late afternoon when I phoned Tayla to come and collect me. Jim the Great was looking tired but happy to have had a chat. The day had given me lots more information about my family. While much was not of the branch that led directly to me, at last I had confirmation from a living relative that traced me back to Annie and her husband. While I had many stories about the extended family there still remained a gap. I could place Sid and his wife, the mother of Grannie J, in Moree, but Annie and her husband's story remained missing. All I had learnt was they were somewhere out west. Perhaps beyond the back of Bourke on a sheep station. Where were they after Annie had posted her letter, and what was the connection to Bessie in Aramac? I still didn't know. My mind was rushing, trying to remember all that I had heard, and hoping I would make sense of the scribbled notes I had written. It did perhaps explain the lack of success in some of my searches for births, deaths and marriages. I may have been looking in the wrong state records. Then there was still the problem of the next step. How could I find out more about the mysterious Annie? Already I was planning how to tackle that problem when I returned to Melbourne.

12 Home in Melbourne

Tony was standing at the gate as I exited the air-bridge and entered the terminal. I had planned to catch the SkyBus into Southern Cross Station and then take a taxi across the Yarra River to my apartment a few minutes from the bus terminal. However in replying to a text from Tony inviting me to a film festival in July I'd told him of my travel plans, and he had then arranged to meet my flight from Sydney. It was a kind offer, and I was looking forward to seeing him again. But I had a niggling irritation that he was taking over my decisions.

As we were driving the freeway into the city the image came to my mind of a spinning multi-coloured vortex that descended into a dark black hole. Tony, I could imagine as the brightly coloured force spinning madly around me, but what was the dark hole that the colours spun into and disappeared. It was an unsettling thought. Thinking about colours I wondered what colours I would assign to my family. Compared to Tony we would be pastels. My granddaughter I thought was pink. No, she was more a darker red, but with a pink shading. My son was blue, a solid mid-blue, neither too dark nor too pale. My daughter was more difficult. I thought yellow or orange but neither seemed to really fit her. My parents were green. My father, a dark reliable green, and my mother a lighter shade with a touch of orange or yellow. Matt was silver. Solid, reliable, and precious. I had no doubts about him.

Coming closer to my home thoughts of what colour to paint my family were replaced by another thought. I'd met many of Tony's family on my visit to Bright. There had been brothers and sisters, cousins, aunties, uncles and all their children. It was obvious that family stories were shared; sometimes loudly and excitedly. In the conversation around the tables old stories of earlier generations were passed along to the younger. While I thought I was close to my parents, I had come to realise how little I, and my brother and sister, really knew of theirs lives, let alone the lives of our grandparents. Yet their past and their younger years had moulded them, and in turn us. Tony's and mine were two different types of family life. Mine was one of reserve and privacy. Much was left unsaid. In that respect, I was little different to my parents. Tony's family appeared to be one of broad inclusion. Yet were all the family secrets shared or did they also have events that were never discussed and passed on?

Tony carried my suitcase into the apartment and I offered him a coffee. I could sense that there was something on his mind and I wanted to let him settle and bring it out in his own time. I waited for the question I knew must be coming. It was another invitation. This time to a family wedding, a niece was to marry in August and he would love to take me. It was his youngest sister's daughter, and it would be a big Italian family wedding. All the relatives would be there. It was a kind invitation and I appreciated how much my acceptance would mean to him. I was also concerned that it perhaps meant that I would be considered as part of the family. I was not ready for that. I made an excuse about needing to check with my daughter about some commitment that I had promised her. It was a weak excuse but at least it gave me time to consider. I liked Tony. I enjoyed his company and I didn't want to hurt him, yet I was hesitant!

After Tony had left I phoned my brother and sister with the information I had discovered in Sydney. I now had more details of Grannie J's life and her parents. As a child, and a young woman, she had lived with her father and younger brothers in Moree and she had cared for her brothers after her mother's death. It was there that she had met and married our grandfather Stan, and it was where our mother, Nan, or Jean, was born. According to Great Uncle James, Grannie J, her husband and their baby had moved south while our mother was only young. Grannie J's father had been a fettler on the railways, and his father, Annie's husband, worked on sheep stations in the west of New South Wales. That could tie in with Warren where the letter had been posted. Western New South Wales is a huge area although the population is not very large. We decided to have another tea and scones session and plan our next line of enquiry. We did agree that it appeared unlikely that there would be any hidden family fortune to find.

At our next family gathering, Meg, my daughter, and her daughter Sass, joined Margaret and John and I. Sass had proved helpful to her mother and me in our internet searches. Together we discussed the information I had learnt in my chats with our Great Uncle James, and we each added the results of our investigations.

Margaret had done some research on the military history of our grandfather. He had joined the army in Wodonga at the commencement of the Second World War and served with the 6th Division of the Australian Infantry Forces.. He had been involved in the fighting in North Africa and the initial capture of the Libyan towns of Bardia and Tobruk. Those battles had been successful and then his division was transferred to Greece in March 1941. It was there, two months later, he had died fighting. She had found out that he was buried in a grave in Suba Bay, in Greece. His enlistment papers named his spouse as our Grannie J, stated his occupation as road-worker, and gave an address in Wodonga. The details matched! We now knew a little more about the grandfather we had never known.

"So was he one of the famous Rats of Tobruk?" asked John.

"No. He was involved in the initial capture of the town but was transferred before the German counter attack and their siege of the town."

Margaret had also discovered more of our father's war history. He had been in the 9th Division and had taken part in an amphibious landing to retake Lae from the Japanese forces in September, 1943.

"Was he on the Kokoda track?"

"No John, I checked. The Battle in the Coral Sea was in May, 1942. The Japanese fleet had turned back but their ground forces had commenced an advance down the Kokoda track in July. The advance had been turned around in September that year but he wasn't involved. His last military service was just before the war ended when his Division was involved in the fighting at Labuan.

"Where's that?" Margaret had anticipated our lack of knowledge and the likelihood of the question.

"It's an island off the coast of Borneo. It's adjacent to the Malaysian state of Sabah and north of Brunei in the South China Sea. It's now part of Malaysia. His occupation on enlistment was shown as labourer. He had also joined the army in Wodonga, but in 1942. He was nineteen when he joined up."

"The same age as me! That really freaks me out. My great grandad in a war at nineteen."

I could understand my granddaughter's concern. I certainly would not want Sass to have to go to war, but nor could I imagine her in a war zone. To her wars were something remote on the television, or a game to be played on your phone. Both her mother and I were concerned about her maturity and her practicality in her approach to life.

"I wonder if they knew each other? Our father and grandfather?"

So far we had no way of knowing the answer to my brother's question. Our grandfather was twenty-six when he had signed up in 1939. Our father would have only been sixteen when the father of his future wife left Wodonga for the war. Perhaps they knew each other, perhaps not. The only people who might know were now all dead.

John had had his daughter doing some more searching on Trove, but so far it had been unhelpful. From what we had learnt I guessed our family was unlikely to be newsworthy. Short of criminal activity or some unusual event I suspected they would leave little trace in newspapers. However we did have a few more dates, and a few more towns to use in our searches. Maybe Annie McGregor and the districts of Moree, or Warren, or Bourke might turn up something. John agreed to put his daughter back on the search.

I also had more dates and information to work with. Now I could try the records in New South Wales. I had also discovered shipping lists and census records. Some were on-line and Sass had offered to help me with the searching. I was looking forward to working with my granddaughter and getting closer to her. Her mother was concerned about the friends Sass was making at university. They were a different group to her friends from school. The new friends were all fellow students studying media and communication courses like Sass. Unlike her school friends they were much more radical in their attitudes and behaviour. Gone were the jeans and loose tops. Now the knees of the jeans had been slashed and brightly coloured sneakers with meaningful names had replaced the plain white sneakers favoured by her school friends. Her new T's showed her commitment to the latest social cause. Changed also were her "formal" clothes. The pretty party dresses were replaced by dark coloured dresses barely long enough for decency and often exhibiting far more of her than her mother and I thought appropriate. So far she had not cut her long blonde hair in favour of the short spikey brightly coloured hair of some of her friends. Sass had always been proud of her long locks and I suspected cutting them would be a step too far. Tattoos might be another thing. They were her mother's and my greatest fear. A few of her girlfriends already had a collection of tattoos, some a passage of a favourite saying, others birds or flowers. Some were discretely tattooed on a foot or where they could be covered if required. The exhibitionists in the group had them emblazoned across their backs or even worse on breasts. I was fearful of what would happen in the future when social trends moved on. Tattoos could not be changed as easily as a new shade of lipstick or a new hairstyle. The thought of fading ink and sagging skin as one aged was not pleasant: the cute little butterfly or frog would become some horribly distorted unrecognisable coloured blotch.

Her mother was also concerned that Sass's attitude to study was not as dedicated as it needed to be. To Sass and her new friends uni work was what you did between your social life and your social causes. A protest in the street, or the latest club, were much more important. I shared her mother's concern. We saw university as an opportunity, and while the social life could be fun and exciting, it was a step to a better life. I wondered what our rural worker/railway fettler/road worker forebears would have thought of the opportunity of a university education for a young woman.

Sass had brought over her laptop and we spent the afternoon searching records of births, deaths and marriages for New South Wales with mixed results. We had found a marriage record for Grannie J in Moree and that had confirmed her parents, Sidney and Jeanie MacGregor. The search for her father had led us to a record of the marriage of a Mary Ann McGregor. The dates looked roughly possible, it was in the west of the state, but the name was a little different. Mary Ann, Annie? That was possible. Macgregor, McGregor? I had a friend with a Scottish name and he told me people always made mistakes in how they spelt his name so that was also possible. The trouble was the date of marriage didn't fit the date of birth for Grannie J's father. I suppose that was also possible?

Together we tried a number of other searches including some for Bessie Buckley, but they were inconclusive. With little to work with, Bessie or Elizabeth Buckley, or Buckly, gave some results, but we didn't have enough information to narrow the search to the person we were seeking.

I had enjoyed the time with my granddaughter. I thought back to when I had been her age. The world she lived in was so different to the one in which I had grown up. For her, things, which my parents had struggled to give me, were today considered as expected. I was fortunate and had lived in years when work was readily available, wages were good and life became better each year. Even the tougher years had not lasted too long. It was hard to convince a young woman that life was not always so easy and you need to plan for a future that may not be so rosy.

Sass left me to meet up with some friends who had organised a film night somewhere in Richmond. It was to raise consciousness for Global warming and the disaster that was awaiting us if we didn't act. We arranged to meet again the following week, and she would bring a pamphlet about the film festival she and her friends were planning to see. Since I'd told her I'd just enjoyed a movie, she'd decided that I may be interested in some of the films at the Festival. It was the same Festival that Tony had invited me to attend.

The evening with Tony had started well. We had finally found a date for the "the little restaurant in Brunswick" and it was everything he had promised. It was a rainy night, and there was a May-time chill in the air when we had returned to my apartment and I had offered him a hot coffee and a port. We sat and talked and talked. Drank more coffee, and port, and the hours passed quickly. Gradually a fear came creeping into my mind. Had I made a mistake? Did Tony expect to stay the night? How was I to hint it was time for him to go? I felt like a teenager on a date that wasn't working. I thought of my granddaughter and how she would probably handle the situation. I doubted I could be as brutal or direct. At last I found the words to suggest we call the evening quits but it did come at the cost of suggesting another date. I hadn't really resolved the situation, merely delayed it to another time and place.

In the days that followed Annie kept coming to my mind. I was sure we had found the Annie of the letter, but we still knew little of her life somewhere in far western New South Wales. I was a city girl. I was never likely to go to Warren or Aramac. Even Moree, although it was on the road to Queensland, was unlikely. These days only trucks and grey nomads used the road, the rest of us flew. I thought my search for Annie and Bessie had reached an end.

13 Noosa

After my return from Sydney I'd received another invitation from my daughter-in-law's Aunt Jane to visit her in Noosa. This time I decided to accept.

Jane was waiting for me at the airport as promised. We'd been distant acquaintances in our shared schooldays but the connection and friendship had become closer since my son's marriage to her sister's daughter. After the confusion, caused by delayed flights and changing departure gates at Tullamarine, the Sunshine Coast Airport seemed small, although still busy and crowded with two planes disgorging passengers onto the tarmac for the walk to the terminal where another three planeloads of passengers were waiting to board.

As she drove Jane explained we were heading north from the airport by the scenic route along the coastline. In places I had views of blue ocean water and rolling white surf breaking onto sandy beaches. Already I was enjoying the sunshine and the warmth of the air that were so different to the approaching winter days in Melbourne. "We don't actually go as far as Noosa. My house is just this side." I was familiar with Noosa. Matt and I had holidayed there on several occasions. Jane gave me a quick refresher of the geography. "Noosa, well what most out-of-towners think of as Noosa, is Hastings Street and the beach. It's quite tiny but that's where the main tourist action is. Very pricey. Then there is Noosa Junction, a little way back from the beach where the locals shop. Then there's the river. Again it's touristy, and finally you have Noosaville. That's where most people live and where the main commercial businesses are based. And of course Tewantin. Not really sure what happens there. My house is in Sunshine Beach. It's about thirty minutes from the airport. We have a lovely little beach, it's much, much quieter and there are lovely walks through the park. You often see some strange sights because the walk takes you past the free beach."

"Free beach? I don't remember there being a fee on going to the beach in Australia."

"Oh Liz. Free of clothes. It's the nudist beach! Some people look quite good without clothes, but I think for some, clothes are definitely an improvement. Even any old shift or denim shorts and t-shirt improves some bodies?"

As we drove through Coolum with its apartment buildings and caravan park you could see the difference in the attitude of the people walking down to the beach to swim or surf. Most looked like tourists escaping the winter weather of down south. Often they would be couples, or young families. Many were grey nomads spending the winter in the warm north in a caravan parked beside the ocean. Our road took us along the coastline past small parking bays and tracks leading down to beaches hidden behind the native shrubbery that covered the dunes. At times National Parks flanked our drive. The greenery of the native bushland and heath between the housing developments gave the area a more human and relaxed scale than the wall-to-wall high-rises and housing estates of the Gold Coast.

We left the David Low Way and drove past some holiday apartments, a few shops and a surf club, and then turned into a street of houses. As we pulled into the garage at Jane's home I realised that her husband must have left her very comfortable indeed. Already parked in the garage sat a red convertible. A station wagon and a sports car! Two cars for one woman! I thought I was comfortable and reasonably free from financial constraints provided I was sensible, but there was no way I could have two expensive German cars in the single parking bay allocated to my apartment in South Melbourne.

My invitation had been timed to coincide with the local wine and food festival. The restaurants were abuzz with locals and visitors all hoping to try the specialities of the chefs who had flown in for the occasion. Restaurant bookings were hard to obtain, but Jane with her local connections had already covered that problem. We dined well and often. She knew how to enjoy life.

The days passed easily. Some days we would walk the path amongst the banksias and paperbarks overlooking the local beach and then return along the sandy foreshore listening to the wind in the she-oaks. Other days we would drive to a nearby beach and walk it. One day we braved the parking in Noosa to have a coffee in Hastings Street and watch the passing parade of holiday makers. The women and girls were generally a fashionable lot displaying their latest resort wear. Whatever their individual style, they all seemed to be beautifully groomed with their blonde hair, immaculate polished nails and smart dark glasses There were lots of slim tanned legs showing from brief skirts or shorts, tanned shoulders from strapless tops, and even tanned backs: on show from dresses and tops with deeply plunging, or non-existent, backs. With my pale Melbourne skin and out-of-date holiday clothes I stood out like a beacon. Jane took me in hand and we visited her favourite shops. Later we walked the beach promenade, checking the bodies stretched out on the sand working on their tans. Then we decided on a long lazy lunch overlooking the beach.

We were never alone in our walks. Mornings or afternoons, there would always be others out running or strolling, sometimes with their dogs on leash or running free if it was allowed. One day our walk took us all the way through the park to the end of Noosa Beach. It was a relaxed lifestyle and I could easily imagine dropping into the local way of life.

On the Wednesday we drove out to the Eumundi markets. I had heard of them but Matt and I had never made the excursion to see them. Together Jane and I wandered the alleys, checked out the clothing and craft stalls and I looked for gifts for my family back in Melbourne and Sydney. We bought coffees, found a seat and watched the swirling crowd of tourists. It was a much more varied gathering of humanity with all their different styles and fashions, and tattoos, than I had seen in Hastings Street.

Some evenings we would try a restaurant that the locals frequented. We were sitting in one having a fish night when I realised it was familiar. The décor of the restaurant had changed but it still brought back memories of eating there with Matt. When we had occasionally holidayed at Noosa we had usually spent most of our time on the beach, or having late lazy breakfasts in cafes as we watched other tourists in Hastings Street. In the evenings we would dine out at a restaurant or buy fish and chips to eat together in our room. Staying with a local I saw a different side of the town.

As I talked with Jane I realised five, almost six, years had passed since Matt's death. Yet I still found myself speaking of 'we' as if he was still there, just absent at present. He was still very much a part of my life. Jane had gone through a similar experience. Her husband had also died but his death had been slow and painful. He'd had treatment and fought the disease for years, but eventually he'd succumbed. An unhealthy lifestyle and stress from the disastrous financial downturn hadn't helped. Fortunately for Jane it was not too disastrous by the look of the cars in the garage.

With her husband dead she had decided to leave Melbourne. Noosa had always appealed. She loved the atmosphere and the climate, so different to the changeable weather of Melbourne with its cold winters. As well, she knew other Victorians who had made the move permanently, or spent the winter in Noosa. She had moved on, made a new life, new friends. I'd stayed in Melbourne. Now, my mother had gone, my son had moved to Sydney. There was only my daughter and her children who were holding me to Melbourne, and they no longer needed me, at least not close by. Talking with Jane, I realised that, unlike her, I had not moved on. An odd feeling that I had ignored re-emerged. What was my future to hold? Occasional visits from kids and grandkids when they had time to spare in their own busy lives? There was something missing in my life. Something I would never admit to, even to myself.

It was after another of our late afternoon beach walks that Jane informed me, "I'm going to organise drinks for tomorrow afternoon. Just a few of the locals and a friend who has a unit in town. She and her husband spend time between here and a property out west somewhere. They're both here at the moment."

"They spend quite a lot of time apart?"

"Yes. I don't think Margie is really the country sort. She much prefers the big cities. If Mike has business in Sydney or Melbourne, or more usually Brisbane, Margie will be with him. I rather gather that life can get a bit terse on the property. She says his kids see her as the wicked stepmother spending their inheritance."

"How old are they?"

"Don't know. Adult. I think they mostly run the property. Mike just has an overview and concerns himself with industry matters. They might have a point. I don't think the marriage is all that solid. It's number three for both of them and Mike is a bit of a flirt. Well more than a flirt, not that Margie is snow white either.

"What's she like?"

"Great fun. First into anything that is a good time. I expect that was what appealed to Mike."

"And what's he like?"

"Charming. I think he is rather good looking with that cute curl in his hair and his dark eyes. He does have a reputation as having an eye for the ladies. I gather he is quite successful at what he does. Cotton farming I mean."

"What about the other guests?"

"They are all locals. Retired couples. No single men. If there was a good one I would keep him for myself. There are a few single men around but it is very competitive. More widows than widowers in this part of the world. But you would be alright. I'm sure you could handle the competition." I guessed Jane's remark was meant as a compliment, but I wasn't sure that it was what I wanted, but again the thought re-emerged: there was empty space in my life since Matt had died.

The three hours of the drinks passed quickly and agreeably. The guests were an interesting mix of people from a varied range of past careers, and they were much more colourfully clad in shorts and light shifts than a similar group in wintery Melbourne. The warm climate and sunshine seemed to create an endless holiday spirit amongst them. Jane had certainly developed a fascinating group of friends. I was puzzled by the relationship between Margie and Jane. There was a politeness but a certain tension. I once noticed Michael and Jane exchange a quick glance at each other. The thought came to me that perhaps Jane had once had a fling with Michael. That could explain her earlier remarks and the tension with his wife. As Jane had said, he was certainly charming and I found myself often in his company. When I asked him where his farm was located he explained it was not far from Emerald, still this side of the Great Dividing Range but further north. That led me to ask him, "Do you know anything about Aramac?"

"Yes. Well not a lot. There is not much in Aramac these days, but I have been through it several times. What is your interest?"

"It's an old family mystery. A letter posted to Aramac in 1877. We have never been able to work out what it is about. One day I would love to go to Aramac and see if I can discover what it may refer to."

"Kandanga Farm is about four hours from Aramac. If you would like to have a look why not come up for a visit? I could drive you out and you could see the town for yourself."

"That would be interesting but wouldn't it be an imposition?"

"No. Not a problem. What's say Friday for Aramac? I'm flying up to Kandanga in the Cirrus tomorrow. There is room for you provided you don't have lots of heavy suitcases. We could have a few days on the property and fit in a day trip to Aramac."

"What about Margie?"

"I think she has plans here in Noosa. A friend is coming up from Sydney on holidays and she wants to see him."

I accepted his offer.

Later in the evening I mentioned the offer to Margie. She appeared a little surprised but quickly regained her composure. I had a similar reaction from Jane when I mentioned it to her after her guests had left. It had all happened so quickly. What had started as a holiday in Noosa with an old friend had become an expedition to a far western Queensland town. The town where a puzzling letter had been delivered one hundred and thirty-eight years earlier. A letter somehow connected to my family but just how was a mystery. At least I would get to see where it had been sent. Perhaps, there, I would learn something. Then there was Michael and Margie. It might not be a comfortable trip.

14 The Farm

The white Landcruiser pulled up outside Jane's house at seven in the morning as arranged, but it was not Michael.

"Hello. I was expecting Michael. Not that you're not welcome. It's just that it's unexpected."

"We've had a change of plans. I've decided to go up to the farm so I thought we could drive up together. Mike has a job to do and then he'll fly up in the Cirrus. I expect he will still be there before us."

It wasn't that I didn't want to make the trip with Margie but I had been rather excited when Michael had suggested I fly up with him in his plane to visit the farm at Emerald. To fly off in a private aircraft piloted by its owner would be a first for me, and I thought it rather exotic. Last night Margie had spoken of her plans in Noosa for the next few days and had seemed agreeable to Michael's suggestion. I wondered about the sudden change of plans and thought of Jane's description of Michael. Then again, I was still unsure about the glance Michael had given Jane. Well they would certainly have nothing to worry them with me. Whichever one might be worried.

I had been intrigued by the thought of visiting an actual farm. I really was a city girl and my only knowledge came from programmes I'd watched on television, or articles I'd read in newspapers. So often it was stories of drought or floods, fires or financial ruin. Rarely good news, yet Michael had been upbeat about his business.

Once upon a time families had uncles and aunts, and maybe even cousins your own age, who lived in the country, but Australia had changed. Those days had already passed by the time I was growing up in the city. I had not even known my forebears had once worked on sheep stations, and of my Great Uncle James who had worked in wool sheds. Nowadays, the most many kids would see of sheep and cattle was on a school excursion to a farm that maintained a group of quiet animals that could be patted and petted. Or perhaps they may have visited The Royal Show in Melbourne. Once when I had taken my children to the Show I had seen school groups, each student armed with a pencil and a quiz sheet, being herded by their teachers through the sheds housing cattle and sheep. Most of them would have much preferred to be on an exciting ride in the side show alley, or looking for show-bags to buy and take home.

Margie explained it would take around nine hours to reach the farm. Probably a bit longer if we stopped somewhere for a break and lunch. We would head up the coast to Rockhampton then turn west for Emerald and finally another eleven kilometres to the farm.

"What's the farm called? Michael did mention something."

"Kandanga. Mike bought it off a family who named it that. We have no idea why they chose that name but once a property has a name they tend to stick. Even if you change it the locals keep referring to it by the old name."

"How long have you owned it?"

"Mike has had it for about twenty-five years. Long before my time."

"How long have you and he been together?"

"Eight years now. Seven married."

"How do you like living in the country?"

"I prefer Noosa. I'm not really the RMs and big hat sort."

"RMs?"

"R M Williams. It's a brand of clothing. Very popular in the bush. In fact almost a uniform. If you don't wear RM Williams boots to a party nobody will talk to you because you are different."

"You're not serious are you?"

"No. It's not that bad. They will talk to you but you're not really one of them. It's a bit like going to a party in Sydney and wearing clothes with the wrong label."

"Do you spend much time on the farm?"

"Probably about two weeks every month. It varies. Depends on what Mike has to do. Actually his two kids run the place on a day-to-day basis. Mike is more just a supervisor. His main involvement is in the financial and industrial side of the business."

"Industrial?"

"Yes. Industry boards, research organisations and the like. He is fairly heavily involved in those sorts of things. It's good because we get to travel quite a lot."

"How did you get to meet Michael?"

"When my ex-husband and I split, I got the holiday unit in Noosa. He kept the house in Sydney. That suited me. I was looking for a change anyway, and there's some lovely people living in Noosa. Michael had friends here and we met at a party. He is very charming and great fun. We hit it off straight away. Then we ended up married. I have tried to get him to sell up and relax and buy a house in Noosa, but he won't leave the bloody farm. He could keep it, and the kids could run it, but he doesn't want to let go either."

"How old are his children?"

"Old enough to know better. Bella is twenty-four and James is twenty-one."

"What are they like?"

"Bella is the smart one. She can be very pushy about what should happen. She's got a boyfriend on a place further west. I wish she would go and live with him. It might make Mike less inclined to stay at Kandanga although I pity the boyfriend. James is a bit of a tear-away. Likes the girls and a good time. Bit like his father I suppose, although Mike is a bit more responsible."

"I get the feeling you are not very happy with his children."

"They see me as the evil stepmother. I think they ruined Mike's second marriage and now they are out to do the same to me. I think they see me spending their inheritance."

"That must make life difficult?"

"Mostly we just agree to be polite. Some of the neighbours

are heavy going as well. The only thing they talk about is cotton, cotton prices, will there be enough water, and bugs. Hardly stimulating conversation."

Margie's description of life at Kandanga was already making me have second thoughts about the wisdom of accepting the invitation. A womanising man, a suspicious wife, two troublesome kids and boring neighbours. What was I doing here! At least at home in Melbourne I had none of those problems.

We drove on. Sometimes chatting, other times silent. After we passed the turn off to Maryborough Margie put on a CD. As we travelled north we passed through the main street of Childers with its interesting old buildings. At times the road ran through forests of native trees, at other times the view out the car window was of gentle rolling hills and valleys with sugar cane and orchards. At Tobanlea Margie stopped to let me admire two beautifully restored old classic high-set Queensland houses displaying the elegance and grace that the style had once been famed for. In places we drove alongside ranges of blue hills, sometimes on our left, other times on our right and occasionally the road ran between two blue ranges.

After three hours we stopped for a coffee and Margie produced a thermos and some slice from a hamper. "It's easier to bring something with us. Besides I am never quite sure of where we can find good coffee on this trip."

"What do you do when you are at Kandanga?"

"I usually take a lot of books and some DVDs. I do the cooking when I'm there, and a bit of cleaning. Unfortunately this time I forgot to stock up as I wasn't planning on going out. There will be some DVDs out there but Mike's are always about cotton or nature documentaries, James likes car chases and superheroes but Bella usually has a couple that are ok.

As we approached Rockhampton the country started to change. Beside the road tall green grass became more prolific, the tips of the leaves already showing a hint of brown. The animals in the paddocks became more obvious and when we drove beside the railway line we now saw electric as well as diesel trains. That had surprised me. I'd always thought of electric trains and suburban commuter trains; never freight trains far from the major cities.

Our road turned west just before we reached Rockhampton. "What's Rockhampton like?"

"It's a city. I never go there. Lots of big hats, fluoro vests and bulls."

"Bulls?"

"Yes. They have statues of bulls all over the town. Cattle and mining are what it's all about. Neither greatly interest me so I rarely go there unless I have to."

Our road west took us alongside double electric train tracks with long, long trains, often with an engine at the front, another in the middle and a third at the rear. At one place I counted over one hundred coal wagons in one train. Again Margie found a spot to stop and this time a quiche and salmon sandwiches appeared from her hamper, along with a glass of white wine. "One glass and we're still legal. Maybe even two, but I would be careful after that!"

I was still puzzled by Margie's behaviour. She was hospitable and friendly. Yet it was obvious she had no great understanding or interest in the country we were traveling through, and I doubted she had any interest in visiting Kandanga. My initial thought was that she was wary of what may happen if Michael and I were left alone, and yet I had a feeling that their relationship was not all that important to her. None of it really gelled for me.

As we continued our drive the road gradually climbed gently upwards and I realized we were entering the Great Dividing Range. Yet unlike the other great ranges of the world such as the Andes or the Rockies our range was more a modest range of hills. We passed through the coal mining country of Blackwater and Moura, and our road west led us through the tiny village of Comet.

I was intrigued by some of the names I had seen on a map at Jane's house at Sunshine Beach when I was looking to see where I would be going. Emerald, Rubyvale, Sapphire. I asked Margie if she knew the reason for the names. She was unable to provide an answer. "Ask Mike. I'd be happy with any of them in a ring or a necklace."

"Have you been to Aramac?" As we were nearing Emerald I realised we were coming closer and closer to the town I had researched on the internet. I would probably never be so close again. I hoped Michael would deliver on his offer. Perhaps I really would get there

"God no! I hardly ever go to Emerald. Aramac is out in

the sticks. Why do you ask?"

I explained to Margie what I had told Michael. "There is an old letter in our family records. It was posted to Aramac in 1877. It's a bit of a mystery. Talking with Michael he said he would take me out there so I could see the town for myself."

"I know it's only small. Nothing like Emerald. I doubt you will find much there, but you're so close you ought to have a look. Who knows? Something might pop up. Ask Mike. I don't know how far it is from Kandanga."

As we came closer to our destination I noticed more and more white dirty scraps of something lying beside the road. I asked Margie about them. "It's cotton. There's a cotton gin near here, and they're bits that blow off the trucks carting the rolls or modules to the gin."

We arrived in Emerald and Margie pulled up at the shopping centre to buy some supplies from a supermarket. "We're only about ten minutes out of town but it's probably best to pick up a few things on the way." The town gave the impression of a busy go-ahead community far from the dying rural centres I had seen on television. The shops were modern, the names on the businesses were familiar, and the shoppers a mix of young and old. I also noticed the mix of fluoro vests and what I had now decided was rural attire.

As Margie had predicted Michael had already arrived. The blue and white aircraft was parked near a shed at the end of a long paddock covered in short green grass. Beside the shed a tattered airsock lay limp in the afternoon breeze.

"Looks like he's just arrived. Or else he has been out checking something. That's James with one of the workmen pushing the plane into the hangar."

"Welcome to Kandanga. I hope Margie took good care of you. I'm sorry you couldn't fly up with me. It is so much quicker than the drive. Do you want to freshen up or would you like a coffee first?"

I accepted the offer of a coffee and the three of us settled around a table on the wide shady veranda. Soon we were joined by a young man. Mike introduced his son. "This is James. He handles the field work around here. You'll meet Bella in a minute, she's just cleaning up. She handles the agronomy and irrigation."

James was obviously his father's son. They shared the same build and skin tones. Both were tanned. Their faces similar, with dark eyes and with the same hair colouring. Perhaps the father was carrying a bit more weight but I could see a young Michael in his son. It was a package that many young women would find attractive. From Jane's comments many women also found the father attractive.

The house was a modern brick home that Margie had told me that Michael's first wife had designed and had built not long after they had purchased the property and started developing it for cotton. It was a spacious single story home, comfortable, but now a little dated in its style. Good years had allowed for some extensions and the addition of a swimming pool. The ready supply of water allowed for expansive lawns and trees but garden beds were at a minimum. However several long hedges of bougainvillea added spectacular splashes of colour to the garden.

By the look of the tables and chairs much of the family's time was spent in the kitchen or the large covered patio. Bella, when she joined us, was a female version of her brother. Slightly older, almost as tall as her younger brother but finer in her features, with beautiful green eyes, perhaps a gift from her mother. She was an attractive young woman. From Margie's description I had expected two scowling unpleasant brats. Instead I found two personable intelligent young people. Both were at ease with their father and obviously close to him. The tension that Margie had mentioned appeared to be held in check with a visitor present.

In the morning Michael, he preferred Mike, took me for a drive around the farm. I asked him if he knew of the reason for the property's name.

"It was what it was called when I bought it. There is a town in the Mary Valley in the south east of the state with that name. I've been told it means 'bend in the river' in the Kabi Kabi, or Gubbi Gubbi, aboriginal language of that region. However that's not the aboriginal language of the tribe that lived around here. They spoke Gayiri. Perhaps the people who named the property just liked the sound of the name or perhaps they came from that region. I don't know."

My next question showed my ignorance. "What's the difference between a farm and a station, or a property?"

"Size. Stations are generally larger, although you may see the original headquarters of a station now on a much smaller block of land that keeps the name station. Stations tend to raise livestock but some also have farming, sometimes large farming operations. Farms are smaller and more involved with agriculture—tilling the soil. However some farms do concentrate on animals. Property covers the total range including specialized businesses such as orchards, feedlots, vineyards. Cotton has farms although there are big stations that have large cotton operations on them. I have probably only confused you. You soon pick up the expressions and usage."

My next question obviously touched a tender spot. "I often see cotton blamed for wasting water and poisoning the environment? What is your view?"

"There have been massive changes in management over the years. Today we are much more efficient using water to grow cotton. We have to be. Water is a limited resource in most years and it's expensive. We have also changed and now plant varieties that are resistant to various diseases and insect damage, so our spraying programs have been greatly reduced and are very targeted. In addition we are now using beneficial insects to assist in controlling pest damage and they have to be protected. You should talk to Bella, she's the expert that handles that side of the management. Get her to take you out when she is doing an insect count. I think these days we are much more attuned to the environment than the backyard gardener in a city. Nowadays there are people who make statements without any understanding of what they are saying. Not just about the cotton industry. I'm sure they say things that make them 'feel good' and virtuous without ever considering the problems of implementation and the sometimes negative unintended consequences of their beliefs. It really pisses me off, sorry, but it does."

We spent the morning driving the farm, checking water

supply channels, pumps, and storage dams. The soils where the cotton was grown were like a rich dark chocolate. Yet the country could change quickly from scrub to prime irrigation fields. I'd expected the irrigation fields to be flat but here they were often undulating. Mike explained that they were carefully laser graded to control the flow of water down the furrows to irrigate the plants. Any excess water would be recycled to the next field or into a storage. At the machinery shed I was amazed at the size and specialized nature of the machinery that was being checked and prepared for service. I learnt the difference between a spray coupe and a four row harvester, between the tractors used for planting and the tractors used to move the modules or rolls of cotton. Looking at the machinery it became obvious that farming required a lot of money, and that was without the cost of the land itself.

We arrived back at the homestead to find a dust-covered four wheel drive ute parked at the garden gate. "That'll be Euan. He said he would call in on his way home. Euan, I would like you to meet Elizabeth Manners, a friend from Melbourne up to visit the bush to find out what we do all day. Liz, this is Euan, Euan Hamish McLeod. He's a sheepman from further out west. He claims his family came from Scotland but I doubt it with a name like that."

The new arrival was a quietly spoken man. With his sandy coloured thinning hair, turning grey at the temples, I guessed him to be in his sixties. I noticed the brown riding boots and the jeans with a symbol of horns on them. I had quickly become familiar with the "horned steer's head" that denoted belonging to the group. Excusing themselves, Mike and Euan went into the house. An hour later they emerged from

Michael's office and Euan drove off.

Sitting around the dinner table Michael told of Euan and his family. They were an old grazing family in the west, maybe even one of the first families to settle their district. I gathered that Michael thought Euan was a bit old-fashioned and out of date. "Bella has a bit to do with his son, Donald. I think she rather would like more to do with him but he is a bit standoffish. She reckons Euan is a good stockman and runs a good property, but I think he is a bit behind the times when it comes to money. At least these days they are more into cattle than sheep. They had to change when the sheep job collapsed, but he still keeps a few sheep. It was a big change for the old school graziers. Once they were the top of the pile but they've had to come down a few steps—quite a few steps actually. These days he has dormers or dorpers, or something. His precious merinos have all gone. I think we might have a bit more to do with Euan in the future. James also keeps wanting to head west whenever there is a chance to see Euan's daughter. Kate's a stunner. Actually you will get to meet them. They're all coming over on the weekend for a party to celebrate Bella's birthday."

On my second night at Kandanga, I asked Michael about his farm. Cotton was their main activity but they also grew grain, particularly sunflowers. Others in the district grew citrus or grapes. The dam on the Nogoa River had made all the difference to the region. It was three times the size of Sydney Harbour. Without it, the country would still be running cattle, and much of the industry in the town would not exist. There had been problems. In 2008 the dam had filled and overflowed, then the river had flooded the town. The citrus producers had also had a major disease problem in 2004 that had affected them for five years. All their orange trees had to be removed and destroyed.

Over a few beers and wines, it was decided that at six in the morning Michael and I would leave to drive to Aramac. We should be back late in the afternoon or early evening depending on how much time I wanted to spend in the small town. Margie decided not to come with us but stay at the farm. Tomorrow I would get to see the town and the surrounding countryside where Bessie had probably lived. The town to which my great-great-grandmother had sent the letter. Perhaps there, somewhere, I could find a clue to Annie and Bessie, and why Annie had made their 'new lives far away'.

15 The Real Aramac

We left Kandanga early in the morning on our drive further west. Soon we had left the cotton fields behind us and were back in cattle country.

Today I would see the places, or the signs to places, that had caught my interest on the map. Emerald, Rubyvale, Sapphire. I took Margie's advice and asked Mike about the names.

"There are sapphires at Sapphire, but no rubies at Rubyvale and no emeralds at Emerald. Emerald was named after the nearby station, Emerald Downs, which the original squatter, Peter McDonald, named because it reminded him of the green of his homeland. I think he had good imagination, or lots of longing for his homeland."

Our road took us through the Central Highlands and to the far side of the Great Divide. Gradually the country changed. After passing through Dingo and Alpha, a neat, tidy and green town where all the business appeared to be closed, we finally entered the catchment of the Cooper Basin. Here was the land of open vistas and far horizons that Banjo Paterson's poem had created in my mind.

Mike made pleasant company for the drive and we chatted about the land and cotton farming. How he had made the decision to leave the city where he had first worked when he had left school, and how he had put his savings, plus some, into developing a property. Underneath the big hat that everybody seemed to be wearing I sensed a shrewd and astute businessman. He was far from the caricature of a farmer chewing straw that is so favoured by cartoonists. He was also very charming in a natural, unpretentious way and I could easily believe Jane's comment about his appeal to women. I thought of how different he was to Tony and realised that with Mike I was relaxed. None of the spinning vortices that I felt with Tony.

At Barcaldine we turned off the highway and took the road to Aramac. I was curious about the huge brown box on stilts in the main street. "Ah, it's the Tree of Knowledge." I didn't get any more comment from Mike, he didn't offer to stop, and I decided that it might be best to let the matter pass.

Our road led us across flat or gently undulating country that Mike described as 'Downs': natural grasslands that were ideal for sheep and cattle provided you had water. However out here the seasons had a way of failing and droughts meant water and feed could be scarce. The road narrowed and each time a huge road train approached we would pull off the bitumen to allow it to pass. The road and its verge were also the feeding ground for crows feasting on the remains of wallabies hit by passing vehicles. As we approached Aramac I spied two dingo carcasses hanging from a tree. Mike also saw them. "Dingos and roos are a real problem. With the greater distribution of watering points on stations roo numbers have increased. They can put so much grazing pressure on country that it becomes damaged. You can control sheep and cattle numbers but then the roos eat everything and cancel out your efforts to protect the country.

Dingos have bred with domestic dogs and they will hunt and kill for entertainment. They can make grazing sheep impossible."

The Aramac we arrived in was a small town of wide streets beside the creek that had given the town its name. But the streets were almost empty and the hotels of its early days had long since vanished and only one remained. The houses were neat and tidy but many years had passed since the town had been the major centre of the region. Closed and empty shops told of better days. It didn't take long to tour the town. Mike pulled up alongside a statue of a white bull. I'd already learnt a little of the story with my internet searching but Mike told me the full story.

"Harry Redford was a stockman working on Bowen Downs Station north of here. In 1870, with some mates, he built a set of stockyards in a far section of what was a huge station. In those days it stretched for hundreds of kilometres along the Thomson River. Then they secretly accumulated about a thousand head of cattle, and drove them through the Channel Country and across the Strzelecki Desert to South Australia. The mob included a special white bull which Bowen Downs had imported. The trip was almost thirteen hundred kilometres and took three months. It was quite a feat. Anyway, the yards and the path of the cattle were discovered by workers on the station and the mob tracked. The white bull and two cows had been sold part way along the route for rations. Then the main mob, which had been sold to Blanchewater Station near Marree, was found. Redford was arrested in Sydney and sent for trial before a jury in Roma, south of here. However the jury were so impressed with his feat driving cattle across country that was unexplored that they found him not guilty. The judge is reputed to have said, 'Thank God, gentlemen, that verdict is yours and not mine'. I suspect the jurors were also a bit anti the big graziers. Anyway the Queensland Government shut down the Roma District Criminal Court for a period."

"What happened to him?"

"He later did time for horse stealing, and then became a drover in the back blocks of Queensland. Apparently he and his team never came too close to southern centres. He also took a mob of cattle to Brunette Downs in the Northern Territory where he was manager. Later he was manager of McArthur River Station in the Gulf of Carpentaria district. Eventually he drowned trying to swim a flooded creek. His fame increased when some of his exploits were used in the novel 'Robbery Under Arms', although he was not a bushranger as such."

"He must have been quite a rustler."

"Rustler is an American term. In Australia you 'duff' cattle and 'steal' sheep."

Mike and I found the local museum in what had been a shed beside the tramway the locals had financed and built to connect the town to the main train line at Barcaldine when the railway had bypassed their town. It was one of a number of projects that the town had made over the years to support their community. The latest was a sculpture trail for tourists to follow. It was a project of a local sculptress living on a grazing property along the trail who wanted to support her town.

While the museum was interesting and I'd learnt a little of

the history of the town and its dreams, and of life for the locals in the early days, there was still no connections that could give me a lead to Bessie.

As we left the town we stopped at a memorial near the waterholes in the Aramac Creek, but it was not the tree of RR Mackenzie, rather a memorial to Landsborough who had explored the area in 1860 and then, with partners, formed the station whose cattle Redford had stolen.

The day was just starting to cool and the sun was commencing a slow decline in the west when we left to return to Kandanga. I'd been to Aramac, but I had found nothing. My thoughts were full of Bessie, trying to image what her life must have been like living in the bush. I'd thought of trees and forests but this region was open grassy plains with the only trees along the scarce watercourses. In our conversation by the waterhole Mike and I had decided that she probably didn't live in the township. If she did, it was likely that the letter would be just addressed to her. Her name had not shown up in any of the records at the museum and for the letter to be held at the post office possibly indicated that she was living on one of the stations in the district. Whoever went to town would go to the post office and collect any mail for people living on the station. The fact that it was not addressed to the station may have meant that they were new to the district or were itinerant workers. Shearers were itinerant but they didn't usually travel with their wives. Then there were the teamsters; they sometimes lived on stations, or on the outskirts of the town where the horses or bullocks could be kept between jobs.

I'd never thought about living in the bush. My parents may have moved to the city from a country town but the only life I knew was in a big city. I asked Mike about his change from Sydney to Emerald.

"I grew up in the country. Near Moree actually. My family had a sheep property there but I was looking for something new. I tried working in a city wool-store. That was working for one of the big stock and station agents that ran the auctions that sold the wool for growers. After a while I had enough of the city and wanted to get back to the bush. That was when I found a block at Emerald and started to develop the property for cotton. The Fairbairn Dam opened up country for cotton and citrus and grapes as well as other crops. Without it Emerald wouldn't exist. I was in the right place at the right time and cotton has been good to me. Unfortunately I seem to be attracted to women who aren't so keen on country life. Then I marry them."

I'd thought that Mike probably had a roving eye, and a need for fresh conquests, but as we talked my opinion changed. Certainly he had roved, but he was still very fond of his first wife, the mother of his children. Unfortunately she, unlike their children, was not happy with a country lifestyle. Nor was I sure where Margie fitted into his life. He admitted that in his marriage failures he had taken consolation in short-term relationships. I suspected that now, given his past experiences, he had decided to ignore any woman who was not a country girl. Yet somehow I felt he was still attracted to city women. My background would certainly count me out as a potential long-term partner.

I'd already discovered my family had also come from Moree. I'd learnt of Grannie J's father who had been a fettler on the railways. I doubted whether Mike's family and mine would ever have had much contact. From the little I had discovered about Annie I suspected her friend would be of similar social standing. It would be unlikely that either Bessie or Annie would make headlines in the local newspapers of the time—unless they did something bad.

Sitting in the car for the drive back to Kandanga I puzzled over how my forebear would have recovered the letter she had sent to Bessie. When we had first seen the letter, my brother had noted there was no return address on the envelope, nor an address in the letterhead, so it could not have been returned as undelivered: yet, somehow it must have been returned to Annie's possession.

"I suspect that they must have met at some stage after it had been received by Bessie. Perhaps Bessie also moved and they met up again? Maybe Annie came to Aramac?"

Both of Mike's suggestions were possible.

"You should talk to Euan. He and his kids are coming over to Bella's birthday party tomorrow night. His family have been around the area forever, not in Aramac, but in the larger region. He's not a newcomer like me and he's a bit of a local historian. He would be good to talk to. He may be able to give you an idea of what life was like back when Bessie was here."

Perhaps continuing my search for Bessie might help in my search for Annie. I realised that while Aramac had given me no answers, it had only made me even keener to find the story of my long deceased relative.

It was late in the evening when we arrived back at Kandanga. Bella and Margie had already eaten and were sitting on the veranda with a beer and a wine in their hands. There was a feeling of tension in the air. Something had not gone well that day. When Margie went off to find some food for us Mike asked where James was. Bella informed us that he'd gone into Emerald early in the afternoon to pick up some parts for a machine, but had phoned to say he'd met some mates and was planning to stay with them overnight. She wasn't happy because she wanted the machine working for a job that needed to be done immediately. Margie wasn't happy because James had promised to bring out some ingredients she needed for the planned evening meal. When Margie had criticized James, Bella defended him and words had been exchanged.

We had no sooner started our meal when the phone rang and Mike left to go into his office.

"Another of those bloody phone calls. It happens every night, before we sit down for a meal, while we're eating, or after our meal, and he talks for hours. I wish he would just tell them to call back in the morning. I would like some private time with him!" Evening phone calls were definitely on Margie's list of 'don't dos'.

When Mike returned to the veranda he was unsettled.

"What's the problem, Dad?" Bella had also picked up the feeling.

"It was George. There seems to be some trouble with the investment down on the Gold Coast. He wants me to go with him and talk with the manager. He thinks they are not telling us the full story and there's a problem. He's very worried. I think he may have picked up some gossip. He has lots of contacts. Anyway, he wants to meet me and for us to go down straightaway. I told him I would pick him up on Monday and we would fly down. At least I will still be here for your birthday party down at the waterhole."

16 BBQ at the Waterhole

It had been another beautiful day. Warm, a few clouds and a gentle breeze.

James had returned from Emerald; much later than his sister and father had considered acceptable. It appeared that he and his friends had made quite a night of it, and he had been slow to start in the morning.

He had delivered the expected machinery parts to the farm workshop and was redeeming himself by helping set up the lights and barbeque, as well as the tables and chairs needed for Bella's birthday celebrations. A large pile of logs had been gathered and left near the fire pit. It was expected that the evening would be cool and the visitors would end up around the pit built of old bricks centred in the cleared area overlooking the waterhole. We weren't the only occupants of the area. In the trees around the waterhole the raucous 'ark-ark' of crows and the screech of sulphur–crested cockatoos constantly filled the air. At least by nightfall they would become silent.

The dark was just settling over the waterhole when the first guests arrived. They were a mix of ages and types. Many of the men were dressed in the jeans I had come to recognise by their logo, and I suspected their boots would be 'RMs' as well. Most were in shirts with thin vertical stripes of blue or green and white. As Margie had said, there was a uniform; it was just a different uniform to the ones at similar city gatherings. Even though it had become dark some still wore their large broad-brimmed hats with dark glasses across the crown. A few of the younger ones wore peaked caps. The caps seemed to be either displaying the logo of a football club or a machinery dealer. I had already been educated in the difference between the Maroons, the Broncos, and the Cowboys. That wasn't too hard. In Melbourne I'd grown up with the Hawks and the Tigers. However I could still never understand the rules of the rugby I saw on television. Nor could I understand wearing hats at night. It didn't seem necessary: the sun had long since set. My father would never have approved. For him hats were always removed on entering a building, raised to a lady and never, ever worn at night.

The women were also a mix of ages and styles. A few of the younger ones were in jeans and pretty blouses. Others wore party dresses. The older ladies were mostly in longer dresses or slacks. For the first time since my arrival I saw Bella in a very pretty dress with shoestring shoulder straps. I had always seen her in jeans with her hair tied back in a ponytail, usually under a cap or a hat but tonight it was piled high on her head and I realised for the first time how attractive she would look in any company.

I also recognised the man who had visited Mike when I had first arrived at Kandanga. Bella took me over to him and introduced the young couple with him. Donald was her boyfriend, and Kate, his sister, was a very close friend. "My bestie", and the two of them laughed. Kate was a stunning young woman. I'd been told Euan's daughter was beautiful but had not given the description the value it deserved. She was tall, slim and fine-featured with large blue eyes and auburn hair, and when she moved you could see eyes following her. Her brother was slightly taller, well-built, and while good-looking lacked the impact of his sister. During the day I'd picked up from comments Mike and Margie had made that they were hoping tonight might be the night for an announcement. From her dress maybe Bella was also hoping, or knew, but from what I'd come to know of her in the few days I'd been at Kandanga I thought a surprise was unlikely. She was too well-organised for surprises on important matters.

I joined Margie and Bella in handing around nibbles and chatted with many of the guests. Most were young people, the same generation as Bella and Donald, but there were also friends of her father's generation. Some were locals, others had travelled some distance for the evening. The younger ones were prepared to stay the night and had come equipped with swags to throw on the ground or the veranda when they were ready to sleep. The older ones had been offered bunks in empty rooms in the staff quarters.

There was a happy feeling about the evening. Lots of talk and laughter. The younger ones gradually becoming louder and louder, the older ones drifting into smaller quieter groups. I found myself sitting next to Euan. At that stage I noticed Mike's son was standing alongside Euan's beautiful daughter and I made a comment about them.

"James often tries his luck with my daughter but it will never happen. Kate is too aware for that."

"Your daughter's very beautiful."

"She certainly didn't get that from me. But yes, and she's smart enough to know it and know what it can do. Fortunately she is also very sensible and knows that good looks are not the most important thing in life. In fact they can be a handicap."

"What do you mean? I thought every woman would like to have her beauty."

"While it is a benefit it can attract the wrong sort of attention. Some people are drawn to the looks and not the character. I think Mike's son is in that lot."

We were looking at James and Kate as we were speaking and I noticed the more insistent James became in trying to monopolise the girl's attention, the more she drew others around her into the conversation. She chatted as brightly with James as the others, but to an outside observer it was obvious he was allowed to come no closer.

"What's Mike's son like?"

Euan was cautious in his reply. "He's not a bad lad. Bit spoilt, which has done him no good. He has a liking for pretty girls, but that's not uncommon with boys. Hopefully he will mature one day."

"I believe his dad had a weakness for pretty girls?"

"Yes. Mike has, or had, a reputation. But I don't think you will find any of his wives speak badly of him. He is actually very considerate and caring. He's just attracted to the wrong women. They're not bad women, just never right for him. Contrary to stories, he is also faithful while the relationship is working."

"How do you feel about Bella and your son?"

"That will be a great match. Bella will make a great mate for Donald, but they will do it in their own time. They're not ready yet."

"So it won't be tonight?"

"It never was going to be tonight. They both know it will happen, but Bella has a few matters to attend to. I think she is worried about her father."

"What will happen then?"

"That's a problem. Donald will take over running Raasay and Bella will move in with him. James will take over Kandanga, but he needs Bella's ability to really make it work. He still lacks some of the skills needed and he isn't showing any inclination to acquire them."

"What about you and Mike?"

"We'll become old pensioners looking after the gardens."

"Are you serious?"

"No. Mike will continue as he does now. I'm not sure Margie will still be with him. I will shift into the cottage so the kids can have their privacy. I did think of retiring to a small farm over near the coast but I like the bush."

I had a question for Euan. It was about the hats and caps.

"Generally the hats belong to cattlemen, or sheep men. Caps are more the favoured headgear of the farmers. They spend their lives in cabins on tractors and harvesting machinery. A big hat gets in the way when you are poking around in the bowels of a machine. However it's not a firm rule. Don't count on it."

I had another question for him. I asked what he knew about Aramac and its history. He was just about to answer when Mike called for quiet and started his speech. It was only brief. The subject was never mentioned, but those in the group who had expected an engagement announcement were soon disappointed. He congratulated the birthday girl, thanked all their friends for attending, and proposed a toast to Bella. Then it was Bella who replied, thanking her father and her boyfriend Donald, and his sister Kate for their help.

The chatter around the fire recommenced, but I noticed Margie having words with Mike. I didn't know if it was intentional, or unintentional, but Bella had not mentioned Margie. True, her contribution had been limited, most of the preparation had been done by Bella and two local ladies, but I felt it would have been diplomatic to have included her in the acknowledgements.

I looked at the people standing around the fire and thought of the 1870s and Bessie. They could be the same sort of people. Station-managers, cattlemen, ringers, rural workers. True the fashion of the clothes and the style of beards may have changed, and cars had replaced horses, but the waterhole, the trees, the log fire burning in the centre of the circle, and the mass of stars above would all be the same. It was a different time but some things were unchanged.

I resumed my chat with Euan. His property was south of Aramac and closer to Barcaldine. While his family had been in the area a long time they had come much later than when Annie's letter had been posted. He was, however, interested in the history of the region.

"These days people talk of the speed of change, but

Australia was also changing very rapidly in the last half of the eighteen hundreds."

"Who were the first people to settle the region?"

"First it was the British explorers who came through this country, but right behind them were the first squatters looking for new land for their sheep and cattle."

"Where did they come from?"

"Down south, New South Wales or southern Queensland. There was a movement of people looking for good grazing beyond the last established run or station. The first squatters to settle the area around Rockhampton, you would have passed through it on your way here, arrived in 1853. Prior to that there would have only been an indigenous population. Within six years there was a newspaper, bank, Court House and a School of Arts. After twelve years, work on a railway westward was commenced, and in just twenty-five years after the first squatter arrived with livestock it is said there was a town of eight thousand people with nine churches, seven banks, three newspapers and nine schools, one of which was a Grammar School. The grazing and mining industries needed lots of workers. Now the population is ten times that, but I'm not sure about the banks or newspapers."

"How did they get here?"

"The squatters walked, or rode. They drove their flocks of sheep and herds of cattle as they came. In the early days the sheep were all looked after by shepherds. There were no fences of course. It would have been a lonely life living in a tent or a hut out near a waterhole with the only company a mob of sheep that you had to yard each night. It could be dangerous too. The shepherds were sometimes subject to attack by natives who found sheep easier to catch than kangaroos. Some of those early shepherds were Chinese. Sometimes squatters had Aborigines from other areas working for them. Later on arrivals came by sea to Rockhampton or Mackay further north, and moved inland from there."

"What were the living conditions like?"

"Basic. The houses were rough huts with timber walls, perhaps even canvas walls, and the roofs would have been strips of bark tied to wood rafters."

"Would women have come with them?"

"Not at first, but very quickly runs were established. Then women arrived and families were started. Those first settlers weren't unskilled or lacking in knowledge or experience. Some were very well-educated and had access to money from their families. Others might have had useful practical skills. They could have been emancipated convicts. All of them were exploring the frontiers of European society looking for opportunity or adventure."

"I saw on my trip to Aramac with Mike that Bowen Downs Station that had the white bull stolen was occupied in 1862. That was only nine years after Rockhampton."

"Yes, and Aramac Station was set up a year later. The spread north and west was very rapid."

Some of the younger guests were imbibing freely and becoming noisier and noisier. James appeared to be the leader of the group. I noticed he once again moved closer to

Euan's daughter and whispered in her ear. Kate stepped away from him, but he again moved closer and attempted to hold her hand. This time Kate spoke directly to him and a look of anger came over his face. At the same time Bella came to stand beside Kate. A few more words from his sister and he left to re-join the noisy group of drinkers.

I looked across at Euan who had also seen the incident.

"James isn't used to being rebuffed. He gets very offended when his charm doesn't work. My daughter has experienced it before. Bella understands, she and Kate are very close friends but it does make for the occasional difficult situation."

We chatted on, rarely pausing in our conversation, and the evening passed without either of us realising the hour. Occasionally others would join us and then drift away and we would return to stories of the early days of settlement and life in the bush.

"Why don't you come to Raasay for lunch? Bring Margie and Bella if Mike is too busy."

I declined the invitation. I knew Mike was planning to fly south in the morning, and it had already been discussed that Margie was keen to return to Noosa and I would accompany her. As much as I would have liked to continue the discussion another day it was not going to happen.

It was late in the evening and the cold was creeping over the last of the hardiest guests who were moving closer and closer to the dying fire. Most of the guests had drifted away, and Bella, Kate and Donald were clearing the remains of the meal and tidying the area. Euan and I were still chatting about the history of the region when we finally decided it was time to part.

The morning was another day of cloudless sky and sunshine. Already Kate and Bella were in the kitchen washing the plates and bowls from the previous night. Mike appeared, ate a light breakfast and together with Donald he walked across the yard to the hanger. He was carrying a small travel bag, a tablet and a folder of papers. I had noticed that, unlike most of the guests, during the previous evening he had only been drinking soda water except for a small glass of champagne as he had raised a toast to his daughter. Soon the Cirrus was airborne. As arranged I would accompany Margie back to Noosa to keep her company. Then I would catch a flight home to Melbourne. I was not going to have my flight in the beautiful blue aircraft

I'd seen Donald and Kate, and I was looking for Euan when Bella told me he had already left for Raasay. He had a truck coming to load four decks of cattle for the meatworks, and he need to be present to draft them. I was sad I had missed saying a farewell to him. I'd enjoyed his company the previous evening and I would have liked to have taken up his invitation to visit for lunch.

Margie finally appeared and we were soon in the Landcruiser and on our way back to the coast—and the life style she preferred.

17 Home Again

It was good to be back in my own home. I'd enjoyed my holiday, and I'd met some interesting people, but it was unlikely our paths would cross again. Maybe in Noosa if I took a holiday, but I doubted I would ever make another visit to Emerald, and it was even more unlikely that I would return to Aramac. I had discovered nothing there that would lead me to learn more of Annie or Bessie. Great Uncle Jim had been much more useful than Aramac.

It was also good to catch up with my daughter and her family, and spend time with them and tell them of my travels. Meg had been interested, my granddaughter less so, and my nine year old grandson had not the slightest interest. My friends had made polite enquiries about my activities and then proceeded to tell me of their own doings, which, to them, were much more interesting.

I phoned Tony to let him know I'd returned and he was pleased to hear from me and was genuinely interested in what I had been doing. We arranged to go to a movie and then have dinner.

I texted a girlfriend and we agreed to meet and visit the Quilt Fair in the Exhibition Building in a few weeks' time. I was back home, familiar places, familiar friends and family, but it wasn't the same. I realised I'd seen a bigger world of far horizons. An empty world, well almost empty—there were people out there and I had enjoyed their company.

The movie with Tony had been interesting but I hadn't really appreciated it. This time it was his choice and he had chosen a movie that was dark and moody. I didn't need that. I was feeling dark and moody myself. I needed something bright and frivolous and happy. The only films that fitted that description were kids' films and they were too silly even for me—unless I had my grandson beside me. His excitement was always infectious. Our meal together had been enjoyable and it was good to be with someone you knew and with whom you could share previous experiences. As much as I liked meeting new people it did draw on my emotional energy.

As we parted Tony suggested another date. When I told him of my plans to go to the Quilt Show on the day he'd nominated he wanted me to cancel my plans. I wasn't prepared to do that. I'd been to the Quilt Show before and I'd loved the beautiful craftwork involved. The quilts were true works of art and I'd promised a friend I would take her when I went this year. Tony and I only parted after I had agreed to go with him to the Film Festival in the city at the end of the month. I left it to him to choose the sessions.

I had decided that my search for Bessie was pointless but I did have some leads on Annie. This time I would look in New South Wales and I would start at her end. I would search for her death certificate.

Great Uncle Jim had remembered his father living in Moree, but he had also told me he thought his grandfather, the husband of Annie, had finally settled in Bourke. From my road atlas that was near Warren, if you thought two hundred and fifty kilometres was close. In that part of the world the locals probably thought it was the next town. Great Jim's grandfather had worked on sheep stations 'out west' and both Warren and Bourke fitted that description. I went on to my laptop to search Births, Deaths and Marriages in New South Wales. Annie had died before Great Jim had been born, so that would be before 1924. If Annie had been eighteen to twenty when she arrived in Australia, and that could be roughly right, then the next question was how long had she been in Australia before she had written the letter to Bessie. There was no way of knowing. I decided to search deaths before 1924. Surely there would not be too many Annie MacGregors who had died in the west of the state.

This time I was lucky. Annie MacGregor, died September 21, 1900 and the place of death was shown as Bourke, but there was much more. Annie had been forty-six when she had died, her occupation was given as housewife, and she had died of accidental death. The details of her death were not disclosed and I wonder what misfortune had befallen her. Now I also had her place of birth in Scotland and her father, John McDonald, a crofter, but more importantly that she had been in Queensland and New South Wales for twenty-seven years. That would make her arrival in Australia around 1873 and if she had been in Queensland then maybe that was where she had met Bessie.

Even more important for me was her marriage in Warren to Rohan MacGregor, when she was twenty-three years of age and the Death Certificate also listed her two children. A boy, Sidney, twenty-five and a girl, Helena, four years younger. Sidney, his daughter was my Grannie J, her daughter my mother, and then me. The chain was formed and now I could go back even further to Scotland.

I paid for a copy of the Death Certificate to be emailed to me and arranged another meeting with my brother and sister to share with them what I had found.

"Are you sure this is correct?"

I looked at my brother. "Why do you ask?"

"Well, the dates don't seem to add up."

"What do you mean?"

"Well, look at the years. Annie was forty-six when she died in 1900, so she was born in 1854. She married in '77 when she was twenty-three but Sidney was twenty-five when she died so he was born in 1875. It looks like we have a family scandal unless there was an earlier husband, or the dates are wrong."

It was a cold wet July night in Melbourne, the television had nothing that interested me, and in a moment of boredom that I decide to follow my niece's example and search Trove. The stories from the old newspapers were fascinating in their content and in the style of their reporting. It was a time-wasting exercise but interesting, and I soon became addicted. I spent evenings and afternoons scouring through old, long vanished, local newspapers for articles about Warren and Burke that might give me a lead on Annie's life or death, but I found nothing. Then one night I decided to type in Aramac.

The headline shouted, 'The Aramac Gold Rush'. That

surprised me. I knew of many gold rushes around Australia. Ballarat and Bendigo, Hill End in New South Wales, and in Queensland I'd heard of the Palmer River Goldfields in the far north. Then there were the goldfields of Western Australia and more goldfields in the Northern Territory. Gold seemed to exist everywhere, but I had seen no indications, or history, of a goldfield on my visit to Aramac with Mike. I read the article. A young boy had seen an old man shaking a dish at the edge of the town dam. When asked what he was doing the old man replied, "Pannin' fer gold", tipped out the water and there lay a few nuggets of gold. The news spread rapidly through the town and soon the area and beyond was pegged with claims with men and women using whatever they could find as pans. So much washing of dirt was happening the dam was almost silted up.

The news of the find spread to the coast and the rush grew. Claims were traded, and syndicates formed, but gradually the realisation set in that no more gold had been found. Finally the story emerged. An old miner from the Palmer field had been camping near the dam. One night he had dropped his few nuggets in the dirt. Unable to find them in the dark he had marked the spot and come back next morning, scooped up the dirt with his missing nuggets and taken it the dam to wash and recover his gold. All would have been fine until the young lad spread his story and the rush started. By then no one was prepared to accept the old man's explanation.

The year was 1888. Eleven years after Annie had posted her letter. I wondered if Bessie would have been down at the dam with a dish.

Another story also caught my attention. It was the Aramac Riot. I found it hard to imagine a riot in the peaceful town I had visited. It occurred the following year during the lead up to the Race Meeting. Shearing was finishing, and Aramac was full of cashed-up shearers out to enjoy themselves. As well a few suspect characters had also arrived in town looking to relieve the shearers of their hard earned funds with crooked gambling games. One was caught and according to the newspaper "given a hiding and thrown out of the hotel". He returned with his mates and the fights began. When the police tried to stop the fights the shearers turned on the police. Then it was on. Paddy, the police black tracker was hit in the stomach by a bottle after taking refuge up a tree.

However Sergeant 'Tiger' Ryan had his revenge. Over the following days he went to the race course with handcuffs and leg irons and arrested about eighteen men. I remembered once reading a story of prisoners 'jailed' by being chained to a tree. I could imagine the outrage in the media and social media if that happened today. Yet, when the lock-up was full, or hundreds of miles away, practical problems required pragmatic solutions.

The newspaper articles had shown a very different town to the quiet Aramac I had visited. Maybe Mike and I were just there on the wrong day.

The Quilt Fair was all I'd promised Barb. Another friend had also joined us for the day and we'd had a great girls' session admiring the designs and the craftsmanship, or as we decided, craftswomanship, and catching up on news of friends over cups of coffee. We had chatted and gossiped and laughed and the day had passed all too quickly. That night I was pleased I didn't have a date with Tony. I was sure the movie he would have suggested, even though it was my turn, would have been a serious film.

The day had been so different to a day with Tony. Even when he was supposed to be relaxing, like playing a game of social bowls, he was still competing. He couldn't help it. When he went to a movie it would have to be a movie with a message. When I was with him I never felt as relaxed or as free as I'd been with my girlfriends that day, or the day I had visited Aramac with Mike.

Tony, as I should have expected, had been enthusiastic in booking seats for the film festival. Not only did he arrange tickets for the opening function but for several other screenings of lesser known films. Again, as I should have expected, the programme he had chosen included films with the themes of global warming, gender issues and the rich/poor divide. It was there I ran into my granddaughter and her friends.

I'd seen Sass and her group disappearing around a corner as we left the cinema after viewing a film about the problems of a village of poor farmers whose land would be ruined by the rising temperature. I hadn't been surprised to see her there. It was one of her favourite issues and I had often heard her expressing her views when I had called at her parents' home. I think she held them personally responsible for all the problems of the world.

The next screening Tony and I went to were films about gender identity and Sass and her friends were also there. I'd expected that feminism would be an issue but evidently I was behind the times. As Sass patiently explained to me during the interval, "feminism could be restrictive of personal freedoms and people must have the right to decide their identity themselves. It was wrong to be identified by the body you were born with. True freedom could only come when an individual could make her own decision." I had a few concerns with the views expressed. To me there were inconsistencies in some of the arguments presented and practical difficulties had been overlooked, especially those caused by the developments in medical science. My protestations were quickly silenced by one of Sass's friends and I was left with an expletive laden assessment of my position in society. The severity of my dressing down embarrassed even my granddaughter. It seemed that discussion amongst some university students could only take place if you believed in the cause. To have opinions counter to the accepted view could make for a lonely, isolated life.

It was the week after the Film Festival when Tony rang me. It was August, and we needed to arrange our plans for his family's wedding. Where did I want to stay? Maybe it was the weather, maybe I'd had a bad day and was feeling cooped up in the unit, but the thought of a large wedding with all its formalities and family intricacies just did not appeal. Even more annoying was the realisation that I had never accepted Tony's invitation. He'd just assumed I would go with him. I decided I didn't want to do it. I knew it would upset Tony and I did feel bad, but I wasn't ready to face all the family, and the cousins and their children. Nevertheless, I felt I owed it to him to be honest and not make excuses so I declined as gently as I could. Maybe Tony had also had a bad day and he didn't take my explanation well. The more he kept asking and the more he kept trying to convince me to change my mind, the more determined I became not to change my answer. The call ended badly.

18 An Invitation

It was the night after my disagreement with Tony, and it was unexpected.

I was sitting alone, a brandy and dry in my hand, looking out the window of my apartment at the bright lights of the tall city office buildings, and trying to make sense of the previous night when my phone rang. I didn't recognise the number but it had a (07) in front of it. I thought it might have been Jane or Margie calling from Noosa but when I heard the voice I knew it was from further north and west. It was Euan.

He enquired about my trip home to Melbourne, and I asked about himself, and Donald and Kate and Bella. We continued the polite chat for a few minutes before he told me the reason for his call.

He had some news of Aramac that might interest me. He'd run into an old acquaintance by the name of Chancy Anderson at a cattle sale. Chancy had lived around the bush all his life and knew many of the old stories. When Euan had enquired if he had ever heard any stories of an Annie MacGregor or a Bessie Buckley living in Aramac, the name Bessie had struck a chord with him. It was an old story from the early days of Aramac. He never knew her himself, but had heard his mother speak of her. Mrs Buckley had lived in the town with a young boy, her son. She'd worked for some of the families who could afford domestic help. She'd taken in washing and did some cooking at a pub. She had been well-respected by the locals and a bit of an identity. Then one day she left town. Nobody knew what had happened to her, or where she'd gone.

Chancy was a very old man living in an Aged Care Home in Blackall, but when possible he liked to attend the local cattle sales and meet his mates. His memory was still good and the more he talked, the more the stories of the past would come back to him. Euan thought it could be worth coming up to Barcaldine and we could drive down and meet with Chancy.

It was an unexpected and strange invitation, but, after all, I did know Euan and his family. It was at that instant that I realised I really knew so little about him. We'd talked for hours at the barbeque beside the waterhole, and he'd told me stories of the early days in the bush. We'd spoken of his children and other guests around the fire, and I felt as if I knew him. Yet when I thought about it, he'd said so little about himself. He had children but where was their mother? She'd never been mentioned. Was she dead? Was he divorced? Was she still in his life? I had no idea, but I did know I'd enjoyed his company and the thought of seeing him again was pleasant.

I decided to make an excuse and turn down his invitation, but instead I found I was making an excuse to delay accepting it. I thought to myself I would phone Noosa and make some discreet enquiries about him with Margie before I accepted. Perhaps Jane also knew of him, or had friends who knew him. I promised to call him back in two days. I made the excuse that I had already promised my daughter that I would house-sit her house while she and her husband were away overseas. It wasn't really the house that needed minding but my granddaughter.

"Bring your granddaughter with you. You told me she is nineteen so she and Kate should be good company."

"But how would we get there? It's so far away."

Euan explained we could fly to Brisbane then catch another flight to Barcaldine. He would meet me, or us, if my granddaughter came. We would need to be careful with our flights or we might have to overnight in Brisbane. Otherwise it would be a drive. A long drive, but an easy drive, and we could make it a holiday. We would see an Australia that was far from the coast and very different to the Australia I knew.

We ended the call with the promise that I would phone back within two days with an answer. I hadn't told him of my plan to check with Margie and Jane, maybe even Mike.

I reached for the phone to call Noosa, but I put it down. Did I really need to check on Euan? I knew that I wanted to see him again.

I picked up the phone and rang my daughter.

19 Discussions with Sass

It was the day after the phone call to my daughter telling her that I had decided to make the trip north. I was stopped, sitting in a long queue of traffic at a red light that seemed as if it would never change, when the words from Banjo Paterson's poem 'Clancy of the Overflow' that I had learnt at school came to mind. 'The sunlit plains extended'. I thought of the drive to Aramac with Mike and the golden glow over the countryside as we started our return to Kandanga. Then there was the evening down by the creek and more words from the poem, 'and at night the wondrous glory of the everlasting stars'.

I had never realised how many stars there were as on that clear, cloudless night, out in the bush, away from the lights of cities and towns. It was so different to the crowded noisy city around me with its hassled pedestrians, and frustrated car drivers, and determined bike-riders; all jostling for space on the crowded roadway. Suddenly the misgivings that had started to creep into my mind disappeared. I felt a longing to see that country again. Euan's call mentioning possible information had given me an extra reason, and I'd enjoyed his company. I had to secretly admit to myself that, unexpected as it was, I would like to see him again.

That evening my daughter called around for a coffee and

chat.   At first we discussed my plan to accept Euan's invitation and visit Barcaldine, but the conversation soon moved on to my granddaughter. Meg was worried about Sass. She was certainly enjoying her first year at university, but Meg was concerned she was enjoying it too much; at the expense of her studies. She had quickly made friends with others doing the same course but Meg was concerned that Sass's new-found friends were like her, and more interested in a good time and 'important issues' rather than study. I pointed out to my daughter that her father and I had had the same problem with her brother, but he had finally settled down to work and had got his degree and good job offers.

"But Mum, I don't think Sass has the smarts of Sam, she's more like me, and I had to work really hard to get through. I'm just afraid that if she messes it up she will drop out and it will affect her chance in life. Graham and I don't want that for her."

I could understand their concern. They had made big sacrifices to give Sass the best opportunities. When Meg and Sam were at school an excursion might be to Canberra to study the nation's capital and see Parliament in action. These days Sass's school was more likely to organise a trip to an Asian country to visit another culture; if not that, then a trip to Europe to practice their French or German language skills.

"What are her friends like?' I asked. The character assessment I had been given at the Film Festival still lingered in my mind.

"They are forever texting or updating their Facebook pages. That seems to be the main way they communicate these days. That, and some form of messaging. I'm sure when they are sitting around together they send each other messages rather than talk to one another. Although that's not really true. At times they will be constantly talking to each other, all at the same time. Unfortunately that doesn't seem to apply to parents. I'm lucky to get a few words out of her sometimes. The other mothers say the same about their daughters."

"What about boys? I suppose we should say men now."

"There don't seem to be many. It's mostly a group of girls she hangs out with. There are a few boys but only two or three girls seem to have an on-going man in their life, and they seem to change them frequently. I'm not sure if that's good or bad."

I thought back to the time when Meg had left school. Life had been full of highs and lows in the Manners household as she had made the emotional change from school friends to new university friends. Fortunately it had not lasted long as she had quickly settled into study. My son had been more of a concern. Not problems with friends, he had immediately fallen in with a group of like-minded students and played football and cricket and spent hours discussing matches at a pub. There always seemed to be a girl in tow, although they had also changed with regularity.

"You had a group of girl friends at her age. You survived."

"I know Mum, but it's different these days. There are drugs and sex."

"There were drugs and sex when I was doing nursing. Especially in the universities, and your father and I worried about what was happening around you."

"You were fairly safe with me. I'm not so sure about Sass."

"Do you think she is into drugs?"

"Well if she isn't, some of the group are, and she goes to the same parties and concerts."

"Does she ever mention anything to you?"

"She says there are drugs everywhere, even when she was at school some kids were into them, but she says she wasn't. I believe her, but I still worry about the future."

I thought back to Matt and my fears for Meg and Sam. We'd had the same concerns and while we suspected they had tried, fortunately they had quickly passed the exploratory state and avoided drugs. When I had left school drugs had been around, although then the main drug was marijuana and not the more serious drugs of today. I had been offered and tried one funny cigarette, felt sick, and avoided smoking for the rest of my life.

"Have you talked with Sass?"

"I've tried to discuss it but I don't get very far. She just says 'Don't worry mum. I'm OK.' And changes the subject. If I push she gets angry and storms out. I'm not sure what 'OK' really means. I'm worried about leaving Sass on her own when Graham and I take Pete to Cambodia as part of his school Asian Studies. I was hoping you would come over. I'm not sure she can really look after herself. She is not very practical or interested in mundane things like cooking. I think she would be at Macca's or some other fast food outlet every night and I'm not sure about some of her friends if she is alone."

That night I decided to ask Sass to come along with me. It would be uni holidays, so it wouldn't interfere with her studies, and a long trip far from home, through what for her and me would be the great unknown, might be interesting. We would learn more of the country that was our homeland, and hopefully I could get to know and become closer to my eldest, and so far, only granddaughter as she grew from a gangly girl into womanhood. At least that was my wish. But first she had to agree.

That was not as easy as Meg and I had hoped. Sass's first comment was that she'd arranged with a girl friend to go to a concert. When asked if she had already bought tickets she had to admit that she had not; it was still in the planning stage. Her girlfriend was having trouble with her parents who were being "sooo unreasonable and unfair". There was also this cool guy that she hoped would ask her. If he did, she wouldn't have to pay for the tickets because he was friends with the band and could get tickets for free, and he could get a backstage pass for them. Asking the name of the band was no help. Neither Meg nor I had ever heard of it, but then we were hardly cognisant of the music that Sass enjoyed. Usually all we ever heard was any sound that escaped from the headphones or ear pods she wore most of the time she was home or on her way to Monash. We even had our suspicions about whether she removed them in lectures.

Meg tried the suggestion that a trip to Queensland would be of benefit to her course in communications and media studies. Again to no avail. It became quite clear that as far as Sass and her fellow students, and I suspected her lecturers, were concerned anything outside the inner suburbs of a big city was feral country of no interest to them. Rural Queensland was definitely off the radar, perhaps the Gold Coast or Byron Bay would be different but where I was planning to go—"no way , but really, the pits, it would be so uncool!"

The matter rested for a few days and I started to look at the practicality of getting to Barcaldine. Could I fly? Could I take a train? The answer to both was yes, with limitations. There was only one flight a day, and that was not every day. I would have to change to a smaller plane in Brisbane. A train was possible from Brisbane but it would be a long trip. The other option was to drive, but that would take days. Still it would be an interesting road trip of discovery about an Australia that I didn't know. However I was unsure, even a little frightened, of driving all that distance on my own. My daughter was certainly against it.

We again tried to interest Sass in joining me for "the road trip of a lifetime" but met the same answer. She and her girlfriends had planned some shopping expeditions into the city to find some new clothes and check out some make-up they had seen in a magazine that the local shops didn't stock. Another night they were planning to go to a pub in Richmond that one of their friends said had great bands and lots of cool guys that could be fun to hang out with. It appeared Sass's uni holidays were going to be fully occupied.

I phoned Euan to ask if I could put off making a decision for a few more days. But I knew if I were to travel on my own then it would be by aircraft. I was just about to confirm suitable dates with Euan and go online and book when I got a phone call from Meg. "Hold off on booking. Sass was talking to her friends today and they think it is cool that her grannie wants to take her on a road trip. 'Awesome' was the word they used. Anyway, hang off for a day, I think now that her friends approve she will decide it's OK to go."

I waited a day and dropped in on my family on the way home from a garden club meeting. This time when I broached the subject of the trip the response was positive. I was so pleased. I loved the idea of just a grandmother and granddaughter together on a trip across the wide expanse of Australia. So much of it was unknown to both of us. We started to make our plans. Together we would share the driving. We would stay in motels on the way. We would pack breakfast and lunches but find some place in town for our evening meal. What clothes would we need? What would the weather be like? Who would we meet when we got there? Was there anyone her age? I told her of Euan's children, Donald who was older than her, and Kate , about the same age as her. I wondered to myself about how they would get on. I had met Kate at the barbeque on the creek and she had impressed me as a practical confident girl but I wasn't sure that she and Sass would have a great deal in common.

Now that Sass had approval from her friends her attitude to the trip completely changed. The girl who rarely chatted at home had lots of questions and would ring me with questions I was hard pressed to answer. Mostly they were about clothes.

Our next question was how to get there. We knew it was north and in Queensland, but what were the roads? Which way would we go? How long would it take? Meg found a road atlas and we started our planning. The obvious route from Melbourne was north to Shepparton, cross the Murray at Tocumwal and across the edge of the Riverina to pick up the Newell to Dubbo. Just over eight hundred kilometres. That would be a big day's driving for the two of us. Then the next day find the Mitchell highway to Bourke, where Annie had died, and into Queensland. We would stop the night in Charleville. It would be another big day. Two long days but where we were going towns were far apart. Finally, across to the Landsborough Highway, into Barcaldine and on to the station. Euan had assured me it would be easy to find, he would email me directions and a map. That would only be a short day of five hours.

As Sass and I, with Meg looking over our shoulders, sat poring over the map I thought of Bessie. I'd driven through Barcaldine with Mike on our way to Aramac where the mysterious Annie had sent a letter to her. How would Bessie have arrived at Aramac? It certainly wasn't in a car with her granddaughter, but was she with friends or family? Where had she come from to get there, and what had her trip been like? So many unanswered questions. At least I would be returning to that country. Also I had noticed on the map we would cross the Lachlan River, somewhere down that river Clancy had been shearing, before he went 'a-droving' in Western Queensland. Western Queensland. That was where Sass and I were going.

20 Travelling North

We were certainly seeing a wide range of country as we drove north. Fields of crops, paddocks of grazing animals, dairy farms and orchards, forests, flat land and hilly rises. We had already driven through many towns, both large and small.

My granddaughter had not been as curious about the countryside as I'd been. Sometimes we'd talked, but she had spent most of the time listening to music, or dozing lying sprawled out in her seat, only occasionally looking out the window. Sometimes it was difficult to know if she was awake or asleep. We'd tried listening to the radio, but as we travelled the stations would fade from reception, especially the FM stations that had the music she preferred. We tried some of the CDs I had brought with me but they were not to her taste, and eventually we decided to turn the radio off so she could listen to her favourite tracks on her mobile while I drove on in silence.

When I'd discussed my plans with my daughter, she had been insistent that Sass should accompany me if I drove. I wasn't sure if it was my daughter wanting me to be there for Sass while they were overseas, or if she wanted Sass to be there for me. I'd been relieved when my granddaughter had finally agreed. I had come to realise the magnitude of the trip and the distance involved, and how far I would be from assistance should we need it.

I was also secretly excited that Sass had agreed to come. The drive had taken on the image of an adventurous road trip together, and much more interesting than being shut in a narrow tube of metal passing from one airport to another. I had also been looking forward to having an uninterrupted time with my granddaughter but so far we had not shared a great deal of conversation.

Once we were away from the city traffic we had planned to share the driving and as we left Shepparton I pulled to the side of the road and we exchanged places. At least now Sass had put away her ear pods and concentrated on her driving.

"This is so different to when I'm driving with Dad. He keeps telling me what I should be doing."

"Well just keep doing what he's told you."

"I've never driven in places like this with so few cars."

I was pleased; at least when she was driving we could chat. Perhaps I would get my wish and get to know granddaughter better.

We crossed the Murray River at Tocumwal and the landscape changed. Now we were in the wide plains country and the traffic became even lighter. Sass drove on for another hour and we pulled into a wayside stop for our lunch. Restarting our travels we swapped positions and I was again driving.

"Gran, why do you want to do this trip?"

I wasn't sure of the answer to the simple question. The

search for Annie was part of it, but I couldn't explain why it was important because it wasn't really that important. It would change nothing. Then there was the invitation to visit Euan. I'd enjoyed his company at the barbeque on the waterhole but he was hardly likely to change my life either. Ever since my return from Emerald I'd just felt a need for change, to find something new, to go to new places, but how would I explain that to my granddaughter? "Oh darling, your Gran is just looking for a new experience in her life. You are probably having so many that you don't want anymore."

"Yes, uni is so much more fun that school. That was a drag but now I've met some cool friends and we have a great time hanging out together. They're goals."

"Goals?"

"You know what I mean. They are really great and I want to be like them."

I thought of my encounter with one of Sass's friends at the Film Festival and I was quite sure I didn't want my granddaughter to see her as a role model. "What are your friends like?"

"We all have the same interests, well mostly. Things like the environment and people's rights. Standing up to the rich who are ripping off poor people. And animal rights. Most of my friends are into that stuff. They're vegans but I'm only a vegetarian. Sometimes we go out and put up stickers on roadside stop signs so they read 'Stop eating animals'. Killing animals is so gross!"

I remembered Meg's complaint about the change in Sass's dietary requirements and its complications for family meals.

I was grateful I'd made curried egg and not ham sandwiches for our lunch. Sass had not made any comment so obviously eggs were ok. I suppose no chooks had been harmed in the process. I hoped they had been free-range but I couldn't recall what I'd bought. Vegetarianism could be problem because where we were going was a farm that bred cattle and sheep for meat.

It was dark by the time we found our motel in Dubbo and we were both pleased to find a nearby takeaway, eat and fall into bed after a long day of driving.

We planned our morning departure from Dubbo so we would arrive in Bourke in time for an early lunch and a break from driving. I'd done some research on our trip and I wanted to see the old wharf on the riverbank, and I had another plan if we had time. Bourke was where Annie had died, so somewhere in the cemetery should be her grave.

Sitting on the high timber wharf we ate our sandwiches as we looked down onto the river slowly flowing by us. It was hard to imagine that this had once been a major port of Australia. Paddle steamers had made their way from South Australia, up the Murray and into the Darling, bringing supplies and taking away the wool from that vast area known as 'Back of Bourke'. It was from here supplies had been taken by teams of horses or bullocks pulling wagons into Queensland. Camels and Afghan cameleers had serviced other remote and drier areas.

The river-boats had not been an easy trade. There was

always the risk of drought and the flow of water could fall so low the boats could no longer navigate the river. Then they would have to spend time marooned until new rains raised the water level. Floods brought their own risks from floating debris and there were stories of boats taking short cuts across flooded land only to become trapped and stranded for years when the flood waters receded faster than anticipated.

Our search at the cemetery for Annie, and her husband who I thought may possibly lay buried with her, had not been successful. We had decided that a McDonald and a MacGregor would be good Scots and would be buried in the Presbyterian section of the old cemetery but we could find nothing. It was sad to think that our distant forebear was probably here, buried somewhere in the red dirt, no longer acknowledged. So many of the old grave sites were unmarked, a legacy of floods or fire and maybe even white ants eating the old wooden crosses used when the family couldn't afford a monumental mason. Perhaps this place would be the end of my search for Annie and her life.

As we drove on I noticed Sass take a photo of the countryside beyond the window.

"Gran, my phone won't work. I want to send a message to Rissa and show her I'm out in the sticks, the boonies, but it won't send."

"Do you have a signal?"

"No. It's gone. Don't they have towers out here?"

"Not everywhere. I found that out when I went to Aramac with Mike. There were places where it doesn't happen."

"I'm dead. How can they live without a phone?"

"We all used to live without mobiles Sass."

"But Gran, how did you keep in touch?"

"If you weren't going to see the person we phoned on landlines or wrote letters. We managed."

Travelling with a teenager I realised how different my world had been at her age. Then, even earlier, Annie had been only four years older than Sass when she had married. If the records were to be believed she was only a few years older than Sass when she had a child.

"How would you feel having a baby?"

"Gran? What do you mean?"

"Your great, great, great, great, grandmother whose grave we couldn't find in Bourke was only two years older than you when she had a baby. It's possible."

"I know, but really!"

"I'm sure you know girls who have got pregnant. There are lots of unmarried mothers these days."

"Yeah, but you don't have to get pregnant."

"They seem to."

"Yes, but they're not careful."

"I hope you are." Sass's mother had kept me informed of what she had heard about the activities of some of Sass's friends and it seemed very unlikely that Sass had been different.

"Well yeah. It happens, but I'm choosey. Some of the guys think I'm cold. I don't just want to have sex with anyone. If a guy tries it on I tell him to get…Well go somewhere else."

Travelling with Sass took me back to my youth. We had faced the same issue. Did you, didn't you? But we were never as direct or open in our activities. Was it modesty, or the need to preserve an appearance?

What would the future hold for her? So much had changed in my lifetime. There were no mobile phones, no internet; aeroplane flights had only been possible for the wealthy. Even the jobs we did were changing. Some were even disappearing. We probably couldn't even imagine the changes that would occur in her lifetime. What does she want from life?

"What would you like to do when you finish uni?"

"I want to get a job in social media. Television and newspapers are so yesterday. They're boring. Nobody reads a newspaper anymore."

She was certainly correct there. The only people I ever saw reading a newspaper were people my age. The young never picked up a paper or probably even a magazine. Nowadays everything came through their phone or a tablet.

"But who will pay you for that sort of work?"

"There are all sorts of new businesses starting these days. They will need someone to blog or tweet for them, and develop marketing campaigns, but you have to get out and market yourself first to get a really great job."

Hopefully she was right, but I kept thinking of once famous businesses, even in the IT world, that had once existed, blossomed, only to vanish a few years later. So much of the world was based on marketing. What in my youth was called selling, but today salesmen or saleswomen was an old term. Now even the sales girl in a dress shop was an associate or fashion advisor or some other trendy name.

The world had once been a gentler place, or maybe I just thought that. Certainly there had been violence but it never touched my life. My friends and I could go out on a Saturday night without fear of becoming involved in a drunken fight, and we girls would never have been in the fight, yet the television had reports of bad behaviour by young men and women every weekend. The nightly news reports showed a level of anger and aggression in the community that troubled me. Some people appeared to drink purely to become drunk. I'd been drunk several times and I hadn't liked the result. I'd quickly learnt what I enjoyed and didn't enjoy! I'd also been to parties where there were drunken men and women and I had found them rather boring and poor company. Perhaps it was a sign of my age and upbringing? I really preferred company that could be entertaining without the need to dull or heighten the senses with alcohol or drugs.

"Do you ever have any problems with fights when you go to a club?"

"Sometimes there are guys who want to cause trouble. You just have to avoid them. It helps if you stick with your squad."

"Squad?"

"Your friends, your group."

"How did you get on at schoolies?"

"There were some idiots there. We just wanted to have fun and party but some dudes were real badass. That, or others just pissed you off. You just made sure you stayed close to your friends and looked after each other."

I was pleased to hear that friendship was still important. Memories of the group of girls I had seen with Sass at the Film Festival came to mind. I thought it would be a brave male who attempted to mess with them. I remembered going to dances and we would always go to the 'Ladies' with a friend, but that was not so much protection as to have a private gossip and make plans.

"What about drugs?"

"Yes, they're everywhere if you want them. You need to be careful, they can be bad news. I had a friend who bought some and she almost died."

I wasn't really sure about Sass's answer. But I thought it may not be the time to push the subject any further. Perhaps another day, after we had spent more time together.

Our driving had taken us northwards to Queensland, to Cunnamulla and then on to Charleville for our second night. It was another long day of driving and it was again dark and we were both tired by the time we found our beds for the night. This time there were no bright signs outside the doors of big-name fast food outlets vying for our custom and we settled for a little Thai restaurant. Driving around the town I had seen a huge two-storey hotel. Once it would have been very glamorous, but now it was a faded shadow of its past. At our motel the receptionist explained that in the days of the wool boom Charleville had been the end of the rail line and *Corones* would have seen the wealthy graziers coming in for shows or race meetings or to overnight before catching a train to Brisbane. I would have liked to have seen inside the hotel but I was afraid the food at the bar would probably be big red steaks that would offend Sass's sensitivities. At least she would be safe with Asian food. I was sorry I couldn't bring myself to ask her to eat there as I would have loved to have investigated the building and its history, especially when she had ordered a duck dish for her evening meal. I was beginning to wonder how rigid her dietary preferences really were.

We were a little late starting the next morning. Sass had slept well, and since the day's drive would be much shorter the later start was unimportant. Only five more hours plus a stop for lunch and we would be at Raasay. Today our drive took us through country with either low shrubby trees or open treeless plains. Sometimes we would pass through areas with more thickly timbered country. Occasionally a small town would appear, but there weren't many and they were always far apart. The drive seemed to take forever.

It was when I saw a sign as we were driving through Blackall that the reality of where we were struck me. Yesterday we had stopped in Bourke, and gazed out at the 'Back of Bourke', we were already 'Beyond the Black Stump' and today in Blackall the sign pointed to 'The Outer Barcoo'. We were in the outback and everything started with a 'B'.

Finally we were travelling the Landsborough. The name of the highway was familiar; I had seen the replica of his initials carved on a monument in Aramac, and each kilometre brought us closer to a town I recognised. Barcaldine. We were almost there.

21 Raasay

Once we arrived in Barcaldine it was easy to follow the directions that Euan had emailed me. He'd said it was an easy drive and that had been correct. However it was also a very long drive. We had been on the road for days and I was looking forward to stopping, a long hot bath, and a relaxing night with no more travelling.

I was relieved when I finally came to the mailbox for Raasay and turned off the road onto a graded dirt track. Five minutes later the homestead came into view. Unlike the house on the cotton farm near Emerald it was an older timber building. It was large and rectangular with a wide veranda running around three sides. Three steps led up onto the veranda. A steeply gabled roof sat over the house rather like a hat, changing to a gentler slope, like the brim of the hat, for the veranda. Beside the main entrance door a series of French windows opened from the veranda into the house. The house sat in a large garden, but it was a garden of trees and shrubs. It was a practical garden for ease of maintenance, not the domain of a keen gardener. On various parts of the veranda were tables and groups of chairs. Some chairs were arranged around the tables while others looked better suited for relaxation.

As I stopped the car Euan came down the steps from one of the verandas to greet us.

"Welcome to Raasay. You've made good time."

I introduced my granddaughter to Euan and he led us into the house.

"Don't worry about your bags, I'll show you your rooms and then get them. You can freshen up then we can have a cup of tea. Or coffee if you prefer that."

The bedrooms were off a long passage that ran to the rear of the house. On one side the passage was open onto a central courtyard; on the other side were the doorways to the bedrooms. Each of our rooms had French windows opening out onto the side veranda. The walls were white painted timber, and the ceiling pressed tin panels stamped with a pattern. A fan was suspended in the centre of the white painted ceiling. Only the trim and the doors were in a soft grey colour. The rooms had a bright airy feel. Each of the bedrooms had a double bed on which lay a towel, a hand towel and a face-washer.

"There's a bathroom next to your granddaughter's room. It's just for your use. We have our rooms on the eastern side of the house. When you're ready come down to the kitchen. It's at the end of the passageway."

After Sass and I had removed the dust that had somehow crept into the car and settled over us, we went searching for the kitchen. On our arrival the house had looked to be a rectangle but it was actually more a square. The wide frontage we had seen on arrival held the formal rooms. Down each side, opening off the passageways, were the bedrooms and bathrooms. Across the rear, beyond the open courtyard lay the kitchen and breakfast room, and an informal lounge room.

"Your house is an interesting design."

"My grandfather built the main house after he had had a run of good seasons and prices. The old kitchen was in this position. That was standard practice in those days in case the fireplace for cooking burnt the house down. Which it almost did. So when my father rebuilt he made some changes, modernised the kitchen, and added two rooms. Then my wife had another go and brought the kitchen into the current age."

I looked at the kitchen. It was well-maintained, the fridge and stove and other appliances were modern, but the style was far from recent. I thought possibly eighties. Although it had been repainted the layout and the cupboards had not been changed.

"Where are Donald and Kate?"

"They are both out working. Kate is checking and cleaning some water troughs, and Donald is on the grader tidying up some tracks and fence lines. Kate should be back soon. Donald won't be back until dark. I was just speaking to them on the radio."

"How did you go drafting your cattle for market? I was sorry I missed you at Kandanga."

"They went well. We'd negotiated a good price at the meatworks and I needed to make sure they went. I'm sorry I had to rush off without saying farewell."

As the sun was dropping we gathered around a table on the wide western veranda for drinks. Unlike the eastern veranda this section of the veranda was screened by gauze.

As well, trees, planted in the garden by earlier generations, broke the harsh glare of the sun as it set in the west. Kate had organised some biscuits and cheeses, and eventually Donald also joined us. When he had first returned from his grading he had been barely recognisable under the heavy layer of dust covering him from head to foot. When he had taken his sunglasses off the paleness around his eyes had stood out from the grey coating of dust. It was later, after we had eaten our evening meal and had moved from the breakfast room beside the kitchen to the adjoining lounge, when I raised the question. "You said you had met an old man that may have known something of Bessie Buckley. Where is he?"

"Chancy is in an old people's home in Blackall. I'll take you to meet him. I think he might be able to give you some more information. I left him thinking about the old days and I hope it will prompt his memory. You're probably over driving, so have a day here tomorrow and I'll take you to meet him on Tuesday."

Later, while Euan was answering a phone call, Sass and I took a walk in the garden. The lights at the rear of the house were hidden by the high roof and the front of the house was in darkness. It was a cloudless night and in the sky the stars were bright and beyond count. I pointed them out to Sass.

"I never knew there were so many stars, or that the Milky Way could be as bright."

Like me, my granddaughter was a city girl. Our stars were hidden by the lights of the city around us. I had seen stars at Kandanga but here they were even brighter and more numerous.

"Gran, is Euan married?"

I had to answer her question by admitting I didn't know. Every time I had planned to phone Jane or Margie and enquire I'd hesitated and put the phone down.

"Why do you ask?"

"I saw a photo in the sitting room. It was Euan and Kate with a woman. She looked like Kate. It must be a recent photo because it was at Kate's school graduation."

"He has mentioned a wife, but I don't know whether he is married, or divorced, or if she is still alive."

"You like him don't you."

"Yes. I enjoy his company but that's all, and he has offered to help me in solving the mystery of Annie and Bessie."

Walking together in the garden the sounds and smells of the bush came to us. Unlike Melbourne there was little noise. Just the sound of a small breeze moving through the trees. In the distance a cow was calling: perhaps for a calf, or perhaps for a mate. There was quietness to the night but it was not silence. It was all so different to Melbourne. At the far end of our garden walk we came upon an old rough building. In the moonlight it appeared derelict and unused. It was a strange garden feature to find.

We returned to join Euan and his family and made plans for the next day. His suggestion was to have a relaxing day on Raasay and he would show us around the property. Then, as promised, the following day he would take me to Blackall to meet Chancy—Clarence Anderson, the Third.

I awoke in the morning to an intermittent roaring sound. When I raised the noise with Kate in the kitchen she apologised, and explained it was the pressure unit that supplied the house with water. The tank and the pump were not far from my bedroom and every time somebody showered or the washing machine started the pump would operate. That was another new experience to add to grading your own roads and disposing of your own waste rather than expecting the Council to come and collect it.

After breakfast the three of us started our tour of the farm. Kate and Donald had already left for their day's program.

We spent several hours driving from paddock to paddock, checking water troughs and livestock as well as the condition of the pastures. Euan explained that the property was once all sheep, but market conditions had forced a change to cattle in order to survive. Markets had changed again and now they were running some sheep, but these sheep were not for wool like the old days but for meat. We stopped at the huge old woolshed and walked through it. Euan explained it was a relic of the past. It was now unnecessary, but it was still very dear to him, and he hoped he could preserve it: sheep had provided for the family for many years.

I asked about the time when Bessie would have been in Aramac.

"The first squatters coming to Queensland mostly brought sheep. The wool industry was growing rapidly. Wool could be shorn and baled and sent to England for sale. It didn't deteriorate with time, and it could take a long time between shearing, transporting by horse or ox drawn wagons to a port, and then shipping to England in sailing boats to be sold. Until canning, and later freezing, became viable beef and mutton were a problem. Meat could only be salted or dried to preserve it. That was a limited market, unless you had a huge growth in demand due to gold miners. Then the animals could be walked to the goldfields and slaughtered when needed. At times, the only value in cattle was for the hide and sometimes the sheep's carcasses were even boiled down for the fat to produce tallow.

"I gather Aramac must have been a very progressive town when Bessie was here."

"Yes. The early squatters first stayed near the coast and that country was not very suited to sheep but the country west of the Great Divide was ideal. So sheep moved west and cattle remained in the country where sheep didn't do well. With the sheep came people."

"What is the old building at the bottom of the garden?"

"That was the first real house on Raasay. The family have kept it as a reminder of where it all started. I say that is where I will retire when Donald and Bella make a decision. Would you like to see it?"

It was a small two-room cottage, more a hut, with a separate lean-to a short distance away from the main building. The lean-to housed an oven built of rammed earth and a small open fireplace.

"You're not serious about living here?"

"No, but it does remind me of how my great grandparents lived."

The walls of the cottage were slabs of timber dropped between round sticks of timber, small branches, nailed to the vertical posts. The roof was of similar round timber over which flattened sheets of bark were laid and tied.

"We added the corrugated roof to protect the bark."

"How old is it?"

"I'm not exactly sure. The family story is that the first MacLeod lived in a tent until he built the hut. The family arrived from Scotland in 1897 and settled here a year later, but how quickly they built the house I don't know."

"So where did the name Raasay come from?"

"Scotland. It's an island between Skye and the mainland. It's traditional MacLeod land. The first MacLeod to settle here named it after his home island and we've been here ever since."

"What about your children? Will they always be here?"

"That's up to them. They will have to make their own decisions, but I hope Donald and Bella will stay. I'm not sure about Kate. She's taking a break from uni this year and is doing a gap year before she goes back. Well, a gap year with some external study."

Euan explained that Kate was studying business management and finance. "Very handy in the bush these days, but I suspect she will move to a city somewhere. In a couple of years she will have to find a job. I doubt it will be here, probably in a big city or a regional city. We lose so many bright kids from the bush. Then I will have to sort out the succession planning. These days you have to be fair to girls. Not like when I was young and girls were expected to marry another property owner. Once upon a time rural families would try to set up their sons on the land. Girls were expected to find a mate on the land. That worked if sons married country girls and country girls married country boys. Times have changed. Nowadays girls must get their share. It can cause the breakup of rural businesses. As well, not all children want to stay on the land, my brother didn't, and there can be problems buying siblings out, or the property not making enough to pay the family member working it plus a share to the absent family members. Sometimes the property doesn't make enough money and it has to be sold up. Then everyone is off the land."

"Do you have many brothers and sisters?

"One brother and two sisters. I had to buy my brother out when he moved to Sydney, he wasn't interested in the land. The estate had to provide for my sisters until they married and then give them a lump sum payment. After probate of course. Fortunately Death Duties had been abolished by then or it would have made continuing here impossible. One moved to Rockhampton and the other lives on a property near Longreach."

"What about Donald? Did he go to university?"

"Yes. He studied agricultural science. Same as Bella, but he did more animals and she did plants."

That evening we again sat on the veranda. Sass and I with glasses of wine, Euan with a whisky and Donald and Kate with beers. Euan was laying back in a large chair, rather like an oversized deck chair with a canvas back and wide arms with wings that swung out and around as extensions of the arm rests. It was an unusual chair. I asked him about it.

"It's called a squatter's chair. Very popular in the old days, and today as well. You swing the extension around and rest your legs on them." He demonstrated. "Try it."

Donald rose from where he was sitting and offered me his chair. I sat in it and lent back against the canvas material. It was relaxing, but the thought of swinging the extension arms around and lifting my legs onto them was out of the question in a dress. Even in slacks it would have been a most unladylike position. I looked across at Kate who was reclining in another of the chairs. She was relaxed, her legs sprawled across one of the arms but even in jeans, she had not swung her legs out onto the extensions.

"I thought all Queensland cattlemen drank rum? That was what I was told at the barbeque at Kandanga."

"I prefer whisky. I suppose it's my Scottish heritage. Rum was, and is, very popular."

I asked him more about the house. When he had shown us around the house I had noticed that the ceiling in each room was different.

"Wunderlich pressed metal ceilings were the fashion when this house was built. Previously there had been small cottages like the one you saw in the garden for family and workers. Another cottage or a lean-to was added as the family grew. The ceilings really date the house but I love them. The one in your room is acanthus; Sass's room has flannel flowers. The dining room is of vines. It's very busy with lots of detail, and the sitting room was called fleur. My bedroom is bluebells. My wife loved it."

The mention of a wife opened up the subject. "Where is

your wife now?"

"I don't have a wife. Donald and Kate's mother and I separated years ago. She was a Brisbane girl and she didn't really take to life in the bush. It can be hard for some people to make the change. Some can, some can't. I would hate city life. I don't think I could adapt. It's such a different lifestyle. I think living in the bush you are closer to the seasons and reality with droughts and floods, life and death. City people sometimes seem to be so removed from reality."

"What happened with your children?"

"When the kids needed to go to school she moved to Brisbane for their education. They would all come home for holidays, but eventually it became obvious that it wasn't working. She still lives in Brisbane and has since remarried. The kids are fond of her and we are still good friends. I'm pleased the kids have returned here, even if Kate will probably move."

I'd been watching Sass and Kate talking together during the evening, and I was unsure of how well they were really connecting. I suspected they had little in common, and that Sass was not interested in making an effort to get to know or understand the other girl's views. When Euan had told us of the possible plans for our visit to Blackall, Sass had decided to come with us rather than accept the offer to stay with Kate. She had expressed interest when Euan mentioned the 'Tree of Knowledge' and 'The Worker's Hall of Fame', which I suspected would be more approved of by her university friends, with their so-called progressive interests, than spending time with a rural 'hick' raping the countryside producing red meat.

I went to sleep that night wondering what I might learn from my meeting with Chancy Anderson the Third. Would he provide some clues to the life of my great-great-grandmother Annie? Tomorrow I would find out.

22 Chancy Anderson III

As we were driving into Blackall to meet the old man I asked Euan about Chancy's name.

"Everyone knows him as Chancy but his real name is Clarence Anderson. Clarence Anderson, the Third."

"Where does the third come from?"

"That's a mystery. Apparently there is no one or two. Chancy reckons his mother just liked the idea. Thought it was impressive, made her baby sound important. Bit like a king or a family with lots of history and money. His father's name was Fred."

"Was there any history or money?"

"None that Chancy knew about. They were always battlers."

"What about the name Chancy?"

"He got the name at school, not that school and Chancy spent much time together. He says he left school when he was thirteen. His dad had died when he was a little kid and he wanted to get a job to help his mum. She'd been a station cook, moved around and then into town so he could get an education. His mum used to cook at one of the pubs. When he was a young fella he was always telling his mates, 'Reckon we're in with a chance here mate!' It might have been racehorses, girls, a business venture. He was always dreaming up some get-rich-quick scheme. I don't think they ever worked."

"Is he a crook, or a rogue?"

"No. No, he's honest. Mischievous, yes. Usually unsuccessful in his plans. He loses his money, and yours if you back him, but he loses it honestly. Just don't invest in any of his schemes."

"What is he like?"

"I've known him for years. He's a bit of a legend around the place. He's had many careers, and interesting ones too. He's worked on various stations in the West and at the saleyards. When he was a young man he worked up in the Territory for a few years. He has lots of stories about those days. His last job before he was pensioned off was working for the local council—on the roads. He is also quite a storyteller although sometimes you have to question how true they are. I hope he gets started. It's always a pleasure listening to Chancy tell stories."

We found Chancy on the veranda of the aged care centre. He was sitting in a cane rocking-chair enjoying the morning sun and watching the passing traffic in the street. He apologised for not getting up. "It's me knees. The doc says me heart's not good enough to replace them."

He was a tall lean man, dressed in a faded checked shirt and blue jeans, and wearing carpet slippers. Euan had told me he was quite an old man but I had never really considered what I would find when I met him. When he spoke he certainly gave the impression of a younger man. Not exactly young, but certainly younger than the ninety-one years that Euan had told me he was.

After introductions he and Euan chatted for ten minutes, discussing the weather, cattle prices, the season and mutual acquaintances before the subject of Bessie Buckley was mentioned.

I'd decided that addressing him as Mr Anderson too formal for the old man, yet Chancy was too familiar for someone I had just met. I addressed my question about Bessie to him as Clarence.

Chancy went quiet when I asked the question. "Call me Chancy love, everyone does. It was only me mum and the missus who ever called me Clarence, and then I was usually in trouble."

It had all been so many years ago when he was only a little fella. He remembered his mother talking with an old lady friend. They went very quiet but he overheard. He didn't understand what it was about then, but later he realised.

"My mum hadn't ever known this Bessie but she'd heard the stories. The old lady had known Bessie. From what I heard from me mum, if I remember it right, was this lady, Bessie Buckley, was married to a stockman who worked on a local station. They'd both come out from Ireland early in the piece. Apparently he left the station and started working as a teamster, carting wool to the coast and bringing supplies back. Don't know where he got the money to set up a team and wagon. That would cost a few bob, even then. Maybe his old boss helped him. The boss might have reckoned he'd get preference shifting his wool. Anyway Bessie and her husband set up camp on the outskirts of Aramac. There they would have grazing for their horses or bullocks when they were between jobs. Then they had a little baby. A boy. Anyway one day there was a bad bushfire going through the country and her husband was out fighting it and a tree fell on him and killed him. Everyone was devastated. He and his wife were very popular in the district. After that Bessie and her baby moved into town and she found a job cooking at the pub. She also took in washing and did some cleaning for the nobs in town."

I could identify with Bessie. Like me she had lost her husband in an instant. But with her it was so long ago and she was far from her family and the services I took for granted. She also had a young child who needed care. My children were adults and I had, at least, been left in a secure financial position. For her, all those years ago, it must have been so hard and frightening.

"All the locals rallied around the poor woman but it got worse. When her son was about five some horses spooked and a coach took off down the street. It hit the little kid."

"What happened to him? Was he badly hurt?"

"Pretty bad, he died a couple days later. The poor woman was apparently beside herself according to the story the old woman told my mum."

I thought of the conversation with my Great Uncle James. It certainly explained why Bessie was referred to as 'poor Bessie'. "So what happened to Bessie?"

"Bit of a mystery. One day she just left town. Nobody ever heard of her again. Guess Aramac wouldn't hold too many good memories for her."

"Did your mother ever speak of an Annie MacGregor?"

Chancy twisted his head and looked skywards in thought before he replied. "Can't say I've ever heard that name mentioned."

"What about a Mary Ann McDonald?"

"No. Don't know that name either. Who are they?'"

"Probably the same person. I suspect McDonald was her maiden name." I explained my story to Chancy, about the mystery of the letter from Annie to Bessie. But he could shed no light on the matter. Bessie had left town after the death of her son and Chancy's story ended. The death of her husband would certainly be distressing and the baby could be 'your precious one'. The story did fit the letter but still left the mystery of Annie. I was no closer to solving that puzzle.

Euan enquired about Chancy's well-being, how he liked his room, and if he had had any luck with picking winners at the recent race meeting. A sparkle came into Chancy's eyes as he told the story of backing a horse at ten to one. I thought it must have been a winner, until he said 'it came in at quarter to four'. Suddenly I realised what Euan had meant about Chancy and his stories.

I asked the old man if he had any family. He replied no, and told me the story of his life. He had married but they had lost their son at birth. "Almost lost me wife too. I was a bit of a flash lad in those days and I'd been on the booze when my son was born. Never touched the stuff again. Ever since then I've been on the wagon."

I asked if they had tried for another child.

"No. It was just so hard on the missus. It could've killed

her. Couldn't do that to her again."

Soon he and Euan began talking about old times. He'd first gone to the Northern Territory when he had turned twenty-one and got a job in the stock camp on Buchanan Downs, near Top Springs. It was there he met his mate Polley. It was a pretty busy life. Most of the times they spent out in the camps: sleeping in a swag under the stars. "You started work at daybreak and finished in the dark. Then sometimes you had to do a turn watching the mob at night. It was a great life. Rough horses and wild cattle and great mates."

When the mustering finished he was offered a job yard building. "Cripes it was hot mate. The sweat poured out like a waterfall. I was on the booze then but there wasn't any in the camp and even in the pub it was hot. It was rum and water in those days. Never liked that very much. There were five of us building yards. The boss, me, me mate Polley, and a couple of the indigenous. They were good workers. The boss, Tom, was a good bloke to work for. He didn't take no nonsense. He was tough but if you worked well, he treated you well. Slack off and you could walk, and it was a long way to walk. It was the same for all of us. The Aboriginal blokes were very quiet in camp. Kept to themselves a fair bit but they could work when the rest of us were buggered. Sometimes used to see them in town with their mates and it was a different story then. They could be very vocal. Very popular too 'cause they had some money and their 'lations wanted some of it."

"What were you building the yards out of?"

It was a question I would never have thought of asking but

it was obviously of interest to Euan.

"We used to go out into the timbered areas and find ironwood for the posts and then cart them back to the site. We'd find some bulwaddy scrub and cut lance wood for the rails. They made pretty good yards provided you looked after them and made sure the wildfires didn't burn 'em down. That used to happen a bit. I hated that bulwaddy scrub. It is evil country."

"Why?"

"It's thick, hard to get through, dry. Just hate the look of it. Grass doesn't grow. Anyway after a few years Polley and I decided we had had enough and came back to Queensland. Then I met 'The Missus', never went back. Polley did though, for a few years."

"Did you catch up with your friend Polley again?"

"Oh yes. We were great mates but he died a few years ago."

"How did he get that name?"

"Always had that name. It was his head, I think he got it as a kid."

Euan explained that a poll, or a polley, was an animal without horns.

"Yeah. Even as a young bloke he had a big forehead, not much hair on top. Reckon he was probably born that way!"

"What about your wife? What was she like?" I was curious to find out more about the woman who had married Chancy.

"Her name was Marie, and her women friends would call her that, but I always called her 'the missus'. Most of my mates called her 'Chancy's Missus' or just 'Missus C'."

I could see Sass who had been sitting back quietly listening to the conversation stiffen and sit up a little straighter. I could imagine the treatment a male friend in her group would receive in mentioning his partner in such a manner.

"She was a wonderful woman. Really strong and capable. She was a great person if you had a problem, not just for me but for her friends and the town. When I had a problem with the drink, she held things together. She didn't make a fuss but you really paid attention when she let you know. Not that she was bossy like, but just she was a woman that you respected."

As he spoke the old bushman's eyes moistened. Euan had told me Chancy's wife had died many years earlier, but it was obvious the affection and love remained.

The time had come to make our farewells and Sass and I left Euan with Chancy who wanted to sort out some private matter that was concerning him. As we were walking back to our car Sass asked me why I was so interested in Annie's story.

It was hard to explain to a teenager. For them it was the past and unimportant in their lives. Even for me, it was not going to change my life, and I had been surprised myself by my interest in the matter. I guess as we get older, and have time on our hands, curiosity about our past increases. Perhaps as we get closer to our own death our interest in those who preceded us grows. Certainly at my age I have more past than future.

"Gran, why does Euan treat that old man with so much respect? He's just an old man who hasn't done anything special in his life."

I suggested that she ask Euan that question over lunch.

23 Barcaldine

We left the aged care home with the old man sitting on the veranda outside his room and Euan drove us back to Barcaldine to see the Tree of Knowledge. I remembered seeing a segment about it on television many years earlier. There was some story about how the tree had been poisoned and was dying. The ageing tree had a place in the history of the union movement and the Labor Party had taken great and expensive steps to save it, or at least the remains of it, which were then encased in a very expensive timber structure. I wasn't sure how you would really describe the structure.

As we sat in the Shakespeare Hotel, eating a counter lunch, with the Tree of Knowledge and the Railway Station across the road from us, Euan told the story of the tree and the Shearers' Strike.

"The late 1880s were a troubling time. Wool prices were fluctuating and the seasons were being difficult. At first the graziers reduced the price they would pay for shearing, but then they restored it back to where it had been. The Gold Boom had ended badly and the entire country was in a very difficult position financially. By the time the shearers went on strike there was a Depression in Australia. It was a time of great social unrest, socialist ideas were popular and even communes were being formed. All around the world workers were demanding an eight-hour day. In 1891 the shearers went on strike and set up a large strike camp on the creek just outside town. There were also other camps around Barcaldine and at other towns. The accepted story is that the strikers used to meet and discuss their grievances and make plans under that ghost gum in front of the railway station. Some old Western Queenslanders I have spoken with question that idea. The tree wouldn't have given much shade even then, and I suspect there would have been a lot of talking in the Strike Camps as well. However it would be a central meeting place in front of the railway station and the pubs on the other side of the road. Although without any pay the strikers eventually ran out of money, so that may have affected their beer consumption. Anyway, that's supposedly how it got the name 'Tree of Knowledge'."

"What happened with the strike?"

"It got very lively. Woolsheds were burnt down and armed guards put on others. Attempts were made to derail trains bringing in non-union workers. People were intimidated if they wouldn't join the strike. It became very nasty. It was even feared that it could break out into civil war. At that time Queensland was still a separate colony and the Colonial army was called in. Eventually it all died down. The strikers were running out of money and getting hungry."

"Did the poor shearers get a pay rise?" It was Sass who asked the question.

"It was never really about pay rises. The real fight was over the Union demand that only Union members could work in woolsheds. The graziers would not accept that condition. They insisted they could employ whoever they pleased. One hundred and twenty-four years later unions and employers are still arguing over that condition."

"So what happened?"

"The strike ended. The shearers went back to work and the shearing rate and conditions were unchanged. However it did lead to the emergence of the Union movement in Australia and from that the Labor Party was developed. Some of the strikers eventually had prominent political careers. The site of the biggest shearers' camp was just outside town on the banks of Lagoon Creek. Just before the end of the strike there was a big May Day March in Barcaldine with over thirteen hundred marchers, including a large number who were mounted on horseback."

"You said May Day. I always think of those big parades in Red Square in Moscow on May Day, but the Barcaldine parade would have been long before Russia became a communist country."

"Yes, Liz. I guess growing up around here I developed an interest in history. May Day was originally an old, well ancient, festival at the start of summer in the Northern Hemisphere. The present May Day traces back to the USA. As I said, there was worldwide agitation regarding workers' rights. In the States a rally of workers supported a strike calling for an eight-hour day. It became violent and a bomb was thrown at the police. Then there was gunfire and police and civilians were killed. It was in early May 1886 and that, and the subsequent legal proceedings, became known as the Haymarket Affair. It led to the establishment of the International Workers' Day in May. The idea came to Australia, as did the name for a new political party. Have you ever noticed the Australian Labor Party is spelt with an 'o' not an 'ou'. That's the American spelling that came over with the American idea of workers' rights and the eight-hour day."

I could imagine Euan chasing up obscure points of history. I'd already noticed a quiet determination to seek out an understanding of whatever caught his attention. I asked him if his family had been involved in the Shearers' Strike. He told me that "No, they had come to the district a few years later." By then the strike had ended, although tensions between the station owners and shearers remained. He told me about the awards which came into force and governed employment. They had even stipulated the size of toilet doors, the type of bed and the mattresses on them, as well as the food to be provided to the shearers. Details that most people, shearers and station owners alike, eventually ignored but for many years Union officials and Government inspectors could cause many problems if the buildings were not painted in an approved colour, or the size of the veranda didn't meet the rules. The last big battle with the Unions was over the width of the comb on the handpiece used to shear sheep. The Union resisted the change that most of its members wanted because it enabled them to shear more sheep and earn more money.

"Some of the strikers had dreams of a 'Workers' Paradise'. Socialism and communes were big ideas at the time, and certainly some things should have been improved, but it was only a few years after the Strike that the wool industry went into a decline and industry profits and wages both fell. Even today some people just don't see the connection between our living conditions and the economic reality."

"What is the big structure over the tree?" Like Sass I was curious about the big box on stilts I had first seen when I had come through Barcaldine on the way to Aramac.

"The tree became quite sick back in the nineties. It was an old tree, after all it was one hundred years after the Shearers' Strike. A tree surgeon was called to try to save it but it was still pretty sick and miserable. Unions and Labor, and trees, can still be a touchy subject for some people in the Bush. Anyway, about ten years ago it is thought someone poisoned the tree. There are a few theories about how it happened but I doubt we will ever actually know the truth. The remains of the tree were taken to Brisbane and preserved then it was brought back here and re-erected. Not only that, this 'award winning structure' was erected over it. It is supposed to have all sorts of symbolism but most of the locals just think it was a waste of taxpayers' money and completely out of character with the town."

After we had finished our meal and were enjoying the last of a cup of tea Sass asked her question of Euan.

"True, he's not an important man but he's a good man. From his stories, and what others have told me, he was bit of a wild lad in his youth. But, as he said, when he lost his baby he changed his life. If one of his mates, or in fact anyone in town, had a problem or needed a hand Chancy would be the first there, and if he told you he would do something, he did. He'd never asked for a favour or payment, he just got in and helped. He believed you should treat people fair and that's how he expected to be treated, but if you took advantage of him your reputation was finished in Western Queensland. Does that explain why I value Chancy's friendship and respect him so highly? To me he is a true gentlemen."

Sass was silent as she thought about Euan's answer. He continued.

"Quite apart from all that, he deserves respect for his skill. Obviously I never saw him working when he was a young man, but even in his middle years he could out-ride most young horsemen. He had a way of understanding horses and cattle that is very special. Plus he was fearless. I have seen him ride horses and bulls at rodeos that the young guns couldn't ride. He deserves respect for that too."

Sass had another question. "It's about the name of the town."

Euan smiled. "That's a common one. Visitors often say Barcal-Deen. It should be pronounced Bar-Call-Din. With a long emphasis on the call. Don't ask me why, it's just the English language. Well Scottish actually. Donald Cameron established a sheep station here named Barcaldine Downs, after his home town in Scotland. The locals just say Barky, although they spell it b.a.r.c.y, with a 'c' not a 'k'."

After our lunch Euan took us around the corner to The Workers' Heritage Centre. It was an interesting museum of old buildings, each with a display devoted to some section of the workforce, or women. I remembered once seeing the big central tent that had been part of the travelling Bicentennial celebrations years earlier. We were the only visitors as we wandered the grounds. I felt a little sadness: the displays were informative, but tired, and even for me the emphasis on labour was too one-sided. In the Police Watch House I was interested to see an article about 'Banjo Paterson's Waltzing Matilda'. I had always thought three policemen accosted the swagman by the billabong, but this article claimed it was only one policeman, whose official police number was 123. Paterson had the number wrong anyway. The correct number of the officer involved was different. Perhaps we will never know the true facts. A depression-era unemployed swaggie stealing a sheep for a meal, shearers camped by waterholes, squatters mounted on thoroughbred horses. In Barcaldine the words suddenly took on a new and much greater meaning for me.

I'd assumed that the Workers' Heritage Centre would have been more interesting to Sass with her concern for social issues, but she had soon tired of the displays and had settled herself on a bench overlooking a pool of water. It was there that Euan and I met up with her.

"Gran, what sort of birds are they?"

Not far from her bench a group of birds with grey bodies and brown wings were noisily chattering away as they flitted around the waterhole. "They're Apostle Birds."

"Why are they called that?"

"You always see them in groups, families, they have another name, 'Happy Families'. Usually there are about twelve in the group. The Twelve Apostles. Count them and see how many you have."

"You're right. There are twelve. Are there always twelve?"

It was Euan who answered. "Not always, but they do live in groups of about a dozen. Their correct name is Struthidea Cinerea. They are also called CWA birds."

"CWA?"

"Country Women's Association."

"Why?"

"I'll let you work that out for yourself. I like the name Happy Families."

Next Euan took us to the local museum. Entry was by a donation to an honesty box at the front door. Here there was no one guarding the box as would have been necessary in a big city. The museum was a less grand affair run by volunteers in the district. Two, whom Euan seemed to know personally, were working restoring an old machine in the museum yard. Looking at the faded newspaper articles and photos I really felt for the first time that I could experience, just a little, the life that Bessie must have lived. With Euan as our guide I could see the changes that took place in the district. The services that once existed that had vanished. The change from rough bush shacks to comfortable housing. The scale of the enterprises that had disappeared. Now the six remaining hotels in Barcaldine made sense. Once the town had even more when a population existed to service the sheep stations, to scour the wool, produce tallow and even to have their own soap factory. Now the main activity of the town appeared to be servicing the needs of grey nomads.

On our drive back to Raasay my thoughts turned to Bessie and Annie. The Shearers' Strike of 1891 would have been fourteen years after Annie's letter was written. If Chancy's story was correct, Bessie's son would have been killed in the accident in Aramac by then, and Bessie had probably left town. In my afternoon as a tourist I had learnt of both the good times and the hard economic times. I was sure Bessie would have known them intimately.

Where had Annie and Bessie first met? Was it Aramac, or

someplace else? Chancy had said Bessie and her husband had come from Ireland to Aramac. Perhaps Annie had come with them? I asked Euan if that would be possible.

"They could have been on the same boat, even though Bessie was Irish and Annie a Scot from her name. The boats leaving Scotland often carried some Irish emigrants as well, and it's probable that the boat came into a Queensland port. Could even have been Rockhampton. In those days sailing boats came into many of the ports along the coast. It didn't have to be Brisbane."

"Do you think that they could have met up on arrival in a port and come to Aramac together?"

"It's possible, but in those days a single woman would be unlikely to travel on her own. Could she have been married? Girls married young in those days. Another possibility is that she could have come out as a servant to one of the wealthy squatters. You told me the letter was probably written on her behalf so she could have been a servant or a nanny. A governess would require a better education. She could have come out to help a squatter's wife. Many squatters were Scots and they could have brought someone from their village with them. If she did come to Aramac she must have left before Bessie's husband was killed in the fire and it still doesn't explain how the letter was returned to her."

It was Sass who suggested an explanation. Bessie had left Aramac and joined Annie in Warren. Annie had sent a second letter, this one with her address on it, written after the one my mother had so carefully preserved. We just didn't have that letter. Bessie had returned the first letter to the writer when they were together. It was a possibility, but it was unlikely we would ever know.

As we drove up to the house on Raasay a black ute was parked under the trees by the entrance gate to the house. It was a vehicle I had seen before.

24 Visitors

"I wasn't expecting this visit."

Euan appeared puzzled finding the black ute with its flashy wheels parked beside the bottle trees at the garden gate. I knew whose vehicle it was from my time at Kandanga, but Euan told me that if Bella came she was usually in one of the Kandanga four-wheel drive utes or her own little Toyota. James must have brought her over.

Donald and Bella were together in the kitchen preparing the evening meal while James was sitting at the kitchen table watching them. Kate was absent. There was an obvious tension in the room and James had an angry look on his face.

Euan introduced Sass to Bella and James and James' expression immediately changed. Suddenly his dark look vanished as he shook hands with Sass. Just then Kate reappeared from another part of the house having heard our return. She was unusually subdued in her manner.

It was only later, having left the younger ones watching a movie, and when we were sitting on the veranda enjoying the soft warmth of the night that Euan told me of the afternoon's drama. Bella had decided to pay Donald a visit. It often happened. They had a very close relationship and it was not uncommon for them to spend time at each other's homes or to go away together on weekends, or whenever an opportunity arose. Both families approved of the relationship and they now shared a bed when visiting each other. Indeed both families were wishing the relationship would take the next step and they would make the decision to marry, or at least live together permanently as so many young people did these days. Euan had already discussed their relationship on our drive around the paddocks. He was sure it would eventually happen, but he didn't think Bella was ready to take the final step. It seemed she had some concerns about her father's business and felt she needed to be at Kandanga.

This time James had decided to join her on the trip to Raasay. That wasn't unusual. He and Kate had once been boyfriend/girlfriend, but that had ended months ago. Euan had never been told any details, but he thought that Kate had called it off. She had never discussed the reason for the relationship ending, and that was most unusual for Kate who was normally very open about her feelings. He had told me he was secretly pleased. His opinion of James was mixed. He was torn between giving the boy the benefit of the doubt and concern about reports he'd heard. James had not been happy with the arrangement. However, Kate and James had remained friends, although becoming more and more distant.

It seemed that since his arrival earlier in the day he had been trying to restart the romance and had been annoying Kate with his behaviour. Bella had taken him aside for a quiet word but he had taken no notice of his sister. Finally Kate had been very direct in her response to his behaviour and a disagreement had developed. Kate had left the room and Bella had defended her friend. James had then been in the sulk that we had seen on our arrival.

Returning to the lounge we found the five deciding on whether to watch another movie. Plans for the morning were discussed, with Bella wanting to make an early start to return to Kandanga, and Euan and I made our goodnights and retired to our rooms. Kate also took the opportunity to make her departure.

Next morning when I arrived in the kitchen Euan was preparing some porridge. Kate and Donald had already breakfasted and left to check stock in a far paddock. Bella was sitting at the table finishing a cup of coffee. There was no sign of James or Sass.

At last James walked in and found some cereal and made himself a coffee. Unlike Bella he seemed to be in no hurry to return home. Finally Sass entered. She was still sleepy.

"What time did you young people get to bed?"

"Don and I left at midnight. I don't know about the other two. They were still talking when we left."

James flashed a look at his sister. "We didn't make a note of the time, we were just enjoying the company."

"Well you had better stop enjoying the company and get a move on. We need to get home. I said I wanted to leave at six and it's now eight-thirty."

As they left I noticed that this time it was not a handshake from James for Sass, but a hug. A hug that she returned, and they both appeared very comfortable with their closeness.

That evening I discussed my plans with Euan. I was very appreciative of his taking me to meet with Chancy, and I'd enjoyed the visit to his property, but I felt we really should make a move to return to Melbourne.

"Can you stay a few more days? I have to go to a bull sale the day after tomorrow, and I think you would find it interesting. You'll see a bit more of country life and meet a range of people. I'm sure you would enjoy the experience. It will mean a very early start. It is about four hundred and sixty k's away. Would you like to come? It will be a big day but if you prefer you could stay here with Don and Kate. I should be back that night but it will be very late. Your granddaughter is welcome to come with us if she wants to, she might find it interesting, or she might prefer to stay with Kate."

I hesitated. Euan had been very generous with his time but I didn't want to impose. On the other hand, neither Sass nor I had to be back to our homes until the university holidays finished. Nor would a few days interfere with a commitment I had given Tony. As Euan had said, it would be a new experience for a city girl, and I thought it would be interesting. I accepted. I also admitted to myself that a few more days of Euan's company would be very enjoyable.

As I passed Sass's bedroom I called in to tell her of our new plans. I had half expected disapproval for the extension but was pleased when she agreed without any dissent.

"Gran, what do you think of Kate?"

I was surprised by the question. I thought it more likely that I would be asked about James. "She seems very nice. She's very beautiful."

"She's very pretty but I think she's a bitch!"

Sass's outburst surprised me even more. It didn't seem like the Kate that I had seen. "Why do you think that?"

"It was this afternoon. She came up to me and talked to me about James, said he wasn't to be trusted. I think she's jealous because James and I get on so well together."

"From what I've seen I don't think he and Kate are on good terms."

"That's what he told me. She thinks because she's so pretty she can have anyone whenever it suits her, and because he doesn't accept it she's really nasty to him. I think she just wants to keep him on a lead"

"Has he spoken to you much about Kate?"

"A bit. They used to have a thing but he had enough of being treated badly and ended it. Now she's jealous about anyone who is nice to him."

"I'm not sure that's the full story. I have seen them together before and I think James was the one making a pass."

"He told me he tries to be nice to her but she treats him badly."

"Maybe you should make up your own mind up about people. Judge them as you find them, not as others tell you. I've always found that the best way."

"I like James. He's really cool and interesting. He's so different to the boys at uni. They are just so full of themselves."

I left my granddaughter to drift off to sleep with her favourite music playing from her phone. James had returned to Kandanga. Another five days at Raasay would not be a problem, provided Kate and Sass remained at a distance.

Next morning at breakfast it was a different Sass who appeared. Gone were the shorts and the t-shirts of her favourite bands, and in their place were jeans and a long-sleeved shirt. I was sure the shirt must have only been packed at the insistence of her mother. It was so unlike Sass and her current style. Gone also was the lack of interest in the land and animals. Today she wanted to get out and be involved. I noticed however that it was always with Euan or Donald; never with Kate.

25 The Bull Sale

It was five in the morning when we left for the bull sale. There was a chill in the air and it was still dark. I'd come to realise that living in the remoter parts of Australia could mean long days and late nights when you needed to travel. It would be a drive of almost five hours to the property where the sale was being held, the sale itself, and then another five-hour return trip to Raasay after the sale. In the city so many people expected to spend an hour travelling to or from work each day, but here work was just outside your door. It was when you wanted to go somewhere else you had big distances to cover.

I'd never been to a bull sale. I had no idea what it would be like. It would certainly be a new experience and I would enjoy spending time with Euan. I had spoken again with Sass, but she and Kate had already made plans for the next day. It appeared that Sass had softened her view of Kate. They would do a horse ride out to a bore where Donald would join them for a picnic lunch. Then they would spend time on their computers updating their Facebook pages.

We arrived at Rometa Park just before ten and joined the other arrivals for a cup of tea at a table spread with scones and biscuits and cakes. The parking area was a mix of four-wheel drive wagons and utes, plus some trucks with stock crates and even two semi-trailers. Ordinary cars were in a definite minority. There were even two light planes parked beside the fence of the airstrip. I pointed them out to Euan.

"There are a couple of pastoral families up north that buy bulls here most years. They are a long way away from anywhere, and they own a few stations so they need a plane to cover the distance and move around between properties and saleyards."

Before the sale commenced there was a brief talk from an invited speaker, on changing market demands and their implications for cattle breeding, then everyone moved to the cattle yards. I wasn't sure what I expected. Perhaps bulls paraded one at a time in front of the buyers like I had seen on television, or perhaps the buyers moving along from pen to pen as an auctioneer sold the animals. This sale was different. Bulls stood quietly in yards as the buyers moved around each yard inspecting them and making notes in their catalogues. Euan joined the men and women in the yards as I waited in the shade of a roofed area in the centre of the complex. When he had finished he came back to me.

"When does the sale start?" I asked.

"It has. This sale isn't the usual sort of loud open cry auction. Everyone inspects the bulls, makes their selection and decides on a price. Then they go over to that board and give the auctioneer's secretary a card with their name and the number of the bull they want to buy and a price. She writes it up on the board. If someone wants that particular bull and is prepared to pay a higher price they give their card and the higher price to the secretary and the buyer's number and price is changed. If someone is prepared to pay more for the bull you want than you're prepared to pay then you go and find another bull and it starts again. At midday a bell will be rung and a countdown commenced. If you want to change your price you must do it within two minutes. Then the countdown starts again. There's usually a bit of a rush at that stage then it settles and eventually no new changes occur. There's a warning call, and the auction is closed."

"Doesn't that make it complicated?"

"Not really. The system is called a Helmsman auction. The advantage is you can change your mind and decide that one bull is too expensive and then find a bull in your price range. At a normal auction you might like the last bull in the sale, you wait for it and find it is too expensive, by then you've missed the chance to buy the bull that was your next preference that came through earlier in the sale. I like this system."

"How do you know how much you should pay?"

"You know what price bulls are selling for in other sales. It's in the newspaper, and people talk about sales they've been to. Here the opening price is set in the conditions of sale so you can start at that price or make a higher offer if you think the bull is worth it. There is a difference at this particular sale because they have a top price limit. Once someone pays that price the bull is theirs. That doesn't apply at all sales."

The bell rang and there was a rush of bids, then the changes to prices stopped. Two more minutes passed and the sale was declared over. The vendor thanked the buyers, the agent and all those present, and invited everyone back to the house for a barbeque lunch.

The lunch was on the lawn of the homestead. Like Euan's it was a large home built of timber weatherboards and had the high roof and verandas that I had so often seen in the older houses in the West. Unlike Raasay, all except the front veranda was screened with flywire gauze. It was the smaller out-buildings that caught my eye and I asked Euan what they were.

"The first is a meat room. Sheep, and maybe a beast, would have been killed and hung in there overnight away from flies, then cut up and put in a fridge or cool room. The next was an egg room. This property once had a large poultry run for their needs, plus pig pens and a large house garden and orchard for fruit and vegetables. The last building must have been for staff. Perhaps a single man or woman who ate at the house. A gardener or cook."

"What about a governess?"

"Maybe, but she might live in the house with the family. I don't know. This was once a sheep station. There was a lovely old woolshed and shearers' quarters further down the road. There haven't been sheep here for years and the shed and the yards were demolished a long time ago. When I last went past the site of the shed there were only a few old sheets of bent-up corrugated iron and a derelict meat house."

The lunch was a generous serve of sausages and steak, and the smell of frying onions filled the air. The tables were laden with salads and bread and against a wall the large eskies sat filled with beer, plus soft drinks for the children. For the few who wished wine was available. Euan moved around the crowd introducing me to his friends. He seemed to know most of the people. I supposed he would have met many at previous sales. Only a few were new to him but all were new to me and I was hard-pressed to remember names.

It was obviously a family day out. Groups of happy children were running around and playing together, young mums fussed over babies, but older children were missing. I soon discovered the reason. Up until high school age many of the kids were on school of the air. Provided they did the assignments sent to their homes it didn't matter when it was done. They could go to a bull sale with their parents and meet and play with other children. That social interaction with kids their own age was a great treat for children often isolated and far from their classmates. Their school work could be done earlier or later, just as long as it was done. Once they went to high school it was a different story. Then they would have to leave home and go away to a boarding school in Rockhampton or Toowoomba or Brisbane unless the family home was near a town with a high school. Emerald would have a high school so Bella and James could have gone there, but Donald and Kate were much further from town and I had already learnt that they had moved to Brisbane with their mother in order to get their education.

In talking with the young mothers I learnt of the distances some would travel to give their children an opportunity to mix with other kids. Several spoke of how they, or the fathers, would travel hundreds of kilometres to take their young sons to football training or matches. Girls might have sport, or dancing, or piano lessons. Hopefully it could all be arranged for the same time.

The crowd at the lunch slowly drifted away. The trucks and semi-trailers went to the yards to load their purchases, and other successful buyers made arrangement to pick up their bulls another day. The two planes took off on their return flights to the north and only a few people remained. It was apparent that Euan and the owner of the property were good friends, and Euan was invited to go with a small group to inspect some heifers and a new stud sire that had just been purchased. I was left with a group of wives. I was certainly the odd one out, and although they were inclusive in their conversation I had nothing in common with them. Our worlds were so very different.

By the time Euan returned it was late in the afternoon and our host invited us to stay for the evening meal. It would only be leftovers from lunch but there would be plenty. Euan came to me and explained the situation. To return to Raasay would be five hours and at the moment the kangaroos were especially bad on the road between Augathella and Tambo at night. We could stay in Augathella. There was a motel and it was only half an hour away. If I agreed he would phone and make sure they had a room. Euan was with his friends and I could see he was happy in their company. It would have been selfish, and probably foolish, not to stop overnight. I agreed.

Without the need to make the long trip back to Raasay Euan relaxed and settled in to chat. The group sitting around the fire, for the night had become cold, covered a wide range of politics and social issues. They were generally conservative in their outlook but not insular. I realized many of them had seen much more of Australia than my city friends. Also they were far more knowledgeable of cities than my friends were of the countryside.

As we drove the narrow single lane road back to Augathella Euan explained not all country people were as widely travelled as the group around the fire, and there were some blinkered attitudes in the bush just as there were in cities. What really struck me was the concern about the weather. For me, and my friends, it was whether the weekend would be wet or dry, hot or cold, and how it would interfere with our plans. Here it was a matter of financial well-being and sometimes the survival of years, even generations, of work.

The motel was right beside the highway and all night I could hear the rumble of semi-trailers and road trains passing. That was the ones that didn't stop with a hiss and squeal of brakes across the road from our rooms. When Euan had arranged our accommodation I had not queried what it would be. When he came back from the office with two keys I knew.

26 Romance in the Bush

The drive from Augathella, through Tambo and Blackall to Barcaldine and on to the station was becoming familiar. It was the third time I had travelled the road. The last sections I had now travelled five times. I was beginning to remember the bends in the road, the corners that you needed to slow down to take safely, where you could overtake caravans, and the lines of trees along de pressions that could fill with water after big rains. For a city girl whose only experience with the bush was a rare drive along the highway to Sydney, or a visit to a park on the outskirts of Melbourne, the vegetation and the landscape were becoming etched in my heart. I could feel for the writer thinking of the Queensland bush when he received a reply to his letter that he had addressed to Clancy of The Overflow.

It was so different to the beautiful autumn colours and vistas I had enjoyed on my visit to Bright with Tony. Thinking of Tony brought to mind Matt, and then Euan. They were all so different but I knew that Tony would never fill the place of Matt. Nor would Euan, but somehow that wasn't so important. I suddenly realised he was already filling a place—a different place.

On our return to Raasay we had stopped off in Blackall again. Euan told me he wanted to show me the old wool-scour as he thought it may help me to better understand the region and its history—and its present. Yet there was something more to his desire to tell me about the pastoral industry but I didn't know what it was. Once the scour had been an important industry in the town with its own railway siding but that had all gone and the scour had closed. In the early days of the sheep industry, the sheep had each been individually washed in a pool, or tubs of water, to remove the dirt and natural grease from the fleece before they were shorn. It had been a terrible job for men to stand, waist deep, in pools, or tanks, of often cold water for days on end. Then new technology enabled the fleeces to be washed after the sheep had been shorn. Removing the dirt and grease reduced the weight of wool that had to be shipped to markets in England. Wool scours had sprung up all over the wool-growing areas but gradually they had disappeared with only a few remaining, and these had become larger and larger and based close to major markets. The selling of wool had also changed and it was now sold 'greasy' and often the scouring process was done overseas. Australia had lost the industry to countries which could do it cheaper. To Euan it was just another example of the poor decisions and attitudes that were destroying Australia's industrial base.

The Scour and its shearing shed and yards had been saved from their fate as scrap and the old machinery returned to working condition for tourists. As we strolled through the yards Euan told of how sheep would be walked from nearby stations to be shorn and where the shearers and workers would live. Then I saw the machinery in operation as the dusty greasy fleeces were transformed into a soft white web of fibre; the first stage of a long process to make the cloth or yarn for our clothing. Euan explained that these days the process was very similar but the scours were now huge buildings with modern and efficient machinery. This one did have an advantage the new ones lacked. Here the water steaming out of the artesian bore was already hot.

"It's the same with any business, doesn't matter if it's a factory or farm, you have to change and stay ahead of the competition. If you don't, you're history, and your business and the jobs that go with it will be gone."

From the way he had expressed his belief I felt that there was a concern about his, and his family's, future. He had already told me how the family business had changed over the years and I suspected he might be concerned about what the future held for his children. I was beginning to realise that with Euan there were often things left unsaid. With Tony I'd learnt to give him time to bring out what was concerning him, but that would only be a few days, and then he would open up and it would all rush out. With Euan, I didn't know. There was a reticence. He could be open and forthright in his views, but when it came to personal matters or critical appraisal of people he would be very circumspect. I suspected that you would need to be close and trusted before he would reveal his innermost feelings.

It was mid-afternoon when we arrived back at Raasay. Donald was away checking some cattle in a far paddock and Kate was working in the garden. Sass was nowhere to be seen. It was evening before we all came together for sundowners. Sass arrived from her room where she had been reading. Euan reported on the bull sale. "I bought two bulls. They should drop them off tomorrow from a truck that is heading north with some bulls for Merry Downs." The conversation continued about the bull sale and our late departure to return to Raasay, and our decision to stop off overnight in Augathella to avoid travelling the road at night with its well-known dangers of kangaroos and accidents.

The day we had left for the sale the previous visitors had returned to Raasay and stayed overnight. Bella had told Kate that James had decided to come back with her on this visit because he liked the city girl visiting. His comment to Bella had been, "It will be good to see a bit of city talent for a change".

Donald, James and Sass had spent the afternoon moving a mob of sheep closer to the yards, and in the evening Kate, Bella and Sass had prepared a meal, then they had all played pool in what was once the old billiard room that was now a games room. Bella and Donald had gone off to bed, and James, Kate and Sass had sat up watching videos until Kate declared she had enough and was ready for bed after her early start that morning. She had left Sass and James to watch another video.

By the time we had arrived back at Raasay Bella and James had already left to return to Kandanga, Donald and Kate were away yarding the mob of wethers they had mustered the previous day, and Sass had retired to her room.

It was later in the afternoon, when the others had gone to draft the mustered sheep and select some ready for inspection and sale, and Sass and I were sitting by the pool in the shade of a pepperina, that Sass asked me about the night in Augathella. "Gran did you really stay with Euan at a motel?"

I explained that, yes, we had. Locals hated driving that

section of road at night for fear of colliding with kangaroos that would come out at night to graze the grass on the edge of the road and would jump in front of passing vehicles in an attempt to get away, rather than jump in the opposite direction away from the vehicle. Euan had told me of the many accidents that had occurred, sometimes fatal, and of the many kangaroos that had died hitting the bull-bars fitted to vehicles to protect the radiator and engines. At the sale he had pointed to the damage on several four-wheel drives and mouthed the word 'Kangaroo'.

"Gran, you rock! What a cool Grannie."

I immediately realised what Sass had concluded. "No, Sass. We had separate rooms."

"Oh. I thought he would find you hot."

"Just a secret between you and I, Sass, I hoped he would."

"You really like him don't you?"

"Yes, he's a very good man. I like him a lot."

"What are you going to do about it?"

"What do you mean?"

"Well if you like him, how are you going to get him to be your boyfriend? Are you going to live with him? That would be so cool, a Grannie living with a cute boyfriend."

"What would you do?"

"I'd make sure I looked good. I'd find out what he liked and sort of take an interest in that, and make sure he saw that. Sometimes it's boring if he likes football. He thinks you should be there all the time watching him and he just wants to show off to his mates. It sucks but if he's really cool and other girls want him, well you have to do it."

I remembered to emotional pulls of my teenage years. The feminist movement was very active and most of us were demanding our independence and rights, but we still had the longing, and fear, if we didn't have a boyfriend. How times had changed, and yet for all the noise females were still looking for mates and males were looking for...sex? I knew I would never want to go back to those years, I couldn't anyway, but what did I want now? Friendship? No, more than that. Sex, well that could be nice but then...at our age that might be problematic? I suddenly realised what I had not allowed myself to consider. I did like spending time with Euan. I could even consider sex with him, and had even felt a little disappointed that it had not been suggested last night.

Sitting on the veranda of the homestead enjoying the last rays of the setting sun and the arrival of a cooler evening breeze, the conversation turned to the bull sale and local customs. "What's the thing about rum up here?" I had first noticed at the barbeque down on the creek at Kandanga and then again at drinks after the bull sale that some of the men were drinking rum.

Euan supplied the answer. "I suppose you could say it's a cultural thing. Most cultures have some form of alcohol made from a local product. In the north it was sugarcane, so the alcohol was rum. Unlike beer you didn't need to cool it on a hot day. In the old days there was no refrigeration or ice out in the bush. The best you could do was put the bottles in a creek to cool them, or you could lay them under a wet bag. That would cool them as the water on the bag evaporated.

That was never really successful either. It was not cold the way we like beer now. Rum didn't need cooling and besides there were more headaches in a bottle of rum than a bottle of beer, and that was a plus if you had to carry everything on horseback or a wagon. So rum became the drink of choice. In the early years it was rum and water. There was no Coke in those days."

"I've never thought of alcohol as a cultural thing."

"Most cultures have some form of intoxication based on a local product. Down south and in England they could grow barley so you have beer. France has grapes so they have wine. Anything that can be fermented seems to do the trick. They are some very strange drinks around the world."

"You sound like an expert, Euan."

"No, but I've been curious. If a tribe doesn't have alcohol then they will have some other drug: chew leaves or smoke something."

"What about the Aborigines?"

"Well some of them certainly have a problem with the booze that came in with the British. It has been a disaster for some. Kava is a recent import and all the other problem drugs of today that are now so commonplace everywhere have very quickly reached even remote communities. There's always someone out to make a quick quid out of another person's misfortune."

It was Sass who made the comment. "Perhaps they were like koalas and used to get high on gum leaves?"

"Actually they did. Some Australian plants contain nicotine, just like tobacco, and they used to chew it. There was also another plant that had a similar effect. In small doses it was a stimulant but too much acted as a depressant. It could suppress hunger and allow you to walk long distances, or fight fiercely, but too much could make you drugged out. From what I understand chewing pitubi has died out. Beer and wine and the new drugs have taken its place unfortunately."

The conversation had lazily wandered over many subjects when Sass asked the question after she had picked up a tape measure lying on a side table. "What is this funny tape measure for?"

"It's to measure bulls' testes."

"What for?"

Kate answered. "The bigger the balls, the more semen, the more cows the bull will get in calf. Well that's not quite true. There are lots of other factors involved as well and really it's not just size, more an adequate size for the bull's age and condition. Small testes are to be avoided." Sass looked hard at Kate.

"How many cows will a bull get in calf?"

Kate continued. "Depends on the bull. Some are shy, others are go, go, go. We usually work on allowing a bull fifty cows per cycle, that's three weeks roughly, but some can do more. It depends on the individual bull, some are keener than others."

"Sounds like the boys at uni. I think some of them would like to be a bull."

I was pleased to hear Euan's reply to Sass. "Humans are different."

"I'm not sure some of the boys I know are! It's good when you meet a man that is more sensitive."

Kate, who had been relaxing quietly on a lounge suddenly moved. We all looked at her, but she said nothing.

On our last day Sass was up early and waiting in the kitchen when the rest of us arrived. Usually she would be the last out of bed and we would be waiting for her.

The first job for the day was to return some of the sheep to their paddock and Kate and her favourite dog took them away from the yards on a motor bike, followed by Sass driving an old Toyota. Donald was in the shed working on servicing the dozer, readying it for a job. Euan took another Toyota and invited me to join him on a run around the bores and stock troughs. As he drove he talked of the country, the grasses, the trees, and the improvements his father and grandfather had made. He talked of how the country changed from season to season, and between good years and bad. He made little comment about the changes he, himself, had introduced, yet it became apparent that Raasay one hundred years ago had been a very different property. Then it had been horses, and more people. It had been almost all sheep and that had required much more labour. Stockmen, shearers, shed hands, and fencers. At first the water supply had been dependent on creeks and waterholes, then an artesian bore and open bore drains had spread it far wider across the station. The bore drains had now been replaced by piping and allowed the grazing to be better managed.

Once there had been homestead staff: a cook, a housemaid, a gardener, plus station hands and a jackaroo. Now it was one workman, Donald, Kate and himself and the workman's wife who helped out in the house. In years past a team of shearers and shed hands had come when they had been needed. Even with the decline in numbers of sheep in the district the shearing teams were getting harder to find and many properties had changed over to cattle entirely. They required much less labour. Where once shearing teams would have moved from shed to shed by horse or push bike or even on foot, now the few teams remaining drove in cars. Today there were girls working in the woolsheds, something once unheard of and forbidden. There were even a few female shearers. His grandfather and father would never have believed it possible.

Driving around with Euan I became aware of a different world; a world that I had never contemplated. I wonder how Bessie would have found it all those years ago? How different would it have been? "How would Bessie have come to Aramac?"

"You say Bessie was here around the late eighteen-seventies? In those days it would have all been horses. Too early for motor vehicles. The train did not come until later so Bessie and her husband could have come by coach. If Chancy's story is correct and they were working for a station near Aramac, perhaps they travelled together as a party with a supply wagon."

"What would the country have been like in those days?"

"The downs country, the flat treeless plains, would have been very similar. Probably covered with long grass, especially if it had been a good season. Any animals, and people, would have been limited by access to water. In those days it would only be surface water and that was not always permanent. There were no bores or drains at that time. The first artesian bore in Queensland was about nine years after your letter was written. Until then, if the water dried up everything and everybody had to leave. That's why good waterholes were so important, especially in a drought, and there were always droughts, always will be. The artesian bores made all the difference to this country."

I asked Euan how the bores were dug.

"They weren't dug, they were drilled. Or really punched in with a bit. In those days the hole was started and water put down the hole, the bit was raised and then dropped down again. The dirt and stone and mud would be cleaned out of the hole and they would repeat the process, again and again. They were called mud punchers. At first it was done with horses and then steam engines were used. Some bores would go down two thousand five hundred feet and it could take several years and a team of men to drill a bore. It was a very expensive project. The good thing was artesian water would flow up the bore and out the top. You didn't need to pump it."

"What would the people have been like?"

"They were all looking for opportunity. Some had capital, some were escaping the starvation in Scotland and Ireland, but all were hoping that the new land would bring them a chance to better their lives. Just like my family."

He told me his family story. They had come a few years after the big Strike when the huge original stations were being broken up. They had hard years and good years. Some very good years, and some tough years, but the country gets in your blood. Some families stayed, others moved on. His family were stayers. He hoped Donald and Bella would take over and continue, but they would have to make that decision for themselves. He didn't have the right to impose his dreams on them.

"So what will you do?"

"I don't know. I love it here but one day I know I should leave. I certainly don't want to hold back Don and Bella by interfering with their dreams. That's if they ever get their act together. It is often a problem in the bush that one generation doesn't know when it's time to move on and let the younger ones have a go."

"What happens to you then?"

"If I'm lucky they'll value my experience and I will still have a link to Raasay. I just don't want to end up an old man on a hobby farm closer to the coast telling all and sundry how it should be done."

That evening, as we sat around the dinner table for the final time, I noticed a change in Sass. She'd come from the paddocks dusty and dirty, and was obviously tired, but she'd showered and changed into clean jeans and a pretty print top. With her hair tied back in a ponytail she looked gorgeous, no longer the silent teenager whose only interest was her mobile phone. Tonight she joined in the conversation and was keen to learn all she could about the land and sheep and cattle. It was an amazing transformation in just a few days.

27 The Crash

The peace of the evening with its quiet conversation was shattered by the sound of the phone.

After some time Euan returned. He was looking worried.

"That was Bella. Mike has problems. Big problems. They all have."

"What's happened?"

"Bella didn't go into the details, but it appears that Mike had made a big investment in a Gold Coast company. Some sort of internet scheme. It was going to change the world. Anyway it's gone belly up. He's lost the lot and apparently it was all borrowed money. The bank now wants their money back. I heard talk at the bull sale but I didn't put too much weight on it. Some people are always ready to chop down tall poppies and Mike has upset a few people over the years."

"Can't he pay the bank?"

"Mike has always been a high-risk, high-return man. Everything he has is always on the line. He thinks unless you do that you're not trying. The bank has told him he has to sell up."

I felt sorry for Mike. During the short time I had spent in his company I had come to realised how important Kandanga was to him. "Will he sell up?"

Euan explained that if he was forced into a sale he probably wouldn't get a good price. All the vultures would be out. "But it's worse. Margie has filed for divorce. Bella thinks she is trying to get hold of as much as she can but half of nothing is nothing."

"It won't be that bad, will it?"

"It seems Mike's second wife still has some interest in the property. Bella didn't say whether it was the land, shares in the company that owns the business, or a loan. She's now demanding he buy or pay her out. As well, all the local businesses are refusing to deal with them unless they pay cash. I guess they're worried they will only get part of any outstanding accounts he has with them. James is also causing problems. Mike and Bella told him he has to stop spending money and he got angry. He accused his father of ruining his future and told them he's going to Sydney to get a job with his mates."

"What will he do about Margie?"

"Mike has always had an expensive taste in women, but sometimes they don't stick around if their tastes aren't indulged. Bella always had her doubts about Margie. It looks as if she was right. She told me quite a while ago that she thought things were on the rocks. Margie didn't really want to be at Kandanga. She much preferred the life in Noosa. Bella was surprised when she showed up with you. She was actually wondering if Margie saw you as another of Mike's possible conquests. You might even be useful in her divorce."

The news of Margie's plan came as a complete surprise to me. I had never given it a thought. I had been surprised with the sudden change of plan and her driving me up to the farm. I had even thought that she may have come to make sure Mike didn't make any inappropriate suggestions to me if we were alone; after all, I had been warned of his reputation. As a result I had been puzzled by the way she had made sure I spent time alone with Mike. I considered Margie as a new friend. I was very annoyed at being used in such a way. "How is Bella coping?"

"She'll be OK. She's a smart capable girl. Her life will change though. She could get a job anywhere in the industry. I wish that she and Don would finally make a decision to get together permanently. They would make a great team. But, in the meantime she will stick with her father."

"What will happen with Mike?"

"Hard to say. The bank wants him to sell up. He'll fight them. I imagine he will try to renegotiate the debt, get it written down. Maybe try to find a new partner. The operation is probably quite profitable, it was the bad Gold Coast investment that pushed it over the edge. I expect he just got too greedy and careless. He may try to hang on and work his way out, and I'm sure there will be court actions. Possibly over the Gold Coast deal. Bella says it's uncertain whether the collapse was genuine or caused by the organisers skimming funds into their private accounts. Mike may even take action against the bank. That could give him more time but this sort of business never ends up well. I'm sure he'll give it a try, Mike's a fighter for all his faults."

Poor Mike's world seemed to be falling apart. I'd enjoyed the time I had spent with him and found him a very charming man. I knew I was not the only woman who thought that way. My suspicions from Noosa about the relationship between Mike and Jane returned. With Margie seeking a divorce, would she be free to move in? Then, was she the sort of woman who would stand by a man who could lose everything? I suspected not.

"What about James? Will he go to Sydney and get a job as he says?"

"What about James?" It was Sass who had just entered the kitchen and had heard his name mentioned. I told her of the news from Kandanga and its effect on the family. She looked troubled and went quiet, then left the room.

Euan continued with his news. "I don't know. His mates liked having him around when he was spending money. I suspect most of them will be less enthused if he is broke. Besides I don't know how smart he really is. Bella often covered for him."

"How do you think he will cope? You know him better than Sass or me."

"James is very like his father, but I don't think he's as smart. He's a bit of a womaniser too. That's why I was concerned about Kate, and your granddaughter. I don't think he is very caring about his girlfriends. He could cause them a lot of grief if they fall for his charm. I've seen him at work at some of the district race meetings. Bella's different. She's more like her mother but she also has Mike's business ability. Strange thing to say considering the current news, but Mike's a good businessman."

"You seem very fond of Bella."

"Yes, she's a great girl. Smart, you probably don't know but when she was at uni she did an exchange to a university in the US for six months and did some business management courses. She also has a good way with people. Treats them with respect and is interested in them. Cares about people. James is inclined to play the rich kid, 'I'm better than you'. James thinks he runs Kandanga but it is really Bella who makes the major decisions with her father."

"What was his and Bella's mother like?"

"She was a lovely person. A very special person. Mike was foolish to lose her."

"What happened?

"The usual thing. Mike has always had a liking for a pretty face. Whenever the marriage got a bit stressed he would wander. I think Angela had had enough. Eventually they called it quits and she took Bella and James to Rockhampton for school. They divorced. The kids stayed with her during the school terms and came out to Kandanga on their holidays. Mike remarried. Then, eventually Angie met a new man and married. It seems to have worked. Bella says he's a lovely man. She approves of him. They live in Rockhampton and I see them occasionally when I'm there. She was a lovely woman, not just looks, although she was very attractive, still is. Mike would never marry a plain looking woman no matter what her personality was."

From the way Euan was speaking, and the look on his face, I had the feeling that it was more than just admiration that he felt for Angela. "Did you ever think of marrying her?"

"Mmmm. No. I was married at the time. It wasn't a perfect marriage but I was married."

From Euan's answer I suspected the idea may have crossed his mind. "What about later?"

"No. The timing was wrong. By then Angie was married. Besides it wouldn't have worked anyway, and how would it be with a stepson marrying a stepdaughter, even though there was no blood connection? I have hopes for Don and Bella."

"What was your wife like? I hope you don't mind me asking?"

"I guess we were just the wrong people but we didn't know it at the time. We had lots of mutual friends, they were all getting married. It seemed to be what you did at that age, and we did like each other. Well, it was more than just that. Anyway all was well until after we had the kids. Then we had a few tough years. They were really hard. Seasons and money. By then Jennifer had had enough. She wanted me to sell up and move to Brisbane. I couldn't do that. Still couldn't, I'm a country boy. So eventually we decided to separate, she would live in Brisbane and the kids could go to school there. That would save money, and I would stay here. It wasn't quite that easy—we had a few angry moments. Some of them were mine. Then a new man came into her life and we divorced. With hindsight we should never have married, but then we do have two good kids. That's made it worthwhile."

"It must have been hard making the break?"

"Yes. Admitting you made a mistake and it hasn't worked out as you thought it would. We were fortunate. We separated, but at least we were both concerned to protect our kids, and we were able to share their growing up. It was so much better than the bitterness and anger where families refuse to even talk to each other. That can be a tragedy for everyone. Plus, when you have a property or a business a bad marriage can destroy the business, and everybody's future. It's the great fear of many rural families."

I felt for Euan. He had regrets about his marriage. And from the way he spoke and the softness in his eyes I thought that his feeling for Mike's first wife was more than just friendship. Timing and opportunity can play such an important part in how our lives eventuate.

"What happened to Mike's second wife?"

"Mike always liked high-maintenance women. He got that with Julie. It lasted about five years then she found someone with a bigger credit card and more money."

"I thought Mike would be wealthy." Considering the evening's news that was a strange thought.

"Well, he is, or was. Probably will be again if I know him. Julie found a really wealthy man, way, way above Mike. Fortunately she wanted a quick divorce, and didn't want to create any concern about causing financial problems. Why hang out for a piece of cake when you can have a much bigger cake? I gather from Bella she must have got something from the divorce but left it in the business. It looks like she now wants it. Perhaps the new husband's a bit tight, or she wants a running away from home account to finance a lawyer if she leaves him."

"You don't seem to have a very high opinion of women?'

"Well I guess it is just my experience."

"We are not all bad."

"Yeah, I suppose."

I went to bed that night with thoughts of Mike and his family, and Euan and his, and mine. Eventually I drifted off to sleep, but then I suddenly woke in fright.

28 The Dream

It was early in the morning when I suddenly woke. The memory of the dream was still strong in my mind. Usually if I dreamt the images would fade rapidly and I'd have little recall of any of the dream, but this dream was different.

I was surrounded by four dogs. Not as a pack. These all seemed to be individual dogs and they were not frightening in any way, but they were still troubling.

One was small, and brown and white in colour. A hyperactive type of terrier of some sort. It rushed enthusiastically in circles around me, often coming in closer and getting under foot. Just looking at it exhausted me. The second was a large, handsome, well-groomed type of retriever. It was a rich chocolate colour with dark eyes and a curly coat. It was also circling around me. Not so close as the terrier, but I had the impression it could move in closer at any time. It wasn't threatening, in fact it was quite appealing, with a look of power and tireless energy. The third was a large silvery-grey and golden dog. An indeterminate breed, a mix of German Shepherd and Golden Retriever and perhaps something else. An original. A one and only. The image of it was less distinct and almost ghost-like. It was sitting quietly at a distance watching over all that was happening. Looking at it a feeling of calm came over me, plus a little sadness.

The fourth dog I recognised. It was the red kelpie, Harry, that I had seen with Kate when they were working sheep two days earlier. He was crouched down silently watching me and other dogs. I had noticed Harry in that pose and then seen him instantly burst into action when called upon to attend to a misbehaving ewe. I had remarked to Kate how well she had worked him and she had replied that really Harry had done most of the work. He had the mob under his control but together they did make a great team.

Suddenly I realised what my dream was about. They weren't dogs. They were men. The men around me. Tony was the hyperactive terrier that needed, and demanded, constant attention. That would be a problem in real life.

I smiled when I thought logic of my subconscious. Mike as a retriever, a water dog, just the right dog for an irrigator. Even the slight curl in his hair matched the dog and he was certainly good-looking and energetic. From the stories I had heard he could even be ready for closer relationships given the opportunity.

I knew the ghostlike dog was Matt, silently watching over me from a distance. It was reassurance and security that I felt looking at him. It had always been that way.

The kelpie was Euan. That's what had troubled me. I'd enjoyed his company when I first met him at the barbeque by the waterhole, and over this visit I had come to realize how much I liked being with him. As I'd admitted to Sass I could even contemplate a closer relationship. But our lives were so different. And what was he really like? There was so much I still didn't know about him. What did he think? Was he quietly watching me and what would he do? Would I be rounded-up like the sheep if I stepped out of line? Or could we be like Kate and Harry and make a great team? That was hardly likely to happen with my life in Melbourne and his in the Queensland bush. Our lives were just too different.

I didn't know the answers to any of those questions. I wasn't even sure that I really I wanted answers, but I knew what I had to do when I returned to Melbourne.

29 Return to Melbourne

The road trip back to our homes in the south was uneventful. After discussions with Euan we had decided to return by a different path, at least until we reached Dubbo. Over our days together Euan and I had talked of the rapid developments in western and northern Queensland that had taken place in the last half of the 1800s, of the boom days of the gold rushes in Ballarat and Bendigo, and of the various boom times in the wool industry, but Euan had told me there were other booms, and busts. The iron ore boom in Western Australia was more recent and if I went home via Roma and Miles I would see signs of the current boom—the coal seam gas.

With his directions in hand Sass and I had driven away from Raasay early on the Friday morning. Our road retraced our steps to Augathella and I pointed out the motel where Euan and I had spent a night.

"Do you think you will see Euan again, Gran?"

It was a question I couldn't answer. We had parted with a quick hug and best wishes and I had promised to contact him when I was safely home, but there had been no other commitments or indications. Barcaldine was so far from Melbourne and our lives so different, it seemed unlikely our paths would meet unless one of us made a major effort. He'd told me he was not a city person, and although I had enjoyed my stay with him, I was certainly not a country girl. He'd remarked about Mike and his taste for city ladies and how it always led to problems, so I put myself in that category: a problem for Euan.

This time as I drove I had a different appreciation of the view through the windscreen. After spending time with Euan I had a new understanding of the countryside we were passing through. Things that had once meant nothing I now understood. The different trees and grasses that identified various land systems, the low depressions that could fill with water after rain, the signs of sheep or cattle. My knowledge was far from perfect but in the few days I had spent under his tutelage my understanding had grown.

I would miss Euan. I enjoyed being with him. The time had passed quickly and I had grown fond of him in the short time we'd spent together.

I was not the only one with a new attitude. Sass was now more appreciative of the landscape around us, and I hoped the trip had given her a broader view of the world than her outlook when we had driven away from Melbourne. She also talked frequently of James. She was worried about him and how he would cope with his changed circumstances. It was obvious that she had become fond of him. How fond I was unsure and I recalled Euan's, and Kate's, warnings. Certainly in her parting from James there had been a physical intimacy, and after our discussion driving from Bourke to Charleville I wondered how far it had gone. Melbourne would be far from Emerald and once she was back with her friends I was sure he would be quickly forgotten.

On the long drive between towns I had time to think, and Annie and the Bourke Cemetery with its bare red soil and thin patches of scraggly grass returned to my mind. The death certificate had stated her place of death as Bourke, but that didn't mean that she had actually died there. Or that it was where she was buried. It could just be the place of registration of death, the locality. Perhaps she had died out on a station and been buried there. Euan had said that some old stations had consecrated burial sites on them. Whether she lay in Bourke Cemetery, or on some unknown station, she had vanished. Well that was not quite true. While her burial site was unknown and all I had was a letter and a few official records, she had not completely disappeared: there was a little bit of Annie's genes in me and in Sass.

Annie, the daughter of a poor Scottish crofter, would have been the same age as Sass, when she had arrived in Australia. I couldn't see Sass leaving her family to travel alone to the other side the world, to an unknown future, probably knowing that she would never to return to her homeland. Nor could I see Sass, even the new Sass, travelling overland to a remote region to start a life in a country so different to what she had known. Then there was the date. I could trace my history back to Annie, but how did I account for the two years between the birth of her son Sidney and the marriage. Was I a MacGregor, or was there another earlier husband, and the child had taken the name of the stepfather? Perhaps Annie had come with a husband and, like Bessie's, he'd died? Each time a little more of the puzzle fell into place another puzzle appeared.

With Sass at the wheel I didn't even have to worry about kangaroos on the road, or cars or road trains. I was returning to Melbourne and Tony would be waiting. I knew how that would end. I'd changed, or perhaps just become more aware of how I felt. I enjoyed his company, and he was a good man, but I could never be what he wanted, and he would never be what I wanted. I thought of Matt. He was a good man and I'd loved him. I thought of Euan, he was good man, but that would lead nowhere.

And Sass. What was her future? Would she find a good man she loved and who loved her? It was question I hardly dared to raise these days, especially with some of her friends around her. Sometimes love and good character didn't always go together. There were plenty of women, and men, who loved someone who was wrong, even destructive, for them.

Driving into Roma I saw what Euan had meant when he had talked of a boom. As we approached the town we passed yard after yard filled with trucks and machinery. Some of which we had no idea what they did but it all looked expensive. On the road we had seen many vehicles with flashing lights and yellow stripes down their sides and letters and numbers on their doors. We'd seen signs pointing off the road to 'Camp Site C' or 'Drill Rig 25'. We decided to stop for the day and find a motel for the night, but it was impossible. Every room in every motel was booked. Not one room was available. We drove on hoping that in Miles we would find accommodation. Something, anything. I was not looking forward to spending an uncomfortable night camped in my little car.

We were lucky in Miles. We got the last cabin in a caravan park. It had everything we wanted: a clean, comfortable bed and a hot shower. In the morning we turned south. Moonie, Goondiwindi and the Newell Highway to Dubbo. When we had discussed my coming north by road Euan had told me I would see an Australia far from the cities I knew. He'd certainly been correct. I had found another world, and one full of interesting places and people.

When I had returned to Melbourne from my trip to Noosa and Kandanga I had been pleased to be back in my home but there had been moodiness and sadness in the air. July had been wet with grey clouds hanging low in the sky. Perhaps it had been the weather, but I didn't think it was just that. Why I'd felt that way I didn't know. This time the sun was shining and the days and nights were warmer. Already the days were becoming longer and soon Daylight Saving would be with us. Whatever the cause, my mood was different on this return.

Back, surrounded by the crowded streets, I thought again of the open spaces and freedom to move, and I thought of the different lifestyle some people live. My parents had been frugal, through necessity. As a child my father had gone barefoot even on cold winter days and my mother must also have known times of little money with her war-widow mother. They had saved and sacrificed to buy their home. A modest house where they had lived for most of their lives. Their children had never lacked but we'd never had a lot either. School uniforms had often been second-hand, but unlike our father we had never been shoeless by necessity, only by choice. A pretty new dress was for a birthday. It was a treat to go to the pictures on Saturday, but we had all the emotional support we could have wanted.

Everybody was the same. You knew there were rich people but that was never part of our world. I remembered the first special Christmas holiday when our parents had taken us to camp at Rosebud. They'd been part of a group, all with kids our age, and together we had fun playing on the beach, in the water, and at night sitting around telling stories and dreaming of the future.

In his later years my father had taken up bowls, and on Saturdays he had moved from the vegetable patch in the backyard to the local bowling green. I was sure he thought playing bowls was a self-indulgent luxury in his retirement. My parents had always lived a modest, quiet life.

Compared to them I suspected my grandparents' lives had been even harder. On my mother's side, my grandmother, a widow, and my grandfather dead in the war. On my father's side, a struggling farm worker with a life from which my father sought to escape. According to Great Uncle James the family had always struggled. A fettler on the railway whose wife had died young, and before that a worker on a station 'out west' with Annie, his wife. When I had been with Euan I had seen photos of that type of life and it would have been very basic and the work hard. There had certainly been no silver spoon or family fortune.

Life had been good for my brother and sister and me. I had done my training as a nurse and after saving my fare had left for England. My skills were in demand and it was never a problem to find work. I had made the most of the two years I had been away and would have stayed longer if Matt hadn't shown up. I returned to Australia in love and we had soon married and rented our first tiny house.

Matt had started his own accounting practice and his business grew. We saved, and finally had enough for a deposit on our own home. Matt had always insisted that we buy a house no matter how hard it may be. That way we would eventually own it and have more security. While rent may have seemed cheaper in the short-term, he assured me that over the years rents would rise in line with the growth in the cost of real estate. My father approved of Matt's opinion. To him security was so important.

Two incomes, long hours, a rising career for Matt and we had been able to move to the other side of the city. A move my parents would never have thought possible or have made. The bigger house in Beaumaris had still required a sacrifice but we had done it. Then the years of paying down the debt. It seemed to last forever. Two children and expenses, private schooling for them that our parents could have never imagined, but we had done it.

We were fortunate with our children. Life had become easier, money more plentiful, but it still required a sacrifice for them to buy a house and raise a family. Especially as expectations changed. There were so many more things to spend money on, children to educate, cars to buy, holidays. My father had been very proud of the first small car he had ever purchased. It was an achievement, one of the greatest achievements in his life, along with marrying my mother and buying a house. Something to be proud of, but now, for my children, cars were something you changed every three years.

I wondered if Annie and her husband had ever owned a horse let alone a house.

Sass's world was different again. To her the goods which

previous generations had struggled to obtain were expected. Holidays, mobiles, clothes, a university education. I doubted if she had ever given thought to the future, apart from how it was being ruined by ignorant and uncaring people. She had never known a time without food, or the worry about where the next meal would come from. She was fortunate, but could it last forever?

To me the economy had taken the shape of an inverted tottering pyramid with the producers of the world, the growers and diggers and makers of things at the tiny apex, if apexes could be on the bottom. On the broad top was a mass of bloggers and tweeters, sports people, baristas and media marketers that could blow away at any time, never to be seen or heard from again. It was an unstable world with so few people concerned about actually producing the durable goods and useful services the world really needed. And that was the economy. The politics looked as bad with people seeking the rewards of a political career for themselves but seeming rarely concerned with what would work best for the citizens. But then, we voted for them, and it would be unlikely they would tell us that we couldn't have good times whenever we wanted them and then expect to get re-elected.

I'd managed to depress myself so much I decided to give up solving the problems of the world but that meant I had to face my immediate problem. Tony.

30 New Leads

Tony. I'd been putting off making the phone call for days. I still wasn't sure how I should tell him. I'd had girlfriends who had always managed the problem one way or another. "Just give him the flick!" "Tell him you want to move on." "Just do the chill." Over the years I'd heard, and seen, many break ups, some painless, others not so painless, but it had never been my experience. When I was young I'd had a few boyfriends but they had never been serious and neither of us was heartbroken when we parted. In fact we had both 'moved on' without the slightest concern. Once Matt came on the scene I'd never been interested in anyone else so it was never a problem. Since he had died there'd never been anyone. Tony was as close as anyone had ever come.

I phoned and arranged to meet for a meal, no movie, just a midday lunch and I chose the place. A public place with lots of people around. I knew that my decision would not be what he wanted and I expected he would try to convince me to change my mind.

Tony might have been excitable and enthusiastic but he was also predictable. He had tried many ways to talk me around but to no avail. I was sure I would miss his company. I'd always enjoyed our times together but deep down I knew that it was over. My life had taken a new path, a path that led nowhere but that was where I wanted to go.

Some evenings sitting alone in my unit I had regrets over my decision. It would have been good to pick up the phone and chat, to arrange a date together and go on an excursion. Then again, I now had a sense of freedom. I hadn't realised how much emotional energy it had taken to spend time with Tony. Deep down I had known that it would never work, and I knew I would only hurt Tony more by continuing.

I'd accepted an invitation to a Sunday roast with my daughter and her family. I wanted to hear my grandson's impressions of their visit to Southeast Asia while Sass and I had been in Queensland. It was to be only the four of us. Sass had gone to spend a week, or longer, with a friend. They were working on a uni project and had decided that they would get more done if she bunked at her friend's flat.

"Sass is quite different since she returned from your trip up north."

"You noticed did you. I think she's in love. Has she said anything to you?"

"She talked about a James. She seemed to really like him but he is so far away. I think she has texted him and maybe even talked to him but she never says much. That hasn't changed."

My James was only nine years old and he had been full of stories about his visit to Vietnam and Cambodia with his parents and the school group. He had especially loved the elephants. The people and the different traffic had also made a big impression on him. The ancient buildings less so, but he was keen to tell me that "You can buy McDonalds there but it's different, sort of."

With time on my hands I came back to my puzzle of Annie and spent hours on the computer seeking some more answers. It had become a personal detective quest to find a life for my vanished forebear. If she had been in both New South Wales and Queensland and had died in New South Wales and had posted her letter from Warren, then it was likely that she had first been in Queensland. That could account for her knowing Bessie Buckley and her husband. Euan had said many Scottish and Irish migrants had landed in Queensland ports and had not necessarily arrived in Sydney and then travelled north. Rockhampton had been a busy port and it had served the Central West grazing lands. Perhaps I could find a shipping list with an Annie McDonald or an Annie MacGregor. Perhaps there would also be an Elizabeth Buckley.

My plan wasn't as easy to execute as I thought it would be.

There was a mass of information available, but finding what I was looking for was time-consuming and I followed up many unhelpful leads. Eventually I found a name. Then more names. I'd expected Annie McDonald would have sailed from a Scottish port, or at least a port in the north of England, but it appeared that she had left from London. Historical reports gave different departure dates in 1873 for the *Countess Russell* with its consignment of Scottish and Irish migrants, but all agreed it was a horror voyage. In late February or early March the sailing ship departed Tilbury Docks bound for Rockhampton. Numbers varied in the reports but before the boat arrived in Australia around five adults and fifteen children had died. Some were babies born during the voyage. Then another passenger died and the *Countess Russell* was quarantined off Sea View Hill on Curtis Island. The deaths continued with five more deaths until finally the quarantine was lifted and the passengers could go ashore in Rockhampton. The five months on-board the sailing ship must have turned into hell for the passengers and crew with death, and fear of death, all around them, but at last Annie, Bessie and Bessie's husband were free to start their new lives in a new land.

The passenger list I had found showed an Annie McDonald, a domestic servant, nineteen years of age from Scotland. I'd also found Patrick and Elizabeth Buckley of Lemanaghan in Ireland, an agricultural labourer and his wife. Her occupation was also given as domestic servant. If I needed a husband for Annie I would have to look for one in Australia. She was recorded as unmarried on arrival. From the passenger list she would have had lots of fellow countrymen on her voyage. The list was peppered with Mac's and Mc's, Frasers, Campbells, Stewarts, Munros. Scottish and Irish names dominated the list but there was no MacGregor.

Nearly all were listed as 'assisted passage'. Searching the web brought to light the migration schemes of the times. In the early days of Queensland there was a shortage of labour and various policies operated to encourage migrants to the colony. One scheme offered a warrant to a parcel of government land. Remain in the Colony two years and you would receive a second warrant. Waiting for you at the departure port would be a shipping agent. He would exchange your warrant for a free passage to the far side of the world. Other migrants could be nominated by a landowner and again have their fare paid. They were earlier versions of the 'Ten pound Pom' program that had brought some of my friends to Australia.

Euan had mentioned the growth in Queensland's population around the time of Bessie and Annie's arrival, but not that the population had exploded by seventeen times in just forty-one years. I couldn't imagine today's Australia of twenty million becoming three hundred and forty million people in just another forty-one years.

Nor did it appear that the fortunes of the *Countess Russell* improved. Leaving Rockhampton after discharging her passengers, and bound for Newcastle in New South Wales to load coal, unladen save for ballast and one passenger, the sailing ship ran aground on a sandy beach in squally, blinding rain on a pitch black night. It was to be her last voyage.

It was one evening, about a month later, as I was sitting alone, thoroughly bored with some inane reality programme on the television, when my phone rang. It was Euan. As promised, I had phoned to let him know we had arrived safely in Melbourne and we'd chatted but it had all been very low key. Nothing personal, just polite chat. Nothing more. I hadn't expected anything more, nor looked for anything more.

"I've had a call from Chancy. He's found an old book. I couldn't work out exactly what it is but he reckons it has something to do with your Annie."

"What does he reckon?"

"Well, from what I could make out it's about Bessie Buckley, and it appears that she had a Scottish friend called Annie. Annie McDonald. That seems to fit your story.

However this Annie had problems. That was as far as I got because then Chancy decided to tell me one of his far-fetched tales and never got back to what her problems were. He did mention that both women had been working on a property called Kinnaird near Aramac. I've never heard of it. Anyway he told me he wants to give the book to you and he will get it to me somehow. Maybe get a mate to drop it off in Barcaldine. That's all I know."

It was good to hear his voice again. The sound of it took me back to the open downs and the big house with its wide verandas, and I knew I really did miss his company. From then on I felt free to occasionally phone him and enquire about the happenings on Raasay, and Donald and Kate. At times I would get a call from him and he would bring me up to date on the local news. Once I asked him about Mike and Bella.

"There have been some changes. Mike has laid off a workman and he and Bella are having to spend a lot more time out in the fields. Bella isn't getting over here very often these days. Actually Don has gone over to Emerald a few times and given her a hand. James has left. He's gone down to Sydney to try and get a job with his mates. I haven't heard how it's gone."

"How is Mike?"

"Don says he's fine. He is trying to save what he can but it will drag on for years. I'm more worried about Don and Bella. She won't leave until Mike is on his feet again and that will delay any plans she and Don might have."

"What about your plans?"

"We'll see. It looks like I will be here for a few more years.

I just hope Kate doesn't decide she needs to stay here with me next year. I want her to go back and finish her course and graduate. An education and piece of paper is so important these days."

The months passed and it was during another of our now more frequent phone calls that Euan told me of his enquiries.

"I've talked to some of the stock and station agents and cattle buyers. They have a pretty good knowledge of properties around the country. None of them have heard of Kinnaird."

"Do stations change their names?"

"Generally no, particularly if it is a well-known property. Some people think it's bad luck to change the name. Others think that you can change the fortunes of a property that has a bad history. However I spoke with a chap I know in Rockhampton. He is into the region's history and he remembers seeing an ad for a property by that name in an old newspaper. He is going to try and find it and has promised to send a copy out to me. It was for an auction around 1886. It was an estate sale."

"An estate. That sounds very grand"

"No the auction was for an 'estate of'. It's a legal term. The estate of Archibald Fraser. It would appear that he had died and the property and its contents were to be sold by the executors. It describes the property and contents in general terms but doesn't say exactly where it was. Only that it's in the region of Aramac."

"Fraser? There were two Frasers on the boat that Annie

and Bessie arrived on."

It was in late November when Euan phoned. "Chancy called the other day, he's been unwell. He asked how my lady was going. You made a hit with him. He hasn't seen anyone to pass the book along but he did say he wants you to have it and he would like to see you again. He has some news he wants to tell you. He didn't say what it was but I think he wants a date with you! I think you should come quite soon. I don't think he is very well."

"Give him my regards and tell him he is a bit cheeky calling me 'your lady'."

"I've already told him that you're not 'my lady' but he reckons a young lad like me would be the last to know. I quite liked being called 'young lad'. I haven't been that in years. I've always thought he was very astute."

"Do you think I should come up?"

"Yes. It could give you some answers. Don and Kate would like to see you again, and so would I."

We ended our call with me promising to check flights and call him back. I rang my daughter, Meg, to tell her of my plans and started checking flights to Barcaldine. It was only half an hour later when the phone rang again. It was Meg. She had spoken with Sass and told her of my plans and Sass had immediately said she wanted to go with me. Meg had been surprised by the reaction but then Sass had been in a strange place lately. It was as if she was very worried by something but would never say what the problem was. The happy girl on her return from Raasay had been replaced by a moody, uptight, silent woman. At first she thought it might have been a broken romance with James, but then if she was planning to go north, perhaps she wanted to see him again.

"The last I knew James had gone to Sydney. I don't think he is at Kandanga anymore. She may not see him anyway."

"She is very definite that she wants to go with you."

I made the bookings for two and phoned Euan with the details, and arranged for him to pick us up at the Barcaldine airport.

Eager passengers had already started to form a queue as we sat waiting in the departure lounge at Tullamarine when my mobile rang. It was Euan with the news. He'd just heard. Chancy had died the previous night. We were too late to see him. In the minutes as the plane was boarding we had to make a decision. Would we call off our trip or continue? I had wanted to talk with Chancy and find out what he had discovered but that was no longer possible. But then, we had checked in, our luggage was loaded, to cancel now would cause all sorts of difficulties. Sass was also most insistent that we continue. And I had to admit to myself that it was not only Chancy I wanted to see. I also wanted to see Euan again.

31 The Funeral

A hot dry wind was blowing across the plain, coating the mourners gathered around the freshly dug grave with a thin layer of grey dust. Outside the cemetery fence the kangaroos stood watching the activity wishing the humans would leave so they could graze on the scant grass growing between the graves. The hoped-for rains had not yet come to this part of Queensland, and the country beyond the cemetery fence was parched and bare. Unlike big cities where space for the dead had almost vanished, out here there was plenty of room for more graves.

The thought came to me that in some way this was like a first date with Euan. It was a strange first date to attend a funeral, and yet, somehow, that was how I felt. We'd now met on a number of occasions, we'd sat and talked over cups of tea and coffee, or drinks. We'd mingled at Bella's birthday party. Sass and I had spent time at Raasay with his family and I had travelled to the bull sale and overnighted in Augathella, but today there was a different feeling. I didn't know if it was me, or Euan. It could hardly be the funeral, but standing beside him I somehow felt different.

Both Sass and I were amazed at the size of the crowd which had assembled for the final farewell to the old man. Euan was not.

"Did all these people know the old man?"

Euan leant towards Sass and quietly answered her question. "Yes, and many more. I once told you that he was a man who was highly respected. This is the proof. He may have been modest in his manner and thought few would remember him but he touched many people during his lifetime."

Indeed another Chancy story was circulating among the mourners. Chancy had known his time was coming and he had told a staff member at the home "that he was planning to visit the Big Man upstairs soon. Not that he'd ever had much to do with him, but he'd heard he was a good bloke and hoped he'd let him in."

There was a simple coffin placed over the grave and on it were a pair of boots and a whip. Beside them lay four war medals. Only Euan, and a few younger representatives of the local RSL branch whose records had named Clarence Anderson as a veteran, knew of his war service. Few of the others present had ever heard of Chancy's time in the army during the Second World War. It was something he never spoke about, he had never attended the RSL functions, nor marched in the Anzac Day parades. When pressed he would say he wanted to escape from any talk of war and would change the subject. I thought of my father and my grandfather. Had they ever known this bushman from faraway Queensland? Probably not. My grandfather would have been dead by the time Chancy was old enough to fight, but perhaps my father may have met him. They were of the same age. There may have been twelve months at the most between them. I wondered what they would have made of each other. They were both country boys, one who wanted to escape from a farm on the Murray River, and the other a bushman, hoping to return to the far reaches of Queensland and venture further north to the Territory.

The service was simple and brief. Nominally Chancy was a Catholic, and so he was buried in the Catholic section of the cemetery. I suspected his attendance at church was no greater than his attendance had been at school, but perhaps 'the Big Man' would overlook that and judge him on his life. I remembered that he had spoken of the church where his wife had found support when their baby had died.

After the service the mourners slowly filed past the grave to pay their respects. They were a mixed lot. Old, young, men, women. A few in suits, or wearing coats and ties, even in the heat. Others were in jeans and shirts, or denim skirts. All wore hats of one type or another, some clean and smart, others battered and dirty and much worn and loved. It was a mix of rich and poor. The entire spectrum of those whose lives were based far from the coastal cities. The car-park reflected their owners. New four-wheel drive wagons were parked next to battered and ageing Holdens and Falcons. More than one dusty four-wheel drive tray-back sported a cage for the dogs I had seen locked in them on my visits to Western towns. There were even some trucks whose owners obviously planned to do a few other jobs while they were in town.

Sass and I stood together observing the crowd as Euan moved from group to group, greeting those he knew and shaking hands with the men, chatting briefly and moving on to the next gathering of people. Occasionally if there was a woman in the group he would lean towards her and brush her cheek. Unlike the women I knew, and even most men, he never looked comfortable in that greeting.

As we walked back to our vehicle he informed us that there were two wakes planned for Chancy. A few friends had arranged for the Parents and Citizen group from the school to provide tea and sandwiches at the Supper Room of the Town Hall. That had been thought appropriate due to Chancy being a teetotaller. However others amongst the mourners had a thirst and had decided that they would meet at the pub to farewell the old bushie 'properly'. Chancy had told the Home that "I don't need a wake. All my old friends have already died, and I won't be able to attend anyway." Euan thought it best if we went to the hall.

It was a smaller, older group that gathered in the Hall. It appeared it was the younger generation who had the greater thirst. A few old men and women sat together in chairs arranged in one corner. Hovering around them fetching tea or coffee were a man and a woman I recognised from my visit to the Aged Care Home in Blackall, whose bus I had seen parked in front of the hall. Euan introduced me to the people he was talking with but the conversation was often unintelligible to me. It was the weather, the SIO, EYCI or words like scanning, buffel, the Mitchell. Words that meant nothing to me but were understandable, and obviously important, to the speakers. From the talk it was apparent the lateness of the rains was a great worry for many.

Sass was displaying little interest in the chat around us and was constantly on her phone. It appeared she was sending texts and receiving replies to them. I assumed she was reporting on her activities to her friends in Melbourne but she was not looking happy. Boredom I could have expected in her but this was different. I asked if everything was OK. She looked at me with a strange look, a mixture of sadness and anger. "It's OK Gran. Don't worry." Then she moved away to send another message.

Euan had said the wake would be tea and sandwiches, but the ladies of the P & C had done much much more. The tables were laden with plates of cakes and slices as well as trays of sandwiches. Rather than a 'quick cuppa and go' those present had started to tell Chancy stories. Each had their own favourite tale of some adventure or misadventure from their time with Chancy. The laughter grew. Two of the old men from the Home repeated stories that Chancy had told them time and time again of his days when he had worked on the huge cattle stations of the Barkley. It had been a tough life but an exciting one that he had loved to relive. Euan added some stories he had been told of life further north and west on the Murranji track. The stories and cuppas continued for hours until Euan excused himself and said he had to leave.

Before the mini bus had left to return the older mourners to the Aged Care Home Euan had arranged to meet the driver and collect some items. He had never mentioned it to me before but I discovered that he was the sole executor of Chancy's will. "Not that there's very much. He knew he was dying and had made all the arrangements that were important to him. I just have a few loose ends to tidy up. All his possessions were packed in a small suitcase, a few cowboy novels, he used to enjoy those, some clothes and his personal effects. I expect your book is in there. He told me he found it on a bookcase in the Old People home and he wanted you to have it. He said you would understand. He also had a few parcels to send to friends and a pair of boots for a young mate."

"He left me a book that belongs to the Old People's Home?"

"I wouldn't worry, he left what he had to be shared by the Home, the Catholic Church in Blackall and Frontier Services. From what I saw of his bank statement they'll do OK."

"He left his boots to someone?" The incredulity in Sass's voice was noticeable.

"Yes. He knew a young bloke who rarely wore boots. Chancy had promised to give him his when he didn't need them anymore. I have them in the back."

"What about the boots on the coffin?"

"Those boots, Sass, were an old pair from years ago. He had worn them when he got married. I guess he reckons he will need them when he meets his wife. There was a romantic side of Chancy few ever saw. That's why he wanted to be buried here in Aramac. This is where his wife and son are buried."

I asked, "What is 'Frontier Services?'" Euan explained it was the outreach service of one of the Protestant Churches. It had travelling padres who visited distant properties and stations. If wanted they would provide for people's religious needs, but if that was not wanted they provided a discreet, outside, ear to discuss problems and offered support to those who wanted it.

"But he was a Catholic."

Euan answered Sass's remark by saying, "Chancy didn't place much relevance on what breed the religion was. He reckoned it was more important what they did."

"Do you know why he left the book to me?"

"No. He obviously thought it important because he wrote a note on the edge of his will, 'Give it to the girl. She'll understand'. That's all I know. Perhaps you had better read the book."

There was not much talk on the drive back to Raasay. Euan's mind appeared to be somewhere else. Sass, in the back seat, was quiet and kept re-checking the messages on her phone. The mood in the car didn't encourage conversation. Euan seemed edgy and uncertain, Sass, troubled and upset but would give no explanation. I was relieved when we finally drew up at the kitchen gate of Raasay.

Next morning when we gathered for breakfast we discussed plans for Sass and I to fly back to Melbourne. There was still an unsettled mood in the room and both Donald and Kate mentioned it, but they received no explanation. Sass asked if she could use the landline. She excused herself and left the room. Euan announced he wanted to check the new bulls that we had bought at Charleville and asked would I like to come with him and see them.

We drove out to a paddock near the cattle yards that overlooked a large dam. In the distance a group of bulls huddled together around a water trough. I thought it strange that if we had come to inspect bulls we had stopped so far away from them. Usually Euan would drive up close to the sheep or cattle when he wanted to check them.

Euan got out of the car and came around and opened my door. I joined him and we walked together to the edge of the dam.

"This may seem unusual and sudden, but I have a question for you. I know you are planning to return to Melbourne tomorrow but before you go will you accept my offer of marriage?"

32 Sass

The offer took me by surprise, but before I could even think of my reply the two-way radio in the ute burst into life with an anxious call.

"Dad. Dad, can you hear me? Can you come home at once? There's a problem."

The voice on the radio was Kate, but not the usual calm and controlled woman that I knew. She sounded distressed and emotional. Euan picked up the microphone and called back. "Hi Kate, I'm here. What's the problem?"

"It's Sass. I think you and Liz had better get back here straightaway."

"We're on our way. What is the problem?"

"I think it's better you get here first."

I was puzzled by her answer. Whatever the problem was it was something that she didn't want to discuss over the radio where others might hear the conversation. It also involved Sass. That was strange. I could imagine some problem on the property that needed attention. Maybe an accident? Although that would hardly require secrecy. Some business transaction that had problems? That was possible, but that wouldn't involve Sass. Yet from Kate's call, it must have something to do with my granddaughter, but I could think of nothing that it could possibly be. Maybe there was bad news about our family? But then that wouldn't be just Sass.

Euan and I didn't speak on our way back to the homestead. It was only a short drive from the dam and a few minutes later we were in the kitchen with Kate and Donald and Sass. It was obvious that Sass had been crying and Kate was trying to comfort her. When we arrived Donald left the room and Kate motioned to her father to follow him.

I looked at Sass, and then Kate, but both were waiting for the other to explain the situation. Finally Kate spoke. "Sass has had a problem. She needs to talk to you. Perhaps you need to take her to a doctor."

I looked at Sass, apart from the tears and the worried look on her face she appeared fine. A little pale perhaps, but that was all. "What is it darling?"

"Gran, I don't know how to say it, but I'm pregnant. I may be losing the baby."

"What do you mean? How do you know?"

"I've got cramping. It's really bad, and I'm bleeding, but it's not like my period. Down here. It started last night.

"How long have you known you were pregnant?"

Through her tears the story emerged. She told of the night when she and James watched videos. Donald and Bella had left to go to bed. Kate had also left. Then she and James had started cuddling and kissing. Soon it became more intense and they had gone to her room and made love.

"How long have you known you were pregnant?"

"Over a month."

"But you saw James here in August. You would have realised earlier if it was then."

"Gran, I missed my period but I wasn't too worried. I thought it would come, but it didn't. Then after a while I got really worried."

"Are you sure it is James?"

"Gran! It has to be James. There is no one else."

"Well that's almost three months since we were here."

"We've met since then. That's when it would have happened."

I remembered her mother telling me that Sass had gone to stay with a uni friend because they were working on a project they needed to finish. It would have been about the right time. "Where did you see James?"

Gradually the full story emerged. After their night at Raasay, she and James had continued to talk and message. James had gone to Sydney hoping to use a mate's connections to find a job. He had stayed in a friend's flat, and when the friend had gone on holidays to Bali with his girlfriend, James had invited Sass to join him in Sydney. She had told her parents the story of the uni project but had instead flown to Sydney. She and James had had a fun week, days on the beach, nights clubbing and long sessions of sex but by the end of the week the friend was returning and James put Sass on a plane back to Melbourne. It was the last time she had seen him. Already he was becoming moody as no job offers that he considered suitable were to be had. They had stayed in touch but his calls gradually became less frequent, and he was less and less interested in talking with her if she called.

After she had missed her period she became anxious and finally visited a pharmacy to buy a test kit. It confirmed what she feared. She was pregnant. Still she waited and hoped the result was wrong, but after missing her next period she had phoned James with the news. He'd denied that it could be his. His rejection had shattered her. When she learnt that I was planning to fly to Barcaldine she decided she had to come with me and try to see James face to face. Suddenly so many things fell into place. The worried texts were not to uni friends about her travels but efforts to arrange a meeting with James. Efforts that had come to nothing. James refused to see her and finally blocked her calls. Her last attempt had been to use the landline and try to get Mike or Bella to put him on the phone. It had all come to nothing.

"Is James back in Emerald?"

Kate answered my question. "Yes, he came back a few weeks ago. He couldn't find a job he wanted in Sydney so he is back working on Kandanga."

"Does he know about Sass?"

"Yes, Gran. He knows I'm here but not that I might lose the baby. He still says it couldn't be his."

"Don't worry, Darling we'll sort this problem out."

I suddenly realised what I had said. "Sort out this problem." That was hardly the way you should think about what should be the joyous news of a new life coming into the world.

My first thought was to get her comfortable while we

made plans. Kate and I settled her on her bed and I went to find Euan. Kate came up to me with tears welling in her eyes. "I'm so sorry. I tried to warn her but she wouldn't take any notice. I know James. I was once there." I saw her father look up from the phone when she said it. "Don't worry Daddy, I was never pregnant, but we did have a relationship for a while. I should know James better than anyone, after all we almost grew up together. He is a very selfish, self-centred man who has little regard for anyone else. He is the opposite to his sister. He is bad news for girls and he treats them badly. Sass is better without him whatever may happen."

Euan had already been on the phone to the hospital and arranged for me to speak with one of the duty doctors about what would be best. My first worry was her safety and to save the baby. It was decided that we would take her to Barcaldine Hospital where she could be examined.

It was a worrying trip to town with the fear that a miscarriage could occur at any time but we made it safely. The Indian doctor in the Emergency Department examined Sass and gave her the good news. At this stage all was well. There was bleeding and obviously Sass was in pain but the good news was that the cervix was still closed. So far it was only a threat of a miscarriage. She could still have a healthy pregnancy, although there was a risk that if the bleeding and pain persisted a full miscarriage could develop. She should be right for now but he suggested she rest and seek medical attention if there was any change for the worse.

Leaving the hospital it was decided it may be safest if we remained in town overnight rather than risk the drive over rough roads back to Raasay. Then we would fly home as soon as possible. Once we had found a motel and checked in Euan left to return to Raasay with a promise to come straight back with our luggage. Kate would stay with us and arrange our airline tickets.

That afternoon was hot and humid and the evening became even more unsettled with distant flashes of lightning across the black sky. The air was charged and finally the first storm of the season broke. The thunder rolled across the night sky from one side to another like some massive never-ending military bombardment and the lightning flashes constantly lit the dark heavy clouds. The rain, when it came, was a solid wall of water. It lasted for hours on end. We all had disturbed nights, apart from Sass. She slept quietly while I lay awake in a bed beside her. My thoughts were on her future, how would we approach her parents, what would happen with the baby? In an adjoining room I could hear the quiet murmur of Euan and Kate talking until Kate went to her own room. Even then I could hear the sound of the television coming from Euan's room. He must have been watching old movies until early in the morning.

As we waited in the airport terminal for the arrival of the aircraft there was a different feel in the air. The gentle rain that had followed the wild storm of the previous night was still falling and the mood of those waiting for the aircraft was of relief: the rains had finally started and the grass would grow. Business would return to the countryside and to the towns. We sat waiting as a group, Kate and Sass, Euan and I, but the question of his proposal was never mentioned.

When the boarding call was made for our departure Sass gave Kate a hug and a kiss. Her feelings about Kate had changed from being a 'bitch' to a deep bond. She then gave Euan a hug and I heard her say a quiet 'thank you'. When it was my turn to make a farewell I was lost. Should I give him a hug like Sass? I certainly felt grateful for his presence, yet I realised we had never really touched. My first meeting had been a handshake, the next was a wave and smile as he had greeted me at the Kandanga party, when we had arrived at Raasay he had held the door open for us and on this trip he had picked up our luggage on our arrival. Should I give him a hug of appreciation? Would he think that was acceptance of his offer when I had not even considered it in the trauma of the previous day? Should I give him a light kiss on the cheek? How could I consider marriage when we had never had any real physical contact, let alone slept together? I felt like an uncertain teenager again. Finally I touched him on the arm and whispered, "I will call you with an answer."

33 Family Matters

It was late in the evening when my son-in-law met us at the airport. Our flight from Barcaldine to Brisbane had first taken us further into the outback, to Longreach, before it had turned south for Brisbane. Then we had a wait until our evening connection for Melbourne was ready. Sass and I were both weary by the time we were together with our family, and that was only the start of the night. Neither Meg nor Graham had any idea of the news we were bringing them.

It was Sass who faced her parents.

They listened in silence as she admitted her deception and its consequences. Her fears and her concerns. The feeling of betrayal and her anger and hurt. Finally her mother came to her and embraced her.

"Don't worry. You must be so tired and stressed. Get a good night's sleep and we'll talk about it in the morning. It's not that critical that a few hours will make a difference. Tomorrow we will see a doctor and have you checked but don't worry tonight. You're home. You're safe. You're with us now."

After Sass has gone to bed I looked to her parents. I'd expected stunned silence with the news, but while her parents were obviously concerned they hardly seemed surprised. I asked my daughter the reason.

"These days girls do. Sometimes they're careless. It is always a worry but that's it."

"So what will you do?"

"First thing is to get her to our doctor and check what is happening. That she's OK. You said she was concerned about a miscarriage. I suppose that's still possible?"

"The doctor in Barcaldine seemed to think she was safe but there was always a risk."

"We'll see what our doctor says. Then we'll make our decisions."

I'm not sure any of us really slept well that night. I kept hearing the low sound of talk coming from the room my daughter and her husband shared, and I was sure Sass was still awake listening to her favourite music playing on her phone. My night was also sleepless as I pondered what the future would hold for the young girl.

It was a different mood as we sat in the lounge room with the morning sun streaming in through the big windows. Beyond the green of the coastal heaths the blue waters of the bay rippled with the breeze, while the usual walkers and their dogs went about their daily business without any thoughts of the concerns in the house beside them.

The shock of the discovery had been replaced by a multitude of emotions, especially in Sass.

Betrayal. She had really cared for James in her naïve

open-hearted way, and he had just used her and dumped her. Mingled with the feeling of rejection was an anger. Not just with him, but with the world at large. Then there was another feeling, less obvious, and hidden by her manner, but I could see a frightened girl wondering about her future, and how she would manage what lay ahead.

Graham had taken my grandson for a long walk and it was just we three women left in the room.

This time tears came, but I wasn't sure what they were tears of. Sadness, relief, worry, regret. They could have been any, or all, of those things.

We were three generations of women but we were close, and Sass had a family to support her. I thought of Annie, so long ago. According to the records I had found she was not much older than Sass when she had become pregnant and she hadn't had her family around her for support. I wasn't even sure if she'd had a husband, at that time. Perhaps Rohan MacGregor was there for her. From the letter I suspected Bessie would certainly have been there.

I drove with Meg and Sass to the doctor's surgery but waited outside when they went in. When she came out Sass was pale and obviously shaken by the experience. Neither said anything on the drive home. It was only when we were back in the security of their home that they told me of the visit.

Sass was fine. There was no indication of new bleeding and her pregnancy should progress normally. There still remained a risk of a repeat occurrence, possibly even an inevitable miscarriage, but the likelihood of that happening was reducing. From Sass's explanation of events, and the stage of development, she was probably close to the end of the first trimester.

The doctor's questions had shaken Sass. How did she feel about having a baby? Did she want the baby? How would she have felt if she had had a miscarriage? How did she feel about being a single mother and committing to raising a child alone? They were questions she needed to consider and answer soon. Any delay would be unwise.

I doubted that Annie would have had much choice in her situation. Maybe in Aramac there was a woman who catered for unwelcome pregnancies. Certainly abortion had a long history, but whether those skills had reached out that far into the west of Queensland at that time I didn't know. Possibly she would not have had the money that was often the necessary precursor for the service. Maybe she had thought of adoption. I'd once heard a story of a family where a woman had conceived and secretly borne an illegitimate child that was raised by another family member who was unable to conceive herself. That way family honour was maintained, the longing for a child fulfilled, and the child remained within the family. That could hardly apply to Annie in her situation. Nor would it apply today. Times were so different. Adoption had vanished as single mothers raised their children. Abortion had remained for those who sought it, but that, for some, could also carry a heavy price far beyond the monetary cost.

What would raising a child mean for Sass's life? The practicalities began to arise. At least she had a home, parents who supported her, but much would have to change. She'd dreamt of a career in media. It was a common dream of many girls these days, but how could she cope with finishing her uni studies with a babe in arms? Worse, how would she manage as a single mum to develop a career while needing to care for a young child? Starting out, and even later, a nanny or occasional childcare would be difficult if not impossible. A mother, or grandmother, could help, but that was not a complete answer. Meg had just started a job she loved. Should she give it up to care for her grandchild? Should I, now to be a great-grandmother, take over the job of raising a baby to allow my granddaughter to develop her hoped-for career? Relying on government support would hardly set her up for a future life. In fact it could almost trap her in the role of mother while future opportunities went to those without commitments. It was a problem faced by others who did not have the good fortune to be supported by a partner for the early years of raising a family. Some managed, some did not.

Sass had been concerned about telling her friends the news. From what Meg passed on to me the reactions had been mixed. There were those who were excited and happy for her. Some were disapproving, and a few were supportive but quietly warned of the difficulties that she would need to overcome.

It was one of her new university friends who was most violently indignant. I suppose, having seen some of them at the Film Festival, I should have expected that reaction. Apparently Meg had overheard the obscenity-laden opinions expressed to Sass that left no doubts about what should happen to James. The more aggressive of Sass's feminist friends agreed. Others took the view that Sass was fortunate. She could now raise her child in a feminist world free from male interference. That group of girlfriends seemed to have no doubts that the baby would be a girl. I wondered what would happen if the poor child was a boy, or how they thought conception occurred without, at least, some male input.

The news had spread rapidly within her circle of friends. No longer did it need face-to-face contact to pass from one person to another. Social media was a far more efficient means of spreading news than telephone calls or letters had ever been.

The days passed quickly and we came to terms with the events that had confronted us. Sass remained withdrawn and troubled by her actions but returned to her studies. Meg told me that a change had taken place in her circle of friends. She was no longer rushing off clubbing or seeking out the latest protest campaign. Nowadays she was more likely to come straight home from classes than hang out with the other girls. Meg didn't know if it was Sass who had made the change or if her previous friends had dropped her. Sass had mentioned that one close friend was ghosting her. Meg had to make enquiries with other mothers to find out what it meant. She had sensed it was a painful subject and hadn't wanted to raise it with Sass until she understood its significance.

After the first emotional days of our return to Melbourne it had been a relief to be back in my own home. Finally I had been able to put the events of our trip north aside for a few moments. I knew I would have to give Euan my answer, and I owed it to him to do it soon. Now it was only Sass and her future that were important to me. As I unpacked my suitcase I found a brown paper parcel, slipped in underneath my clothes at the bottom of the case. My first thought was,

"What's that doing there?", and then I remembered Chancy's gift. Euan had told me he had packed it when he had gathered up my effects from Raasay but I had given it no more thought. I unwrapped the parcel and there was the book that Chancy had been so insistent I receive.

34 The Book

It was a very old book. Not what I expected. Although honestly I had not really considered what it would be. Perhaps a history of Western Queensland with some photos of old homesteads. Maybe a diary of an early squatter with a few sketches of his run. Chancy's book was an old writing book, the sort with a buff hard cardboard cover and a multi-coloured pattern on the inner side. The sort of lined book once used for many purposes, writing recipes, recording events, recollections: anything that need to be written down. This book was filled with a handwritten story.

After I started to read it I could understand why it had appealed to Chancy. His passions in life were the bush and the people who lived in the bush. The page upon page of words met both his passions.

The spider-like script was not the copperplate style that I had seen in our early letter, rather it showed the effort the writer had made in producing the record of her life. As I read the reason Chancy had left it to me became clear.

The writer had never had any schooling. It was only when her nieces and nephews commenced school that she had acquired the skill to put pen to paper and record the story of her life.

It began:

I was born Elizabeth Mary Edmonds near the village of Lemanaghan in County Offaly in 1834. My father was a herdsman for the local squire. My mother, a washerwoman. I had seven brothers and sisters but two had died young.

Life was hard in our village and my beloved heard of a scheme where we could migrate to the Colony of Queensland in Australia. He said the government of the colony would give new immigrants a parcel of land if they paid their boat fare. We had no money to pay for our berths. However he had heard the shipping company would exchange the holding for a berth in the third class.

The thought of a life in a warm clime, far from the hunger and cold of our village and with the excitement of youth in our blood we made our decision. I married my love Patrick Buckley, and we left our village and our families. We would never see my parents and some of my family again although one of my brothers had gone to New South Wales and another would soon follow us.

First we had to travel to London to find a boat. O, I had never seen such a place. The people and the noise. Finally we found a man who could arrange our passage but it was hard. What little money we had was spent waiting til the boat would leave.

The boat we found was an old sailing boat. We could not afford the luxury of a new steamer. The Countess Russell looked sea-worthy enough but what would we know about the sea. It was after three months at sea that the first passenger died, and then it began. More and more. I was so glad I was not with child for of the six babes born on the voyage two died before they ever saw land. At last we reached Australia but then another of us died of the fever and the authorities locked us away on the boat and would not let us ashore. It was a happy day when at last we set foot at Rockhampton. It was so different to County Offaly. The skies were blue but the heat was too much and the trees were so different.

On board the boat was a squatter, a Scottish gent

and his new bride. They were in the saloon and they had a cabin, not the steerage like us Irish. He held a farm so large that we could not imagine the size of it. We were lucky, or believed we were, for he offered my Patrick a job. And a job for me on his station.

Waiting for us was a wagon, a dray and horses and as soon as we had loaded our supplies we were on our way to his station out west. There were eight in the party. Mr Fraser, a teamster and his wagon, a man to drive the cart, my Patrick, Mrs Fraser, me and a girl, a little younger than me, Annie McDonald who was his wife's servant. I had seen her on the boat but we had not spoken much.

Mrs Fraser was a pretty girl, she was about my age who had married the Master when he had returned to Scotland looking for a bride. She was with child and Annie was to be the servant for her while I would care for the house and cook. My mother's instruction were a benefit else ways I would never had got the job. I learnt from the teamsters that Mr Fraser's first wife had died in childbirth many years ago but he had a son who was twenty two years old who was in charge of the run while his father was away. They didn't talk well of him. They were wise men.

Each night we would unload the dray for the Master and the Mistress to sleep up high. The rest of us slept on the ground. But it was dry and the nights was warm.

It was old Mick the teamster who told us the ways. He was an old convict from County Clare. He had his papers and was emancipated. He was good to Pat and me. He taught Pat how to work the big team and keep em working cause Pat had only worked a horse and plough in the fields. It was a long time till we reached the station. First we had to climb the hills. The gullies and creeks were a problem. The road wasn't a road at all it was just wheel tracks through the trees but at last we looked out and the land just went for ever. I never seen so far cept when we was at sea but here it was land for ever.

When we got to Kinnaird we had a hut. It was tiny but it was ours, no one to share but Pat and me. It was old with a roof of bark and the walls were slabs of timber between the posts. Mr Fraser said it was once his house before they had built the new house. His was bigger and it had a veranda out the front. It was so different to Offlay, here the sun was hot and the sky was blue. I missed the grey sky of home and the mists but we was warm and we had food. Not that it was flash. Mutton and damper, damper and mutton. Some tea and sugar. There weren't much else.

The big house was near the creek cause there was a waterhole that no one knew dry so even when the creek went dry there was still water for us and the horses and the sheep and the cattle.

With only us three women on the run, and we had always to be so polite to the Mistress, yes Marm,.no Marm, so Annie and I became good friends. She was a lively happy young Scottish lass and that could be a problem. Our Master was a serious, religious man, severe, and of the old Protestant faith. It did not make for a happy house. The boss's son name was Robert and he was waiting at the station. He was twenty two then and he was called by Rabbie. He thought he was flash and important and he liked to let you know he was too.

When he sees Annie he gets keen and is always around her and nice to her and she reckons its real good. I did na like the way of it and I warned her that them with the money is not for us lot but she reckoned he was a braw man.

It was me Pat's job to help with the cattle and he had a horse to ride when they went musterin. Then he had to go with Mick and the wagon for more supplies so he was away for months.

After q while Annie starts to reckon Rabbie is in love with her but I warn her again not to be with him. It won't come to good. Anyway one day she says he wants to marry her but I tell her he won't, ever. I knows that sort and a pretty girl.

Me and Pat are happy in our little hut but then the rains start and its leaks leaks leaks everywhere. Then I find out I am to hav a baby.

That's when things go wrong. Rabbie doesn't like
Pat and he's always giving him trouble. One day
Pat has had enuff and hits Rabbie. That was it.
The boss comes and says we have to go, and sends
Mick to take us into Aramac.

I was afraid that nobody would employ Pat but
there are them who know Rabbie and reckon it
was good he was hit and Pat gets a job on
another station real fast. This place is a sheep
station. After Kinnaird this is a good place for
us and the mistress is like a mother to me The
new boss reckons Pat is good with horses and
woud make a good teamster so he lends us some
horses and a wagon but we got to cart his wool
first and give him some of what we earn. He took
Pat to meet another teamster cause he reckons its
better thay work together and help each other.
We set up a little hut on the waterhole in
Aramac cause we can feed and water the horses
and I will be near help for our babe when it
wants to come.

We is so happy when our little boy arrives. He
has dark eyes and the hair just like my Pat. I

call him after my dad Daniel. Then one day Im
in to town and I hear Annie is looking for me.
She tells me she is pregnant and she has been
kicked off Kinnaird and carn't go back. It was
Rabbie who got her that way but he claims she
has been running wild with some man who
came through on the road. But that isn't true.
Ther are some who don't like Rabbie and they
say he raped her. But I know that weren't true
either. So Pat and I make a little lean too and
she comes to live with us beside the waterhole.

When the baby comes he's a cute little thing and
she calls him Sidney but Rabbie and his father
start rumours about who the father is and it
makes life difficult for Annie in town cause some
people believe them. It got real bad for Annie
and her little one. Cause they blacken her name
so bad.

My thoughts went out to Annie, alone, so far from her
family. Bessie had been right in her understanding of some
men and I was so grateful for her being there for my
forebear. And it seemed like history was repeating itself
almost a hundred and fifty years later. I could see Sass in
Annie, although times and attitudes to sex and illegitimacy
were so different. I thought Sass may have been more
worldly in some ways, yet she could also be just as naive as

Annie.

Bessie continued the story of my family.

Then me brother Joe comes through Aramac with a mob of sheep. Hes got a job with a drover takin sheep down south cause the feed is scarce where they were. One night we decide he will take Annie and her babe with him and they'll say she is mrs mary ann brown and her husbands died and she is looking for her brother in New South Wales. There were lots of dead men in the west and lots of scots were called Brown so nobody will know and she can be a widow and she will be a respectable woman with a baby Then she can try to find a job as cook or house maid down south.

Bessie's story continued to tell about her life, and of her husband and baby in Aramac . Then came the sad news.

Things were going good until the fire. There was a fire north of Aramac and they needed some help to stop it. That was when I lost me Pat. It was a tree that fell on him and he was killed. There was anither man killed in that fire too. A kanaka from the islands up north. They bought them in to work on sugar but some came out to

258

the sheep and cattle as well. Not many but a few.

The towns folk rallied around Bessie and she found a job cooking in one of the hotels and doing washing and cleaning for anyone who could pay. She and her baby managed but from her story life must have been difficult. Finally they moved from the hut on the creek.

Then I got a place in the town and we was set. It was the best house I ever had. Annie must have heard about the fire cause she sent me a letter and told me she knew and she told me she was alright. I was so glad that things had worked out for her.

I thought of my first visit to Aramac with Mike. Bessie's Aramac was so different. Then I thought of Chancy's wake. There I'd had a glimpse of the real community and real people. On my first visit I had passed though as if it was some stage set or theme park. I'd had no connection with the real life of the place.

Things didn't go so well for Bessie.

Then one day when Danny was five there was an accident. A horse spooked and the coach took off down the street and ran over my boy. He never got better. He was so beautiful that the angels wanted him. A dark shadow came over my life. It drove me mad. My Pat and now my Danny. I *had nothing left.*

I felt for poor Bessie. So far from family, poor, a husband killed and now her young child taken. Alone except for a brother far away, and maybe another somewhere else in Australia. It must have been frightening.

Then the story became happier. It appeared Annie had written again to Bessie and they had started to exchange letters. Annie wrote to say that she had met a man and he had married her and her son had taken his name. Now the dates on the Death Certificate made sense: my forebear was not Rohan but Rabbie. That saddened me, but I now learnt that Annie had found a good man. Blood may be one thing but nurture was another and I was pleased by Rohan MacGregor

Annie had admitted her past and he had still accepted her and married her. They had worked on a sheep station, then he became a manager of another station. Bessie had written about a letter she had received where Annie spoke of the vegetables and fruit the station's Chinese gardener provided. Compared to the early days after their arrival, and even her home in Scotland, it was paradise.

But there was more to their bond. Annie had learnt of the death of Bessie's child and of her terrible suffering, and she sent five pounds and an invitation to come and join them on the station. Bessie's diary, for that was what it amounted to, told of the trip to Warren, and then her job as a cook for the jackaroos and staff on the station. I was so pleased to read Bessie's comments about Annie and her child. Apparently she had been a great mother, loving and caring, but still allowing her child the freedom to explore and grow in the bush environment. She had retained the happy vibrant nurture that had first attracted Bessie to her, and had never become bitter about the events that had led to her pregnancy. It must have been so hard for Bessie to see the young child when hers had been taken from her so early.

Eventually Bessie had moved to Bourke and found a job, once again using the skills her mother had taught her. She had made a new life but had never married again. One brother, the drover, based himself in Bourke and together they had set up a house. The story also told of the younger brother who had finally followed Bessie and her husband to Australia. By the time he had arrived in Queensland Bessie had left for New South Wales. He had found work on western stations in Queensland and eventually he and his family had settled in Blackall.

The last twenty pages of the book were in another hand. The script was rounder and heavier, and a niece told of the last years of Bessie. Bessie had written the story of her life for the children of her brothers.

My auntie had lived with us in our house at Bourke for many years. My dad was a drover and he was often away and Auntie Bessie worked in the town. She and my dad had shared the cottage and when my dad married she lived with them. I never knew a time when she was not there.

Her life had been sad. Her husband had died and so had her baby. It was something that stayed with her forever. I don't ever remember laughter from her yet she was fond of people and always ready to help anyone who needed it. Not with money because we had none but with caring and practical things.

She had a special friend, a Scottish woman, that had come to Australia on the same boat and they were as close as sisters but her friend had been killed young in an accident and my Auntie lived for another thirty-five years. I know she missed her friend badly.

The story continued but it was now of Bessie's brothers and their families. Bessie's last years were as a very elderly lady with nieces and nephews scattered across Australia and even living in the big cities. She had died at eighty-two, never having returned to her homeland.

The final page was in yet another hand. A much later addition in biro.

"I only knew my great aunt as an elderly lady. Bessie Buckley, nee Edmonds, was a strong, capable, gentle, and sometimes ferocious woman. She faced all the challenges and hardships that life placed in her path, and there were many, with a stoic fortitude. But more importantly, no matter how hard *life may have been, she always had unbounded love for her extended family and the people around her. I am proud to be a great niece of Bessie. I hope I, and my family, can live up to her standards."*

I could see why Chancy had valued the book. It was a story of people he could identify with and relate to. It was a story of survival. How it had ended up on a bookshelf in an aged care home in Blackall I would probably never know. It was a long time since Bessie had left Queensland for her new home in New South Wales but her two brothers had large families who had spread widely across rural Australia. Some had settled in Blackall and it was probably there, maybe from a old box of books that had been thrown in a waste bin and rescued, or sold in a box at a garage sale and eventually given to the aged care home where Chancy had found Bessie's diary. At least Bessie's story had survived.

I was so grateful to Chancy for his gift. He had given me the missing parts of Annie's life and it had answered many of my questions. I now knew I did not come from Rohan McGregor but Rabbie Fraser. Not that I held him in great favour. My respect for Rohan had only increased. I hoped that my children, and their children, would hold me in as high and dear a place as Annie and Bessie deserved.

35 Decisions

I waited until the evening before I phoned. I thought Euan would be in from the paddocks and I wanted to thank him. Thank him for all he'd done, and for the support that he and Kate had been when we'd had our problems at Raasay. I felt I owed it to him to let him know that all was well. Or, at least, that the family were supporting Sass. I still wasn't sure just how 'well' that was going to turn out.

I also wanted to tell him about Chancy's book. I thought he would have assumed the parcel was the book Chancy had spoken about, but I doubted he would have been aware of exactly what it was.

He was interested in Bessie's story and especially the bits about Aramac, Kinnaird and the west. They were areas he could associate with and knew. The stories of the south, and Bourke and Warren, were not familiar to him. I told of my gratitude to Chancy for providing me with the missing links in my family history. I also told the story of Annie's baby and who the father really was. I had a family history that traced back to Aramac and to Rabbie Fraser and his father on Kinnaird. I could acknowledge it, although I couldn't respect those particular forebears.

Our call had lasted about half an hour and it was the same Euan I had last seen a few days earlier in Barcy. His manner was unchanged and he made no mention of his proposal.

Finally I broached the subject. I had been honoured by his offer but my family, my life, was in Melbourne. Even more now that I might have a great-grandchild, and a granddaughter who may need me. Besides I remembered he'd once said city girls were a problem in the bush and I was definitely a city girl. As much as I had grown to appreciate the countryside I knew I could never become part of it like the women I had met at the bull sale.

We hung up on our phone call and I suddenly felt very lonely. I hadn't expected that when I had made my decision. I knew Euan would never replace Matt but he was a special man and I would miss him. If only there were not the differences in our lifestyles. If only the timing had been different, and if only my family were not facing a difficult moment. So many 'if onlys', but then that was life.

36 A New Year

Christmas came and went but there was none of the traditional excitement of the season. I had the usual round of Christmas drinks and end of year celebrations with friends, and I took my grandson to the city to see the Christmas decorations and treat him to a huge ice cream sundae at his favourite shop. As a family we had gone to the carols in the Sidney Myer Music Bowl. However, for me, this year the festivities lacked something, something that I could not place, or didn't want to acknowledge.

Our family Christmas morning had also followed the pattern of other years. We had gathered around the same imitation pine tree and opened the gifts we had bought for each other. We'd drunk a glass of champagne and sat down to a very traditional roast although, as usual, we had celebrated our Australian heritage by first sharing a large platter of prawns.

The New Year arrived. Looking back it had been quite a year. Little had I known when we were emptying my mother's room at the retirement village where it would take me, or the news it would bring my family. I thought of my visit to Sydney and Great Uncle James. My son had rung to give me the news of his death just prior to Christmas. He had been our closest link to the past and now that had gone.

Friends had invited me to a party on New Year's Eve but I

had declined and spent the night at home alone with my thoughts. I decided I had to make myself a New Year's Resolution. I really needed to make a change and look to the future and not back to the past. That was easy to say but not so easy to do. Sass and Annie kept coming into my mind. I couldn't move on until I sorted my understanding of their lives. How alike were the two women? Were they really in love, or was it just lust? Just a natural, unchecked, human appetite? The Sass I had known had been very self-centred and never looked beyond her own immediate interests or to the future. She was not alone in that attitude. Many of her friends held a similar view of life. I didn't know if it was because of their uncertainty about the future, and a conscious, or unconscious, decision to live for the present. Maybe it was the result of a sheltered life where they felt no need to consider the future. At home Sass had been surrounded by love but that had not been enough and she wanted more. I guess we all want love and sometimes we seek it in unwise places. From Bessie's book I had the feeling that Annie had wanted love, but she also had love to give. What the family that she had left behind in Scotland were like I could have no idea, however I'd developed a picture of a young girl who was full of love, ready to give and open to receive. It was sad that her generosity of spirit was abused. Annie had moved on. I suppose she had no choice, but she had made the best she could of her life. Sass had made her decision and was moving on. I was confident that she too would be a survivor. Already I could see a once carefree and careless girl becoming a woman.

I had to move on from the past year. Sitting looking out at the lights of the city I decided my resolution would be to live life as fully as I could, give the love I knew I had, and be open to the wonders of the world. Just thinking it made me felt better.

I decided that travel would be the answer. A holiday, different places, different people. That would be the change I needed. I started to make a list of places I wanted to see, things I wanted to do. Over the days the list grew and then I put it aside and lost it. Perhaps later in the year I might consider it again, but then later in the year my priorities may have changed.

Next I decided I should, like Bessie, write my family's history for the future generations. It wasn't full of important people. Indeed there were no important people, but they all had lives and loves and it would be so sad to lose what I had discovered. The brave and adventurous Annie may lie in an unmarked grave, its exact position lost due to the floods that had washed over the red soil of Bourke, but she had been a survivor. That would be an example to those of us still alive and for generations to come.

I commenced my writing but I soon discovered that while I could trace names and dates and places, I could never find emotions. Without their dreams and fears, loves and hates you could never really understand a person. For history such things required some recorded remarks or letters. I had so few, a brief letter to Bessie and a few letters of my mother and grandmother. Very little to work with. My family were not letter writers, or the sort of people whose words were recorded by others. They were part of the multitude who just got on with their lives, did what they had to, or could do, whatever that may have been, and left no record. Not that the written record was always to be relied upon: some could be very self-serving.

The desire to understand drew me to research the times in which the people had lived. The hard times in Ireland and Scotland could explain the actions of Annie and Bessie. Growing up in uncertain times could explain my father's desire for security, but other people sharing the same experience would respond quite differently. Events would show the results, but not always the reasons. My own life had taken a path when I met Matt. What would my life have been if he had not come to London and gone to the same pub that my friends and I frequented? If I had been on the continent travelling with girlfriends at that time I may never have met him. Sometimes we make our lives with our decisions, sometimes life makes decisions for us.

It was one evening in May when I was talking with my daughter that I learnt that James had contacted Sass. Meg told me the conversation had been polite and amicable, but had only lasted a few minutes. Sass had moved on and this time she'd heeded Kate McLeod's warning. The regret and betrayal she had once felt had been replaced by acceptance and caution.

Meg had also told me of other changes in Sass.

She'd altered the list of the courses that she was studying. Gone were the dreams of a glamorous career of blogging and becoming a social media personality. Now her emphasis, while still communications, had switched more to human relationships and the practical communication of information and ideas.

More importantly Sass had also changed personally. She was now less shrill and argumentative in her beliefs and more open to consider the views of others. Indeed I had noticed the changes when I visited their home for our regular Sunday lunch.

Her friends had also changed. Gone were the spikey hair and torn jeans or brief skirts of her more 'out-there' friends with their extreme views and clothes. The new friends were a quieter, and I thought, more sensible group. Some old friends from school days had reappeared and some were new. In some ways I was sorry to see her extreme friends disappear. They had certainly been an interesting, although often difficult, bunch but I was also concerned that some of the new were, perhaps, too conservative; too inward looking.

At least Sass appeared to have come to terms with the events in her life.

On New Year's Eve I had made my resolution, but the days had passed and I'd really changed nothing. My life had settled into a comfortable groove. I had returned to my previous activities: joining the garden group on excursions, going into the city for a movie, long lunches with friends, volunteering with Meals on Wheels. I had even thought of contacting Tony. I had picked up my phone, hesitated, and then didn't make the call. I'd moved on and so had he. I later learnt from mutual friends that he had found a friend who enjoyed movies and dinners, had a passion for bowls and loved large noisy gatherings and spent nights at his house. I was pleased for him.

I flew to Sydney and spent a week with my son and his family. While there I contacted Colleen and returned to her house where I'd once had morning tea with Great Uncle James and told her of my research and travels. Perhaps one day someone on her side of our family would seek to know their background. The more widely that information was spread, the more likely it would be preserved for those who sought it. I promised to send her a copy of my efforts at recording the family's early days, if I ever finished it.

37 More Discoveries

Euan's news of the possible location of Kinnaird had me immediately booking my flights to Barcaldine.

I wasn't sure what I expected, or even wanted to find, but I did know that I was looking forward to seeing Euan again. My refusal of his proposal had troubled me. I knew he had been disappointed, but then he had not broken off contact with me. In the time I'd spent back in Melbourne since I'd last seen him my thoughts had kept returning to Raasay and our times together. Yet the thought of my family held me in Melbourne. Should he ever ask again I knew I would still want to remain in Melbourne with them. I had hesitated about accepting his invitation to come north but the thought that I could see where Annie had lived and our Australian family had started was too tempting.

Euan had discovered that what had once been Kinnaird in the late eighteen-hundreds was now split into a number of smaller properties. The original house had fallen into disrepair after a new brick homestead had been built in the nineteen-fifties and eventually the old timber building had been destroyed by a bushfire that had ravaged the countryside. All that remained of the homestead that Archie Fraser had built for his new wife were a few ageing trees that had been planted in the garden. The earlier slab cottage where Annie had conceived and begun the line that eventually led to me had also vanished. Euan's informant had mentioned two graves overlooking a creek not far from where the house was thought to have stood.

"Whose graves are they?"

"From what I have been able to learn, they are Archibald and his first wife. Apparently that was where he buried her, and when he died he was buried beside her."

"That must have been an insult to his second wife. What happened to her?"

"I don't know. The station was sold and Robert and his stepmother and her child left the district."

From what Euan had learnt the locals seemed to have almost forgotten the Frasers. The original homestead area of the property had changed hands a few times over the years, each time getting smaller, and then one day the site of the original house was added back to an adjoining property.

Euan continued. "I gather it was not a happy family. After the old man died and the property was sold, his son, your whatever grandfather, and his stepmother vanished from sight. Nobody knows what happened to them. Perhaps you should put your detective skills to work on them."

"I'm not sure I really have any empathy for that side of my family."

I called my daughter and told her of my plans. This time there was no mention of Sass accompanying me. She had matured and now had a sense of responsibility that previously she'd lacked. She was also careful in who she allowed into her life. I hoped that the shield that she had built around herself would not be impenetrable and that one day there would be room for someone.

It was six months after Chancy's funeral when I returned to Raasay. When my flight landed at Barcaldine Airport the weather was so different to my last memories of the town. That had been the day of Sass's confession, the night of wild storms, and the morning of gentle rain as we waited for our flight to front Sass's parents with our news. Already the grass had turned to brown and the storms of my previous visit were long forgotten. The season had been kind, and now paddocks were full of grass and the livestock contented.

We spent the first night at Raasay. Neither Donald or Kate were to be seen.

"Where are Kate and Donald?"

"Kate's gone back to uni. She decided she really needed to get serious about her course. I'm so pleased she made that decision. What will happen after that I don't know."

"And Donald?"

"He's over with Bella."

"What's happening on Kandanga?"

"Mike has two new business partners. It won't be the same as when it was just him and his family but he's still in business. He's told Bella she should leave and marry Don. She has taken some of his advice. She and Don are going to take over here once they've finished picking cotton. They haven't gone as far a marriage but that's the way it is these days."

"What do you think of that?"

"It's good. It's what I want. They'll get around to marriage one day. They are a great couple and they should be together."

"So what will happen to you?"

"They've told me I'm welcome to stay here. Bella says they'll always be a room for me and I can look after the garden and the chooks. She can be a cheeky bugger sometimes."

"Does that suit you?"

"Yes. I think they should have the opportunity to do their own thing and now is the right time for them to start. I should move over. I've ordered a mobile home. It should be ready to pick up in two weeks."

I had an image of an aging V Dub Combi with a surfboard on the roof. It wasn't the Euan I knew.

"You're not serious? Are you?"

"Yes. It's not a combi or anything like that. A bit bigger, but not real big. I can stand up in it. It's got a double bed, fridge, stove and a shower and toilet. Everything I need. I'm going to explore Australia and see all the things I've read or heard about. I will be a grey nomad."

"What has happened about Mike's Gold Coast investment? Is that resolved?"

"No. That will take years. The two people behind it

should be in jail but the lawyers are involved so who knows what will happen, and it will go on and on. Justice can be a funny thing these days."

"What about James?"

"He went back to Sydney. I don't know how that will go but this time he will have to make something work. He's engaged. The wedding is in three weeks. It will make or break him. I hope it's not the latter."

I thought of his phone call to Sass. It had only been six weeks ago. "That's very quick."

"Bella tells me it needs to be quick. This time the family are not so understanding as yours. They're involved in the fruit and veggie trade, that's how he got to know them. It's third generation, but they are still very traditional in the ways of their old country. One day they may decide they don't need him anymore."

"You make it sound like the mafia."

"No, it's not that bad, but he will have to work with lots of brothers-in-law and probably a few cousins. One day they may decide divorce is acceptable and he is no longer needed. I don't think his position will be an easy one."

"How is Mike taking James's behaviour?"

"He's livid. Mike may have had a wandering eye but he was always considerate to the ladies in his life. He's re-organised his business affairs, had to anyway, and much of it is now in trust for Bella. Eventually James will get something but he really will have to work for his living."

"And Margie?"

"Divorce is looming. She has money of her own and just wants to move on. Maybe she's afraid Mike will make a claim on her money, but he wouldn't. He'll soon be available if you are interested."

"Euan!"

38 Old Kinnaird

As we drove through the gate leading to the homestead Euan told me more of his conversation with the owner of the property. The family had owned the property for eight years. When they purchased it they had not known of the graves by the creek. From the palms, the bottle trees and the bougainvillea they realised that a house had once stood there but they'd been told the building had long ago been bulldozed and buried in a pit. That agreed with Euan's information that the original house had become derelict and eventually destroyed in a bushfire. When they had found the grave site they had erected a fence to keep cattle from trampling the graves but they had no knowledge about the people who lay buried there.

At the new homestead we met the wife of the manager who invited us in for a cuppa and gave us directions to the site of the old house.

We drove through seemingly empty paddocks until we reached a line of trees and followed our directions to the waterhole. Euan explained that the paddocks we had driven through had been heavily stocked and were now being spelled. The cattle were probably in other paddocks, 'on camp' near water, or in the shade.

The country had changed greatly since Annie had lived there. New grasses had replaced the native pastures and water was now reticulated to all corners of the property. Fencing had changed the way livestock was managed. Markets and work practices had changed, and so had lifestyles.

Standing in the hot midday sun I looked at the two lonely, neglected graves we had come to see. Around us the paddock was bare and brown, the good grass of the previous season had been heavily grazed and was now waiting for the first of the next season's rain so it could once again spring to life. I could understand the choice of place for the graves. In an often dry land the thought of spending eternity overlooking water shaded by the coolibah trees that lined the edge of the creek would be as close to heaven as a local could find. The other choice would be a bare, dry cemetery like the one where Chancy now lay. There you would spend your time with the rustle of the winds and the dust they carried rather than the morning and evening calls of the birds watering in the creek.

The two graves lay side by side. On one the headstone sat crooked, leaning backwards away from the body buried at its feet. The other headstone had fallen to the ground. It appeared that each grave had once been enclosed with low wrought iron rails and the ground within covered with stones, but the rails were now rusted and lay crumpled at the feet of a nearby tree and the stones had long since been trampled and spread.

On one headstone was the name Archibald Fraser and the

date of death: February 28, 1879. It appeared he had not enjoyed many years of life with his new wife and their young child. On the other headstone I could just make out the faint inscription 'Mary Margaret Fraser, beloved wife of Archibald Fraser, mother of Robert'. Her date of death was no longer legible. Archibald had made his decision to be buried beside his first wife, the mother of Rabbie, the father of Annie's baby. I could understand the feelings of his second wife. I think I would also want to move on and away from Kinnaird.

I had found my distant relatives in a distant place. I shared the blood of the man and the woman buried here, yet I could feel no empathy for them. I could respect the efforts they had made to create a life in the bush far from their birthplaces. I could admire the energy that had gone into developing what had once been a prosperous cattle station. Yet I could never forgive Archibald or his son for the treatment of Annie.

My thoughts were of her. A poor girl, illiterate, travelling to the far reaches of the world in search of a better life than the hardships she knew she would face in Scotland. When she had sailed away from Tilbury as a nineteen-year old girl she probably knew she would never see her family again. Life in the new land must have seemed strange and just as hard as the life she had left behind. Not cold as in Scotland, but the heat of a Queensland summer must have seemed worse. And then, to be taken advantage of, and cast out, would take away any security she may have thought she had. I was so grateful to Bessie and Patrick.

I hadn't agreed with Euan. He'd once suggested the Annie may have been a girl who saw a chance and was prepared to give her body and her soul for a better life, only to find that it was snatched away from her. That didn't fit the character of the woman that I'd discovered. Her strength and resolve in keeping and raising her baby on her own, and later her support for the man who became her husband. That wasn't the action of a woman looking for the easiest way of life. I was glad to be of Annie's blood. It was only for Annie that I had respect. She had been a strong woman and I felt she had passed on her strength to her family, to her son Sidney, to her granddaughter Jessie, my mother and to me. I hoped it would flow on to my granddaughter. Then I thought of Sass and her decision. Times were so different now.

I stood there lost in my thoughts. Annie had made her decision. It had been difficult and hard. Today attitudes had changed. Unlike in her day single mothers were no longer shunned by society but were supported by the government and families. Some women even choose to have a child without attachment to any man. The world was certainly different. Different even from the days of my mother. Yet having a child limited the opportunities available to many women seeking to build a career.

I looked across at Euan. I'd also made my decision. Unlike Sass, it wasn't a question of life or death, or commitment to motherhood. I thought of Matt and our years together. I was sure he would approve. I could almost hear him saying, "Always do what you think best".

As we were walking back to our vehicle my mobile gave its familiar double tone for a message.

I looked at the screen.

There was a short text.

It was from Sass.

It started with a smiley face, then the message.

"2 wks prem, all well. Annie is beautiful. XXOO"

39 The Text

The news from Sass was wonderful. I was so glad all was well and I had cried when I realised that she had chosen Annie as the name for her new baby. To be standing at the place where our family journey had begun had made it even more poignant. It was as if a circle had been completed.

At least my great granddaughter would have the full support of a close-knit family around her. Unlike the first Annie who had been cast out by the father of her child and his family.

I turned to Euan and told him the news.

"I suppose we had better get back to Barcaldine and make a booking for you to fly south. I'm sure you will want to see the new baby as soon as possible. It might even be quicker if we drive to Longreach. At least there is a flight out every day. In Barcy you might have to wait a day or so for a flight."

I was grateful to Euan for his thoughtfulness. I liked being with him and wished we could have more time together, but somehow events always intruded, and my family was calling me.

Sass was looking beautiful sitting beside the bed with the tiny infant in her arms. As her text had said, all had gone well, although Annie had surprised everyone with her rush to get into the world. I thought of Bessie's description of Annie McDonald as "a lively happy young lass". It could have been the description of the little Annie in Sass's arms, although the occasional gurgle gave no hint of a Scottish accent. She had her father's colouring but the eyes were of my family. Most importantly, Sass was happy and radiant. She had already adjusted to the role of mother and I knew she had made the right decision.

Twelve nights later we had a family celebration in the house in Beaumaris to toast the new arrival. Sass had come home to a place where she was loved and surrounded by those who valued her. That was the way it should be but I was only too aware that not all mothers would go home to a loving household.

The days passed, the weeks passed and little Annie grew. The routine of the house developed and I was sometimes called to do duty when Sass had to attend classes but much of the time she did her work with a small bundle wrapped in a cot beside her desk. It was a hard job but she stuck to it. It was so unlike the Sass of earlier days.

Then one day I got a call from Mike at Kandanga. Euan must have given him the news. He was interested and concerned. It was only while I was talking to him that I realised that Annie was also his grandchild. We had never considered that. His was a difficult position. He knew that James had denied paternity, yet he knew the truth and was prepared to accept the responsibility. I had lacked empathy for the Frasers and yet, unthinkingly, I had cut out any connection of the baby to another family. If the situation had been reversed I would have been heartbroken. Bella would be an aunt, whether it was legally recognised or not.

40 Time

My brother was finally true to his word. It was almost eighteen months after his bet with us. The bet he had made on the night when we'd first discussed the letter and its possible connection to our family. As agreed, we three Finlay siblings were seated in the restaurant of my choice. In our hands glasses of champagne to toast the lives our family— past. present and future.

It was strange how an old note written almost one hundred and forty years earlier and found in a simple cardboard box had affected our lives.

We had known nothing of Annie. I doubted that my mother who had saved the letter knew much, if any, of the story. That was the past, and my family had always been more interested in the present. Yet surely a little of earlier generations still lingers in each of us. For some to be embraced, for others to be rejected, and perhaps, for a few a source of shame or cause for rebellion. For many, the past is probably an unrealised or an unacknowledged influence in their lives.

Yet time moves on. It is so easy to blame others for the problems in our lives and be a victim, expecting someone else to solve our difficulties. While we may not control all the events affecting our future, our decisions today shape our tomorrows. That was true of Annie, and it is true for all of us.

For my family, my journey had led to a greater understanding of the preciousness of life, and the importance of having good people around us. Plus the realization that when life throws up hardship and challenges other have been there before and survived. So can we!

For Sass it was a child. I knew that she had matured, and, like Annie, would take responsibility for her own life and that of her baby. In time I hoped she would find a good partner to share her love as the first Annie had.

For me, it had been almost another chance at love, but that had never eventuated. The time never seemed right.

Thinking back, I had wasted hours, days, weeks. I'd wasted months with my unnecessary worries about Sass. Time I'd lost forever. Time I could never regain. Sitting in the restaurant with my brother and sister we all decided that we should make the most of every moment of our lives.

Then my phone rang. It was a grey nomad in a mobile home parked far away, overlooking a waterhole at Warlock Ponds.

In another three weeks he would be in Melbourne. This time I would show him my home, my family and my city— then together we would explore Australia. This time I knew the time was right.

ABOUT THE AUTHOR

Valverde Maclean has a passion for Australia.

He has travelled widely throughout the country and has lived and worked in both the southern and northern areas of Australia. This experience shows in the way he writes of an Australia far from the big cities.

Australian history, particularly the development of the inland, and the ramifications for the economic life of the nation form a backdrop to his stories.

However it is not only the past and the outback that appear in his writing. He is also interested in present day Australia. His stories travel from the big cities to regional communities and on to the far distant corners of the vast continent.

He is a keen observer of human behaviour, and of the present day changes and challenges to Australian culture. Observations of both appear in his writing.

His first novel, "The Disappearance of Merry", was well received by readers who enjoyed the combination of romance and mystery. This was continued in his second novel "Magenta". Readers of both books also had the pleasure of travelling today's Australia and discovering, or for some rediscovering, an Australia they had heard of, or remembered.

He now lives in Queensland, Australia, near a small village in the beautiful Sunshine Coast Hinterland.

All Valverde Maclean novels

are available in eBooks or print formats

To find out more about the author and his novels

Visit www.valverdemaclean.com

or

Follow the author on Facebook

The second novel by Valverde Maclean

Magenta

The story follows the twists and turns of their lives and their travel adventures as Suzie Benedict and Peter Jamison seek to understand their relationship.

VALVERDE MACLEAN'S
Magenta

In a remote region a young woman's body vanishes—only to re-appear fifteen hundred kilometres away. A road trip across the North and the West of Australia brings unexpected revelations, romance, danger and uncertainty that change relationships forever.

The *follow* up to the well-received first novel
"The Disappearance of Merry."

The thoughts that had been with me on my flight from Melbourne returned. What was I doing here? Worse, at the front door there was a posy of bright red roses and a note.

As we drove up to the parking spot near the beach we could see the vehicle. It was a small van with a painting of Elvis Presley on the side, but it was empty. There was no young woman with magenta hair on one side of her head.

The airstrip was a cleared strip of graded red dirt. A sign board proudly proclaimed "Mitchell Plateau-Arrivals and Departures Lounge". Around us the rocks of the gorges carved out by the river showed a variety of colours: reds, yellows, various greys and brown.

"Where are they?" Inspector Adamson's question took us by surprise. "Where's what? What are you talking about?" "The diamonds?" Adamson ordered coffees for three and told us a story of diamonds and drugs.

Visit **www.valverdemaclean.com**

www.ingramcontent.com/pod-product-compliance
Lightning Source LLC
Chambersburg PA
CBHW051522050726
47503CB00014B/856